let there be light

A.M. JOHNSON

Editing and Formatting: Elaine York,
Allusion Graphics, LLC/Publishing & Book Formatting
Proofreading: Payne Proofing
Created Design by Murphy Rae
Music design on cover by Noah Hood

let
there be
light

To those who have been taught that love is only two-dimensional, lift your heart to the light and bask in all its beautiful facets.

For Kirk S.

Love: noun
An intense feeling of deep affection, a warm
attachment or devotion for (someone).
Merriam-Webster

Camden

An essay of sound kept my world cloaked and bruised black under the ivory. A composition of notes strung together by my fingers, the music in my head was private— isolated. It's dark here. I counted the numbers, the beats, the measures, and nothing I created matched the sound I searched for.

Turbulence and chaos.

The white rush as the wave crested, manipulated by his palm. Pushed to the side as if the current wouldn't dare to hold him.

It's the sound light made as it sliced through the crystal blue water, touching his skin and illuminating my world. It's a spectrum so loud and beautiful that going back to the dark felt like a prison sentence.

Thick strands of golden blond trickled through my fingertips. I breathed the summer scent of his skin, sunshine and chlorine. Reveled in the straw color of his lashes, as they dusted the tops of his cheeks, and I allowed the heat of his skin to press and mesh with mine. His back to my chest, my hand in his hair, and my nose in his neck. These were the luxuries I dreamt about in my pursuit of sound, of sanity. My heart was too heavy in my chest, my sins a burden I bared to the keys, and the keys alone knew all of my secrets.

The shadows I'd played in all day turned to dawn as his voice started my heart. The familiar scent of sweet and sour chicken drifted through the crack of my bedroom door, and my fingers hovered silent over the keyboard.

"Hope you're hungry," he said to my roommate and I heard him laugh.

The smile he infused into those three words tickled at my memory, and I could almost sense that perfect note, the one I'd searched for all week. I kept my eyes on the keys, and ignored the way my lungs suddenly felt too big inside my ribs.

He was not made for me and I was not made for him.

I repeated this as I heard him, his footsteps, always nine, leading him to me.

Royal

I liked words as much as my sister, Indie, liked paints. She'd take odd colors, blend them together across the canvas, and I'd lose the ability to breathe as I watched the brush in her hand unveil all of her mysteries. I wasn't any good with words, though, but I collected them regardless of my inability to string them together. Words like cerulean and puddle jumper. I liked definitions and the way one word could set off a series of feelings inside me. Reading was my escape as much as art was for Indie. And today, the word precipice had become the weight inside my right foot as it pressed against the gas pedal, had the asphalt in front of me yawning and stretching like an indolent cat, long and slow.

The dry desert landscape had finally given way to the lush greens of Oregon as my sister toyed with the dial of the stereo. Our family data plan had run out about three hours ago and we'd been forced to listen to the twangy guitars and static of some middle-of-nowhere radio station. The temperature felt cooler here, and the scent of the trees, the fir, it washed away the last bits of home. A few hours ago, I'd eagerly rolled down the windows once we'd passed over the state line, Indie and I screaming like lunatics.

Fall semester.

Freshmen.

Freedom.

Friends.

"Just leave it, Indie. There's shit for miles." I smiled even as I worried over her scowl from my peripheral vision.

"It's not funny, Blue. I hate it when it gets too quiet." Her soft voice vacillated between anger and fear, making my shame form into four letters. Jerk.

I dropped my hand from the steering wheel and reached into my pocket for my phone. "Here." I handed it to her. "I'll pay for the data overages for the month."

My sister eyed me. "You don't have to do that. I can draw, I have a sketchbook in the back and—"

"I got you, Pink." My lips responded to her small smile.

She was my mirror.

Indigo and I were born on May twenty-second. Twins. Blue eyes. Blond hair. And names to this day we get razzed for. My sister was technically older, by two minutes, but I'd been the bigger baby. Once I was old enough to understand what it meant to have a sister, a sibling, a twin—I ran with that extra ounce. Played the protector role very well, I'd like to think.

"Mom won't let you spend any money, and you know it, besides, you don't have time. I doubt your coach will let you work any extra hours at the library. You're going to have to prove yourself. You're a newbie."

"I swam the fastest hundred-meter butterfly in the state."

"And?" She laughed softly. "This is college. A clean slate. Everything before won't matter to them if you're too tired to swim. I bet your coach will keep you guys on a strict leash." Apprehension settled her brow into a deep crease. "Don't overdo it, Royal. Last season you ran yourself ragged. Work, swimming, grades. Don't waste away inside the library. Live a little."

I chuckled. "Says the girl who never leaves the art studio."

"I leave."

She turned and faced the window. Her quiet whispers bounced off the glass and guilt caught my breath again as I listened to the hollow sound of her loneliness.

"What are they saying?" I asked, watching her shoulders shrink inward.

Like always, she didn't answer right away. She took a minute and breathed through it like Dad, and all those years of therapy, had taught her.

"I'm not lonely."

"What did they say?" I asked again. My tone taking on a firm brother-bear quality she knew all too well.

"They said I'm a loser... that I'll always be alone."

She faced me with glassy, light blue eyes.

"You're never alone, Pink, never. You'll always have me."

I took my eyes off the road for only a moment, but her smile was well worth the small distraction. She plugged an adapter into my phone, chose a song, and hit play. The wind rustled the corn silk strands of her hair as she closed her eyes, resting her head back against the worn leather seat of my well-used Subaru. An old family favorite played through the speakers and a rush of nostalgia washed over me as I brought my eyes back to the open road. I had a great family. Parents who actually gave a damn and were present. They never made me, or Indie, feel like we weren't the most important things in their lives.

Mom and I were close. I'd inherited her patience and penchant for self-doubt. It was why I'd started collecting words when I was younger. A ploy to seem smarter than I'd felt, to steal a little of Indie's limelight. Dad and Indie were always whispering together, painting. Mom was an artist, too, but she never seemed to mind I had no talent for it. Instead, she'd read to me all the time. Helped me look up words I didn't understand, encouraged my fascination with useless synonyms and terms no self-respecting pre-teen would ever use. She'd encouraged my loud, free-spirited behavior. And, over time, I figured it had been her way to help quell the silence that sometimes descended on our home when things went dark.

Where I was the wild child, Indie was the silent, fragile piece of glass. She shared our father's demons. She struggled with depression like he always had. Voices. Hallucinations. Schizoaffective disorder. Indie was higher-functioning and hardly had internal stimulus, but I'd never stop wondering if she'd just become really good at hiding the voices in her head. The link Dad and Indie shared, though, wasn't a wedge between him and me. It was a balance. Dad and I had our own world, too, but it was different. Our time together was like that deep breath I took when my head broke through the water as I swam. Relief. We talked about sports and chicks and made fun of my uncles. He and his brothers owned a tattoo shop in downtown Salt Lake, but Dad's art paid the bills more than his ink skills, which had given him more time at home with Indie and me. Dad went to every one of my swim meets. A steadfast presence that pulled my limbs through the water fast and strong. He'd once told me I was like his own personal butterfly.

After we'd finished packing the car this morning, and Mom had cried again for the tenth time, he'd handed me a small canvas. The eight-by-eight square was covered in waves of aquamarine, cut down the middle with a bright streak of gold. He'd said, "I painted this after your first swim meet, and it's an image I'll paint over and over again while you're gone. It's a reminder, son, of the pride I feel every time I see you in the water."

Those same words, mixed with the lyrics from his favorite song tightened my throat as I sped down I-84 toward an unknown future. A chance he and Mom had gifted to me with every late-night study session and early morning practice.

"I wish we were in the same dorm." Indie's whispered lament made me chuckle.

"Don't you want your privacy? Spread your little wings." I teased and pinched the denim fabric of her overalls.

She stared at me, the deadpan expression on her face made it difficult not to laugh.

"I have three suitemates. Privacy isn't part of my vocabulary this semester."

I hid the excitement bubbling inside my stomach with a shrug. A single dorm at St. Peter's College was reserved for seniors and athletes. St. Peter's was an elite, private Catholic College known for pouring its money into recruiting the top athletes in the nation. Apparently, they took sports very seriously. It was a good thing their Art department was top notch, because being separated from Indie would be like someone saying, "Here, let me cut out your left lung," and then expecting me to breathe. No matter how weird it seemed to outsiders, she was a part of me, and I was a part of her. She was my best friend, and if I had to do this on my own, I wasn't sure I would've ever pulled out of the lot behind our apartment back home.

"You can crash at my place anytime," I offered and she rolled her eyes.

"Thanks, but sneaking into a men's only dorm is the quickest way for both of us to lose our scholarships."

"You think they're that strict?" I asked.

She chuffed. "Did you not read the Code of Conduct?"

"No, nerd, I didn't."

She shoved my shoulder. "Read it, Blue, or you'll be kicked out on your butt in a week."

"Hey." I laughed. "I'm perfectly behaved."

She gave me the side eye.

So maybe I was kind of a troublemaker, and, maybe I might've given my mom and dad a few heart attacks. But wasn't that part of being a teenager?

"Rites of passage must be attained."

"Now you sound like Uncle Liam," she said with a sharp grin.

"The man drops some killer advice."

Indie giggled as she flipped through another playlist on my phone and the warm sound of it was infectious. Contagious. She was a pandemic of warmth when she let the clouds part from her eyes. She decided on another family classic and smiled as she asked, "Do you think Quinn and Ava will try for St. Peter's, too?"

"I hope so. All the O'Connells in one state again would be pretty epic."

Quinn was my Uncle Liam's son and Ava was Uncle Kieran's daughter. We were all close in age and in soul, and while losing Indie was like losing a lung, leaving them behind was like losing a limb. We were all connected, our family, one big, living, breathing, beating heart. They still had a few more years of high school. Years of parents. Years to figure out what the hell they wanted from life. A lump formed in my throat at the thought. Homesickness, heavy and swift, snuck its way into the muscles of my shoulders.

Did I even know what I wanted? Was this year going to be everything I hoped? Would I fail? Would I screw up and end up costing my parents money, forcing them to fork out cash they didn't have to send me to some shit state college back home?

I swam the hundred meter faster than any other incoming freshman at this college, and academically, I had never let my GPA drop below a 3.8. The side job I'd acquired in the library at St. Peter's through the work-study program, no matter how much my parents or my sister protested, was mine. I was nineteen, and I wanted to prove to myself I could be the man my father had taught me to be. Be the brother who could support his sister in this new environment at any cost.

I'd left my adolescence back home, wrapped up in my childhood sheets, and I was moving forward. I was becoming something more, I was on the verge...

A precipice.

Royal

St. Peter's was nestled halfway between the Pacific Ocean and Portland, Oregon, in a town called Pines Hollow. Sitting on the gentle foothills of the coast range, just on the western edge of the Willamette Valley, surrounded by trees and clouds, some could argue it was remote, and too far from civilization, but the clean scent of rain and evergreens had held my mood steady since Indie and I had arrived about five days ago. We'd found this hipster coffee shop a few miles off campus yesterday, during a break in the weather, and the views of Mt. Hood were pretty stellar. The walk from my dorm at Warren House was about five minutes to the library, ten minutes to Vigrus Hall, my sister's dormitory, and only three to the pool and gymnasium. And even though the fresh air had cleansed the last bit of homesickness sticking to my ribs, I wished for that same, clear view of Mt. Hood right about now.

My bones ached and my soggy hair flopped into my eyes, water trickling down my cheeks, as I made my way to the gym. I was meeting the team for the first time today in the weight room. Five-thirty in the morning was earlier than what I was used to back home, and it only made it worse... dry land training had never been my favorite. Lifting weights, running on a treadmill were nothing like sinking into the rhythm of the water, forgetting the outside world in the waves. But as I glanced up at the tall glass windows of the Everley Platt Gymnasium and Aquatic Center, my heartbeat took on a life of its own, sprinting and jumping in irregular intervals, lodging my breath somewhere behind my Adam's apple.

At the age of two, my mother once said I was better at eating the paint than actually getting it on the canvas. Indie, Mom—Dad, art was their thing and swimming was mine. It had been a way for me to set myself apart. Mom had put Indie and me in swim lessons after we'd started kindergarten, and after Indie had almost drowned, she never wanted to go back. Me, on the other hand, I was a fish. I could still remember the humid air inside the pool room at the local university where our lessons had been held. Vividly, I recalled the ash-colored hair of my swim instructor, how he'd smile at me every time I came up for air and, how at the age of five, I'd finally felt like I'd belonged to something.

I could be good at something, hell, I was an amazing swimmer, but I never wanted or needed to break records, I needed to swim. I needed the water to remember who I was, and what I could become. My parents weren't rich, they were comfortable. We'd never wanted for anything, but I'd be a liar if I said I'd never heard them whisper about the cost of things. Cars, college, food—clothes. Two children with the same needs at the same time. Two tuitions. The day I slipped on my goggles and Pioneer Lake High swim cap, I'd made a plan for myself, for Indie. I'd do this and I'd kill it, make it mine and own every race. If I could get a scholarship, then I would be one less burden for Dad, for Mom. When I'd been recruited by St. Peter's College, I'd jumped at the opportunity. But as I stood in the rain, staring at the doors of the gym, everything felt too real, and I worried I wouldn't meet everyone's expectations.

I tried to take comfort in my surroundings. Every building on this campus had been created to blend into nature. All dark wood, glass walls, and metal roofs. The square and industrial-looking architecture, instead of being in juxtaposition to the tall trees, flowed seamlessly, fitting neatly next to the lush, green nature surrounding it.

Harnessing my courage, I finally opened the door, giving a few lingering students in the lobby halfhearted smiles. I'd toured the facility during orientation so I knew the weight room was on the third floor. My feet moved with the muscle memory and ascended me each step on shaky legs. I was a pretty chill, laid back, confident guy, for the most part, but I was a part of a competitive college swim team now, and I'd have to show them I had what it took to be a part of their success, and not the one lame duck who would drown them.

The weight room was packed, and as soon as the familiar smell of sweat hit my nose, my nerves faded into my wide smile. I nodded my chin at a few guys as I walked past the weight equipment toward the locker room. Once inside, I found my way to the locker I'd been assigned at orientation and pulled my bag off my shoulder, setting it onto the bench. The pool was housed in another building on the west side of the gym and had its own locker room, too. Both facilities had been recently renovated. Everything was brand new and smelled like cedar instead of dirty socks. Shiny blue and silver lockers, and private shower stalls. This place made my high school look like a dump, and Pioneer Lake High was the nicest school in Salt Lake.

"It's Royal, right?"

The deep voice startled me and I laughed as I turned. "Yeah."

A guy, maybe a little older than me, with dark hair and equally dark eyes peered at me, his lips rising slowly at the corners. "Don't let them see how easy you are to rattle, they'll eat you alive." He chuckled with a smirk as he opened his locker. I stood there feeling like a fish out of water. "Kai Carter," he said and gave me his full attention. "Team Captain."

"Royal O'Connell."

He shook his head. "I know. Fastest freshman ever to swim for St. Peter's." My eyes widened. "Don't look so surprised." He grabbed a pair of headphones out of his locker and shut it with a slam that echoed off the marble tiled floor. "I like to know who I'm swimming with." He held out his right hand and I took it.

His grip was strong, but not stronger than mine. The silence thickened as he assessed whether or not I'd back down, if I belonged here, if I'd fit in. His strong and sharp features softened as he smiled.

"We'll be racing the four-hundred medley relay together," Kai explained as he dropped his hold on my hand.

"Yeah?" My confidence grew about as big as my smile. Uncontainable. This guy looked like he was made for the water, long, powerful arms, broad shoulders, and if Coach paired me with him...

"Freestyle is my thing, but I'm pretty fucking fast on the fly." He nodded his chin. "And this jackass, he swims the fly, as well, but don't worry, you'll swim circles around him."

"You wish, asshole." The voice belonged to another guy, this one much shorter than me, maybe even by three inches. His blond hair was shaved tight to the sides of his head, and buzzed short on the top. His foggy, gray-blue eyes narrowed as he sized me up. "Aren't you the scholarship charity case?"

Kai's shoulders went rigid. "We're lucky to have him, Ellis. Don't forget, you're only a sophomore. Royal, after you've swam here a few years like me, you'll realize the local talent..." Kai took a step toward Ellis. "Isn't all it's cracked up to be." He smirked. "Well, except for me."

Ellis laughed without humor. "You're a townie, Kai. You and this charity case will get along well." His shrewd eyes locked on mine and I clenched my jaw.

This kid had insulted me twice and I'd allowed it. Pride leaked from my skin as it beaded along my brow in the form of cold sweat. I wasn't about to get into a fight and lose my spot on the team. The tension was unbearable. I could almost feel it vibrating between us. I wanted to assure this guy I had no intention of being his verbal punching bag all year. I wanted to shove him in his chest, and make it known he couldn't mess with me, secure my dominance, but Coach's command stifled my chance.

"Let's go, ladies, we don't have all morning."

Ellis snickered as he walked toward the back of the room and I let out a long breath.

"Known him my whole life. Rich little shit, gets everything he wants, but it doesn't matter..." Kai spoke, his eyes on the wall, lost in some thought, some memory I was sure I was eavesdropping on. "You can't buy talent." He cleared his throat, the hard edges evaporating as he looked at me. "Don't worry about Ellis. He's going to pretend his dick is bigger than yours all season until you prove him otherwise. Want to shut him up? Do it in the water. Show him what real ability looks like. Show him what his daddy's money can't buy."

Without another word, Kai walked toward the locker room door, leaving me behind with a lump in my throat and hands that wouldn't stop shaking.

Sunshine spilled through the clouds as my feet hit the pavement outside the gym. Sweat coated my skin, and the cool air prickled the back of my neck. I wasn't more than five paces away before I heard my name.

"Royal... wait up."

Kai jogged toward me, his smile, I'd surmised, was more like a suit of armor. Being part of a family where mental illness was the norm, I'd had to adapt, learn to read moods, people, and Kai wasn't an easy read. I'd met the entire team today and heard a few rumblings about who was who, what events they swam. Who was up to par and who wasn't. Corbin and Max, two juniors Coach had paired me with this morning, had spoken about Kai and how he was shoo-in for captain again next year. Kai was also a junior and one of, if not the best, swimmer on the team. He was a scholarship student like me, and I guess that ruffled some silver-spooned feathers. I had no idea having a scholarship would put a target on my back.

"Hey," Kai said as he came to an abrupt stop in front of me.

"What's up?"

"Listen..." He ran his hand through his hair. "I'm sorry about—"

"Nothing to be sorry for. You're not an asshole."

He chuckled. "According to you."

"Politics. I'll find my way. Rich kids with a chip on their shoulder don't scare me. I'm here to swim and get an education, the rest... it's all bullshit." My words were woven with a concrete foundation and I almost believed them.

"Good. Because Coach wanted you and that's all that matters to me."

A couple of girls walked by. One blonde with long, slender legs poking out of a pair of small gym shorts, the other a redhead with eyes only for Kai.

"Hey, Kai." She practically purred as she strolled by.

"Ladies." Kai's smile turned up a notch, and I choked on a laugh when he swatted the redhead's hip with the gym towel he held in his right hand.

"You owe me for that," the redhead called over her shoulder.

"God, I hope so," he said under his breath, as he tucked the towel into his back pocket. He stared at their retreating figures for a few seconds longer before he asked me, "Hungry?" I laughed and he gave me a goofy smile. "What?"

"You seem to be a popular guy."

"Stick with me, and you'll get laid at least three times a week."

I raised my eyebrows. "You have time to get laid three times a week?"

Swim training was brutal, and if he was a scholarship kid, I bet he had a job, too. I'd always blamed my grueling schedule on why I never had a steady girlfriend. Time was precious, and I'd never found a girl who interested me, who lit me up. I'd been raised by parents who loved each other with every drop of blood in their veins. Anything less than a love like theirs was pointless. I admired my dad and how he and my mother, at times, were one person. I wanted that. Another person to blend with, to become one part of a whole and watch everything snap into place around you. My friend, Natalie, was the closest thing I'd had to a girlfriend. We'd fooled around together, but it was mostly for need and release. She'd been my best friend in high school and understood my crazy life, my family. Nat never wanted more from me and it worked for us.

"At least three times." He shrugged. "Balance, Royal... it's your first year, you'll get it all figured out eventually." He ruffled my hair like I was a freaking five-year-old and I punched his shoulder.

"Dude," I barked, laughing too hard for it to hold much of a bite.

"Can we eat now? I'm starving."

"I'm meeting my sister."

"Off campus?"

"Nah." I tilted my head toward the Beckett House dorms where the main cafeteria was located. "We eat in the dining hall."

"She's a student?" he asked as he started walking again.

I followed alongside him. "Yeah, we're twins."

"No shit? She a swimmer, too?"

"Painter."

"She hot?"

He laughed when I pushed him harder than was necessary, and he stumbled over his own feet. "Don't be a dick."

"I'm messing with you, man. Family... it's off limits... I get it."

"You got a sister?"

He shook his head. "Nope... only child." The silence expanded for a few steps and he drew in a deep breath before he said, "Which makes having a roommate even shittier."

"I thought all athletes got singles?"

"Wasn't sure I was coming back." His dark eyes fell to the sidewalk. "By the time my paperwork went through, all the singles were filled. I'm in Garrison Hall with a goddamn music major. The guy hides in his room like a hermit all day playing the piano. I've only seen him once and that was on move-in day, and you know what he said to me?" His brown eyes cleared as his smile reached and touched the corners of his lashes. He spoke with an uptight and proper sounding tone. "'You're going to want to purchase some ear plugs.'"

My head tipped back as I laughed. "At least he was honest."

"Asshole."

I gave him a wounded look as I raised my hand to my heart.

We both laughed as he twisted my words right back at me. "At least I'm being honest."

The cafeteria was brimming with students by the time we got there. The scent of bacon and coffee greeted us as we entered through the glass doors. Like most of the other buildings at St. Peter's, the cafeteria, too, was shaped from hardwood beams, and bright, open spaces. I scanned the room and found Indie in the same seats we'd acquired on day one.

"That's my sister, Indie," I said and waved when her eyes met mine.

It was a sense of relief, seeing her sitting there, her usual small smile bringing me back home. Everything Ellis had said, I hadn't realized how much it had affected me until one look from her washed it all away. People have said twins have some higher sense of being, a deeper connection, and I'd have to agree. She mitigated my mood, and I'd like to think I'd always done the same for her. Some days, though, she'd get lost to the ghosts in her head, and I hated that she'd had to find her own way out, her own way home.

"I grabbed you a coffee," she said as we approached the large, circular table. Her light eyes bounced back and forth between me and Kai.

"Have I told you how awesome you are?"

"Not today."

Indie's smile turned shy, and I was about to introduce her to Kai when he interrupted me, "Hey, man, I forgot I have somewhere to be this morning. I'm gonna grab some grub and go." His eyes lingered on my sister for an awkward second before he clipped me on the shoulder with his knuckles. "Look me up in the directory, a few of us are going down to that shithole bar off Beech Street tonight, you should come."

"I don't have ID."

"Good thing they don't check." He grinned as he took a few steps backward. "Call me, or meet us at Stacks at ten."

Kai glanced at Indie before he turned to leave, and the confident smile he'd worn so well all morning had fallen a little at the corners.

Camden

The fast pace of clicking heels on the cement, the way the tree branches creaked and groaned in the roaring rush of wind, a high-pitched squeal as the clouds opened, weeping fat drops of rain around me, around them. The world laughed and screamed, running for cover as I walked slowly with my head down listening, to the symphony surrounding me. Where most college kids travelled across campus lost inside a conversation, or the latest pop culture hit on their headphones, I listened to the loner's soundtrack, the weird renditions of the campus pulse. Everything, *everyone* had a unique sound—a certain cadence or resonance. And it was sad and beautiful and secret.

It was mine.

I ignored the tickle of sweat and rain as it dripped down the back of my neck, under the thin, hooded shirt that did little to keep the weather from my skin. The cotton had clung to my shoulders by the time I found myself walking through the front doors of Garrison Hall. My anxiety peaked as I entered the small vacuum of silence between the front door and the main door that led to the lobby. A small antechamber, a security measure. You had to have a key or a code to get into any dormitory at St. Peter's College, but the tiny vestibule between the outside and the inside, I guessed, was a way to let you find your way in without standing in the elements. An inaudible nostalgia squeezed my throat, and I purposely clanged the brass of my keys together as I pulled them from my pocket.

Once inside, I could breathe again. Breathe the stale pizza and hear the heady hum of voices hiving their way through the walls. My heart found its beat again, and I found the tune I'd listen to as I made my way to my room. One of the residents, a senior, I think, greeted me from the front desk with a smile. The corners of my lips twitched with effort, and when the man's smile twisted into a smirk, I recognized him from last year.

"What's up, Cam," he said holding his hand up for a high-five.

I stopped and stared at his palm, unable to remember his name. My fingers clenched the straps of my backpack. Most people never talked to me, I was merely a piece of furniture to move around. I did my thing, they did theirs. It wasn't abnormal for me to go days without speaking. Music was my language and most people didn't speak it.

He chuckled and lowered his hand as he shook his head, drawing his voice down to a whisper. "I'm an RA this year… so… if you need help sneaking in the ladies, I'm your guy."

For the second time today, the sharp pinch of anxiety dug its nails into my spine. His smile waned as I stood stock-still. Most guys would have laughed, or punched him in the shoulder with a spirited "hell yeah," but like I'd said, I wasn't normal. I didn't have friends. I loved my solitude and how it heightened my ability to hear things others could not. Call me crazy, but I *liked* going to class. I hated coffee and television. I loathed sports and beer, and as a sophomore, I'd never once been on a date. Tom… or maybe his name was Mike, stared at me, waiting for the typical reaction I'd never give him.

I managed a swallow, but my sandpaper-dry tongue would not move.

He backed away as he said with a grim smile, "I see you're still as talkative as ever."

I shifted the weight of my bag, and turned toward the stairs. I let the white noise fill my head as I climbed the steps. I hit rewind and started the last few minutes over, queuing into the background notes that followed me to the third floor. I pretended it didn't bother me, that my inability to fit in, to have a simple fucking conversation, was the last thing I needed to worry about. I didn't need friends to be the best pianist I could be. I didn't need relationships to hold my hand and make me feel good about myself.

I'd been playing the piano since I was three years old. Raised by a mother who sounded like Beethoven's *Symphony No. 5*, powerful and dominating, while my father was more like a Chopin Nocturne, sleepy and unwilling to rise to the occasion. I'd been groomed to become something worth talking about at the PTA. Talent and spectacle. Love was given at the end of the performance with soft applause and a pat on the shoulder. Every step I took was written on sheet music, and my parents, they held the pencil.

My mood was as dark as my dorm room as I let my keys fall with a furious thud onto the table by the door. I exhaled, another attempt to steal away the muted moment, and switched on the light. A soft yellow glow spread across the small living room I shared with another student. Last year I was lucky enough to have a suitemate who was never home, and I hoped for the best this year. But I realized quickly that my luck had run out. We'd only moved in a couple of weeks ago, but you'd think Kai, my suitemate, had lived here over the summer. I'd barely set up my keyboard when he strolled in like he owned the place. He was the typical jock with a penchant for competition. His smile was practiced, but if you listened closely enough, his bravado sounded more like a chip on his shoulder.

If it was possible, I would have packed my stuff and moved out the night I'd walked in on him and some redhead making out on my couch. My scholarship only covered so much, and my parents sure as hell wouldn't give me a penny to live off-campus, not like I'd take their money anyway. I made my own plan. It was the only way I'd ever be able to live my own life.

That next morning, I'd enlisted the rules. No girls and no parties.

Kai had laughed at me, gently shoved my shoulder and said, "How about no girls in the living room, and if I promise to never have more than three friends over at a time for beers, I'll buy those ear plugs you told me to get on move-in day and stop whining about your classical shit."

My classical shit. The guy was a real lyricist.

Kai lived up to his word. He wasn't home much. His job and training schedule kept him busy and, I held hope, once the swim season actually started, I'd have the place practically to myself. A rare smile formed on my lips as I dropped my bag onto the floor and grabbed a bottle of water from the small fridge I'd shoved under my desk to give myself more room. My bedroom consisted of an uncomfortable mattress, held up by a noisy metal frame, a wooden work desk, bedside table, and my keyboard. The fingers of my free hand pressed down onto the cool keys. They moved in a fluid sequence, drawing out a scale to hang in the air as I wished for the baby grand piano I had at home. As if my thoughts were capable of reaching great distance, like ghosts communicating to the dead, my phone vibrated in my pocket.

A call from my mother.

I unlocked the screen and refused the call. She didn't wait more than four seconds, and again, the phone came to life within my hand. I set my water on the desk, gritting my jaw.

I answered with a sharp, "Hello."

It had been forty-eight hours since I'd heard my own voice.

"Your father and I were disappointed you never called." My mother's tone was weaved with threat and thunder. Proper and cold, it set my teeth on edge. "Are you settled?"

I wanted to crush the phone in my hand. The words *disappointed* and *settled* hollowed my stomach, eating through me like termites in a sweetly aged piece of wood.

"School started three weeks ago," I answered with as little feeling as possible.

One thing I'd learned, being raised by a mother who was a psychiatrist, feelings, emotions, they were weapons she'd use against you. Evidence for all the things you hated about yourself. Proof that you were twisted—that you were wrong. And who you had become ruined any hope for what she'd wanted you to be.

I heard the whoosh of her breath as she exhaled and the sound soothed me. Not because it was her breath, a mother's "concerned" attempt to calm her worry, but because it was better than the intermittent silence she'd punished me with since I was sixteen years old.

"When is your first performance?" she asked.

"October tenth."

"We'll be in Bali."

"Maybe next time then?" I offered, but didn't actually mean.

She hummed into the phone. "Possibly..." It was faint, but I heard her hesitation. "It's so quiet without you here."

Melancholy, strung together in six notes, and I wondered how I'd never heard her sing this song before.

A lump of heat lodged itself inside my throat at the pure quality of her tone. "Your father is restless at night without your playing." Again, the harsh sound of a swallow.

I wanted badly to ask her if she meant what she'd said, if this was some manipulation to make me feel guilty for the impenetrable wall between us, but the front door of the suite opened.

"I have to go."

My gaze lingered on the phone in my hand for only a moment, unanswered questions danced in my head as laughter spilled through the apartment. The smell of fried food drifted in from the living room, carrying with it an unfamiliar voice. I took a tentative step toward my door, the low harmony drawing me to the threshold. I slipped my phone into my pocket and gripped the wood of the door as if to shut it, but his rich and warm timbre wrapped around me like a blanket. The phone call from my mother now a forgotten riddle I'd work out later against the keys.

It was Kai I noticed first, his large body blocking the view of the couch as he set his open container of Chinese food onto the coffee table. I was inching my door shut, curious, but still not willing to engage in conversation, when Kai finally moved. Golden blond hair, wet with rain, fell across the stranger's forehead in a way that had my fingertips itching to move the wayward mop so I could see his eyes. His long arm draped over the back of the couch with ease, comfortable in his own skin. His confidence played like a Gershwin piece as his full lips spread into a crooked smile, and I wanted to hold my breath, make it easier for me to hear him over the rapid beat of my heart. Keen, bottomless, blue eyes, collided with mine, and I let a few perfect seconds scatter and unfurl, his gaze holding mine as I closed the door.

Royal

"That was weird."

"What?" Kai asked, but it sounded more like "Waah" as he shoveled chicken lo mein into his mouth.

My gaze hesitated on the closed door. "Your roommate, he was staring at us."

Kai flopped down next to me on the couch, kicking his feet onto the coffee table.

"I don't even try to understand that guy. Camden's probably a freaking serial killer. I check our freezer for frozen body parts every afternoon."

I laughed. "You don't have a freezer."

"It's proverbial."

"Do you even know what that word means?" My grin held no mercy as it spread across my face and he shrugged. "You're an idiot." I laughed, and he gave me a goofy smile, loading his fork full of noodles.

"On my best days."

I slowly brought my attention back to the door, half expecting to find the same pair of intense, gray-green eyes staring back at me again. "You said he plays the piano?"

Kai groaned. "That's all he does. It's why I never chill here. I can only handle so much moody bullshit in a twenty-four-hour period."

I chuckled. "I actually like the piano. I listen to it at work or when I'm studying."

I caught Kai mid eye-roll as I turned to look at him. "Of course, you do."

My head tilted to the side as my brows furrowed. "What the hell is that supposed to mean?"

"Nothing."

It didn't matter he was the only real friend I'd made since school had started, the superior attitude, that smirk, and whatever assumption he was making pissed me off. "Asshole."

Kai's smile turned repentant. "I didn't mean anything by it... You're... you..." He sighed and let his fork fall into the to-go container in his lap. "You never go out with us, you're always with your sister, or in the library—"

"I work in the library."

"Don't act like you don't like working in the library, dude."

"So, what if I do?"

Kai's eyes darted to the door of his roommate and then back to me.

"Aww, man... I am nothing like—"

"Just saying, you're a step up from serial killer." Kai pressed his lips together, and for two seconds, I was incredulous.

He was lucky, though, I wasn't good at holding grudges, and as he barked with laughter, I found myself falling right along with him. My hand clutched the stitch in my side. Breathless, I muttered a curse and punched his shoulder.

Kai's lips spread into a devious smile. "Come with us to Stacks tonight."

"Can't. I have to work."

"Doesn't the library close at eleven?" he asked as he stood from the couch.

I stood, too, as I reminded him, "Yeah, but we both have weight training at five-thirty in the morning tomorrow."

With a nonchalant raise of his shoulders, he threw his garbage into the trash can near the small entertainment center. "Think about it, you don't have to drink, but you should get to know the team. They're decent guys, most of them."

"I'll think about it."

"Come for one hour, I'll let you use my employee discount."

"Maybe I'll ask Indie to tag along."

He raised his eyebrows. "You want to bring your sister to a bar with a bunch of drunk jocks?"

He had a point.

I chuckled as I said, "Yeah, bad idea."

"The worst." He shook his head. "Come on, Royal, it's only one hour, no big deal. Make an appearance. You're the new guy, they want to know you."

I loved being part of a team, but I was used to spending my time with my sister. She was my best friend, and beyond meals at Beckett House, I'd hardly seen her since school had started. Being apart, it was an adjustment. It wasn't normal to want to be with your sister all the time, but I worried about her. I worried if she was making friends or hiding like a recluse in the studio.

I gave in with a sigh. "One hour."

"Yes." He drew out the word. "I have to meet Corbin near Beckett, I'll walk with you. Just need to take a piss. Wait for me?"

"Sure."

Kai disappeared into the bathroom, and as the door shut behind him, the silent apartment filled with soft and haunting notes. I stared at Camden's door, my eager ears straining to hear. I didn't recognize the song, but it knew me, pulled me, with quiet steps closer to the unique sound. The music was lazy, at first, and under the surface, I could feel the build as each note became more powerful. I didn't know much about music, only my favorite parts, and as the notes soared higher, they reached that peak of perfection. I absentmindedly placed my palm on the cool wood of the door, seeking a connection to the sound. My lips parted into a smile as the music suddenly turned sweet and low. Completely distracted, like I'd get sometimes when I was listening to music while I studied, I'd almost missed the loud flush of the toilet. My hand fell quickly from Camden's door and I took a step backward.

Kai flicked his gaze to his roommate's door when he emerged from the bathroom, an air of annoyance pulling his lips into a scowl as the song I'd been eavesdropping on ended.

Disappointed, I asked, "Ready to head out?"

He nodded, and I grabbed my bag from the floor by the couch. Another song began to filter through the room, and I stole a glance toward Camden's room, wishing instead that I could stay and listen.

Lost to the music playing in my ears and to the scent of old paper pulling into my lungs, I was able to sort through the thoughts in my head as I shelved the remaining books on my cart. I balanced a full-time schedule of classes, mostly general courses, and a few prerequisites I'd have to fulfill if I indeed decided to take the social work route like I'd wanted to. Indie and I hadn't necessarily gotten into a fight about it at dinner tonight, but she'd stubbornly maintained I'd chosen social work because of her, instead of "following my heart" with a major in English. She didn't understand, and I'd never outright call her selfish, but I might've slipped up tonight and told her everything didn't revolve around her. After the words had left my mouth, she clammed up and made her escape, claiming she had to work on a big project for her sculpture class.

I liked books. I liked words, but I was a voyeur. A reader, not a writer. It was a hobby. I'd never been able to master words like she had with paint. I wanted to be a therapist because I liked helping people. The past two summers I'd volunteered at the women's shelter my aunt owned, offering some of the residents free swim lessons for their kids. Working there, I realized how much I loved giving those kids a break from the grim realities of their lives. Homeless, abused, depressed—most people ran from them—I was drawn to them. Indie and my father sharing the same mental illness, I conceded, might have driven me in one direction, but I embraced it because I loved it. I loved being someone to somebody, being a length of rope to hold, or a wall to lean on. Feeling needed, doing, instead of watching.

Thinking about it all over again, I pulled my phone from my pocket and paused the music app. I typed out a quick text.

Me: My twin senses are tingling.

Indie: I'm fine.

Me: I'm sorry.

Indie: For what?

Me: You're not selfish.

Several long seconds ticked by as I stared at my phone.

Indie: Neither are you, it's why you'll make an amazing therapist.

She'd dropped a white flag and I smiled.

Me: I'm going out with a few of the guys on the team after work, text me if you need me to walk you home from the studio.

Indie: I will.

She wouldn't

Me: You promise?

Indie: Have fun tonight.

My laughter at her blatant display of avoidance was cut short as I looked up from the screen, sucking in a breath, I almost dropped my phone. Kai's roommate was right in front of my shelving cart, staring at me.

"Shit, you scared me," I said in a rushed whisper and removed my earbuds. It took me a second longer than it should have to recognize him. I'd only seen him the one time today, through a crack in a door. But those gray-green eyes were unforgettable. I chuckled, feeling a little unnerved as I fumbled my words. "I know you... well, I don't know you, know you... I mean... I saw you..." The valley between his brows deepened. "Today..." I laughed again despite the way my stomach flipped. His face was a sharp, stone mask, and to my chagrin, he seemed a bit bored. "You're Kai's roommate... Camden..." I offered him my right hand. "I'm Royal, I'm on the swim team with Kai."

His gaze moved from my right hand to my left where my headphones dangled around my fingers and cell phone.

"What are you listening to?" he asked.

Camden's voice was graveled and unsure, sleepy and deep as if he'd just woken up from a nap or hadn't spoken in a while. I tried not to be offended by the way he'd left my greeting hanging in the empty space between us.

I lowered my right hand and slipped it into my pocket. "A playlist. My sister put it together. She has a thing for cover songs, mostly stuff from the eighties, but..." An anxious smile spread across my lips as I realized I was rambling. He made me nervous. "It's just a playlist," I repeated. "Piano cover songs."

Camden's eyes met mine and his Adam's apple bobbed. "Piano?"

"Yeah." My pulse quickened as his pale eyes assessed me, and I blurted out the first thing that popped into my head. "I heard you play today..." His cheeks and neck flushed with color. Confused by his reaction, I worried I'd embarrassed him. I pulled my hand from my pocket and rubbed the back of my neck as I lowered my eyes to the cart of books at my side. Color flooded my own cheeks as I admitted, "It was the best thing I've ever heard."

When he didn't say thank you, or offer any sort of proof he'd heard the compliment at all, I looked up. Warmth filled my chest as I took in the faint smile tilting the right corner of his mouth. My eyes drifted over the curve of his bottom lip, witnessing what I was sure had to be a rare and beautiful thing. It lasted only five, maybe six seconds, before the hard line of his jaw clenched.

Still water, lake-gray eyes refused to connect with mine and the air stirred with a sad familiarity. Like my twin, he was screaming inside that head of his, I could feel it. I couldn't force him to tell me what his voices were saying like I did with Indie. I didn't know him, but I wanted to. Strange as he was, I didn't care. My entire family was unusual. Peculiar. An atypical—anomaly. It made sense that he also intrigued me.

Hello, there.

Like... meet like.

He swallowed, and the rich sound of his voice settled itself inside my chest as he said, "I'm looking for *Leaves of Grass*, the lady at the desk said it was being shelved."

I rapped my knuckles on the dingy looking brown leather copy of Walt Whitman's classic before I lifted it from the cart and handed it to him. "I love this book."

Camden's flat expression pinched, and I almost laughed at his irritated tone as he said, "I have to read it for a class."

"Not a fan of reading?"

"I'd rather play music."

"Fair enough."

I let the silence stretch, waiting for him to elaborate, but he never did. Awkward, he simply lowered his chin and turned, leaving me, a little bewildered, watching his tall, broad form fill the space between the narrow stacks as he retreated.

Royal

The light in the library was too low, and the soft tap—tap—tap of my sister's pencil against the desk made it difficult to keep my eyes open. My heavy lids fluttered in fifteen-second intervals, and I was about to doze off when my stomach growled.

"Hungry?" Indie giggled, and I sat up straight, giving her a rueful smile.

Lifting my arms over my head, I stretched, arching my back with a yawn. My muscles ached as they pulled past their desired flexibility, but I groaned with a weary satisfaction. "Shit, I'm tired."

Indie shook her head. "You have no one to blame, Blue, but—"

"Myself, yeah... yeah."

I crumpled the outline I'd been working on into a small weapon and threw it across the table with a chuckle. It didn't make it very far, rolling to a stop at the edge of Indie's textbook.

"Did you have fun, at least?" she asked as she unrolled the bunched piece of paper, spreading it out in front of her.

I smiled as I watched her read the five sentences I'd managed since we'd gotten to the library.

"I don't know if fun is the right word... it's always... educational."

She lifted her eyes from my outline. "Educational?"

I ran my hand through my hair and leaned my chair back onto its two legs. "I don't know. It doesn't really feel like my scene, I guess. The guys on my team are cool, but besides Ellis—"

"We hate Ellis Weston, right?"

I huffed out a laugh. "He's irrationally unlikable."

Her mouth curled into a smile and I couldn't help but mirror it. I'd missed this. I couldn't believe it was already October, the swim season was about to start, and I was already feeling disconnected and exhausted. I'd hardly had a moment to breathe since we arrived at St. Peter's in August. My mornings and evenings were dedicated to swimming. Depending on the day, I was either in the pool or at the gym or both. My days were filled with classes and the ongoing struggle to keep my eyes open. Indie was right, these last few weeks had begun to blur together, and I had no one to blame but myself. I was overwhelmed, inundated—swamped by my one-man circus. Instead of taking time to myself, I divided my nights between the library and spending time with Kai and the guys, trying hard to find where I fit in with the team. The only thing I really looked forward to lately, besides time with my sister, were the afternoons I'd found myself sitting on Kai's couch, listening to his suitemate play the piano. Camden was a mysterious enigma hidden behind wood and sound. The music always floated through his shut door and snuck through the air like a ghost. Being there, feeling present, it had become the only time of the day I actually felt peaceful, felt at ease in my own skin. His music was haunting and beautiful, and I couldn't deny the fact it was why I'd preferred Kai's place to my own private dorm. I hadn't seen Camden again after the night he'd borrowed *Leaves of Grass* from the library, but in some weird way, it was like I'd gotten to know him through his music.

"Besides Ellis..." she prompted, pulling me from the menagerie of thoughts in my head.

A small sigh escaped past my lips. "I'm the only freshman. It's like I'm naïve or too young, and I feel like I'm on the outside looking in. I'm a part of the team, but it feels like by default. They're established, most of them have been swimming together for a couple of years. Fitting in, it's not worth staying up till two in the morning, pushing through training like a zombie."

"You've never had a problem fitting in."

"Maybe *problem* isn't the right word either." I exhaled and she laughed.

"You're struggling today..." Indie paused, hesitant to ask her next question. "What about Kai?"

"What about him?"

"You guys are always together."

"I like Kai. He seems to have it all balanced, but I don't want to party and hook-up with girls every night either. I'm here to actually learn, and swimming is a means to an end, not the end all-be all of me."

She slid my nearly ruined homework assignment across the desk, and I picked it up, reading the bold letters scrolled across the top to myself.

In five-hundred words, explain the difference between post-adolescence and maturity.

"I think you just figured out what to write for your essay." Indie's smile reached her eyes, and the pale color of her irises deepened to a rich, ocean blue.

"Feeling smug?" I asked and she shrugged. I leaned forward and poked her math book with my pencil. "Not like you've gotten much work done either."

She exhaled a long breath, and the blonde wisps of hair covering her forehead shifted. "I hate math."

"Missing Mom?" I asked, knowing the answer already.

"She's so good at this. I swear all I got from her was the color of my eyes." Indie's smile faded into a flat line and her eyes lost focus.

"Hey..." I lightly tapped her foot with mine under the table. "Don't forget about the talent you inherited. It skipped me... And besides, you got all the best parts of Dad. All I got was his good looks."

A lazy grin tugged at the corner of her lips as she idly played with the end of her side braid. Her soft laughter faded, and her eyebrows lifted in surprise as she stared over my shoulder and said, "Hi."

Puzzled, I turned to see who was behind me. Camden stood next to the nearest aisle, staring at us, his hands white knuckled around the straps of his backpack.

"Long time, no see," I teased, but he stood there like I hadn't spoken a word.

"Aren't you in my art history class?" Indie asked as a smile of recognition grew across her face.

"You guys know each other?"

"I wouldn't qualify sitting across a classroom from another person as actually knowing someone." Camden's deep, scratchy voice surprised me. Was that sarcasm?

By the slight upturn of his cheek, I might've thought he'd made a joke. I liked how the faint smile softened his features, made him seem almost vulnerable. His jaw pulsed and my eyes fell to his mouth as he wet his dry lips. I wondered if that had been the first thing he'd said all day.

"How do you guys know each other?" Indie's question pulled me from my thoughts, and I noticed he was just as preoccupied with me as I was with him.

I blinked twice, finding my voice. "He's Kai's suitemate. We only met once... well... twice. Kind of." My lips spread into a genuine smile as I allowed my eyes to fix on his. "Camden is a piano genius."

"Prodigy," he corrected and Indie laughed.

"Uh-oh, don't insult my brother's word choices... it will only make him try harder to one-up you next time."

"Genius, prodigy, phenomenon—savant..." I smirked. "Consider yourself one up-ed."

Indie threw her pencil at me and I dodged it in time, letting it fall to the floor. Camden bent down and picked it up. He rolled it between his thumb and forefinger, as if he was cataloging the feel of it. His long fingers held the pencil captive and I tried, unsuccessfully, to pry my eyes away from the motion. His hands were instruments, just as my legs and arms were. He created music and I bent water. We were talent in all its forms wrapped inside flesh and bone.

A few seconds passed before he handed me the pencil. The air around us thinned as he reached for me. My heart sprinted inside my chest and I didn't understand why. Camden's thumb grazed mine, and a visceral heat filled my stomach, a fluttered feeling invaded my space, taking over my ability to feel anything but jittery. Gray-green eyes stirred a swarm of butterflies inside my stomach.

What the hell?

It was like I was attracted to him.

Was I attracted to him?

His scent weaved its way into my lungs, clean and...

Holy shit.

I was attracted to him.

I was attracted to *him*.

He was tall, and I liked that his shoulders were proud, even if he seemed to hide behind them. I liked the strict line of his nose, and how those ghostly gray eyes made me forget every word I'd ever collected. If breathing was a race, I was winning it. Every lungful of air I took came faster than the last. Was I seriously checking out my best friend's roommate right now? A guy. Maybe I was more tired than I'd realized. Or maybe it was just an admiration thing, his music had been my only saving grace this past month. That had to be it...

"See what I mean..." Indie, clueless to my internal crisis at the moment, continued, "He always has to have the last word. He's a word connoisseur."

I made myself laugh, dragging my eyes to the wrinkled piece of paper on my desk. The awkward tension palpable. Could he feel it, or was I going insane? The last and only conversation I'd ever had with him, that night when I was at work, ran through my head. I'd stumbled over my own tongue like an idiot. I was sorting through my revelation when my stomach growled again. Indie shut her textbook and started to gather her things.

"Where are you going?" I asked, my voice more alarmed than I intended.

She frowned, sensing my mood. When it came to Indie, it was impossible to hide what I felt. She knew me better than anyone. "It's getting late. We should get something to eat before your stomach eats itself."

"Kai wants me to stop by, go over the schedule for our first meet."

"Eat first." Indie's Mom voice was in vain.

"Kai's grabbing Chinese. You should come."

Her gaze bounced between Camden and me as if deciding something. She allowed several seconds to tick by before she answered, "I can't, I have—"

"To go to the studio..." I finished for her as I grabbed my pencil and incomplete assignment, tossing them into my bag. "Come on, Pink."

"I have to finish this piece by next week." She slipped her phone into the pocket of her jeans, giving me a small smile, and I shouldered my bag. "I'll see you at breakfast?" I nodded. "It was good to see you, Camden."

"Indie—"

"I'll text you when I get home," she cut me off with a roll of her eyes.

"Is she older or younger than you?" Camden asked as we watched Indie leave through the front doors.

"Twins."

The flame ignited again as I gave him my full attention, and as unsettling as it was, it wasn't a negative feeling. Bemused. Befuddled. Shocked. I'd never looked at a man like this, with something hot growing underneath my skin. And in truth, not even with Natalie, had I ever experienced such a natural attraction. Camden's soulful silence had to be the appeal, at least, that was what made the most sense. I wasn't a person who lived inside the four corners of a box, but it was hard to wrap my head around the fact I was curious about him in ways that didn't just involve his music or what he was thinking. And I couldn't explain the questions popping up like little worm holes inside my brain. I wanted to know what his hands felt like. If his lips were rough or soft. What would the hard planes of his chest feel like under my palms? Would I even know what to do if I had the chance to answer any of this level of crazy?

I was in the middle of debating the merit of why it mattered, if I'd be picking apart my feelings if I'd met some hot girl last night at the bar, when Camden mumbled, "See you around."

He'd slipped back into his mask of indifference, his eyes to the floor as he began to walk away. All the crap in my head could wait, and besides, it was a moot point anyway. Camden was most definitely not attracted to me.

"Hey," I said a little too loudly, and one of the ladies I work with shushed me from behind the reference desk. I chuckled, and that smell of soap and spice and something I couldn't decipher pooled around me as I fell into step next to him. "I'm headed to your place, if you're headed there, I'll walk with you."

He didn't give me an answer or object, in fact, he didn't say yes either, but it was the way his posture changed that made me think he didn't mind my company. Camden's shoulders broadened, the tight grip he had on his bag relaxed, and he let his arms fall to his sides. For a moment, he didn't look like, as Kai would say, a reclusive serial killer. He looked like a normal guy, walking with his friend across campus. Friends.

I could handle that.

Camden

One... two, three... four. One... two, three... four. Royal's steps had a rhythm. On every other step, along the concrete sidewalk, the sole of his shoes dragged. I tried not to listen to him. I wasn't ready to categorize all of his sounds. He was different than most people. Most people were loud and predictable. Big bass with brass-trumpeted laughter. But Royal, he was too many instruments all in one, too many intricate notes, and I needed more time to hear each one.

The smell of his detergent tickled my nose and made the tips of my fingers tingle. He was talking about something, but I'd become distracted by the soft cadenced sound of the way he moved. Royal's long limbs cut the air, dispersing the space around him, fluid and elegant. The sun dipped his hair in gold, and I'd noticed his jaw and chin were smattered with the same hue. Wanting stitched itself inside me. I forced my eyes down to the damp ground, unwilling the allowance of one more look.

"It's hard for most people to understand, I think," he said, and the smile in his tone lifted my eyes.

He smiled from the inside out. I'd heard that smile in his voice, every time he was at the dorm, when I'd take a break from preparing for my recital, and his words had drifted under my door. In general, I avoided eye contact. There was something too personal about another person's eyes. They held too many secrets for casual, social interactions. I couldn't keep my eyes off of his, though. Pale blue, lined with silver, crystal clear and open. I'd wanted to see them, every day since the first time, but I'd spent too long behind closed doors to give in to the temptation.

Royal held my gaze as he chuckled. "It's weird, right?" he asked.

I had no idea what he was talking about and went with the safest option possible. A noncommittal shrug of the shoulders.

"Indie and I are close, always have been. I'm protective of her, I guess," he explained, letting those open, honest eyes map my features.

"That's not weird." Protecting your family was admirable. "I don't have any siblings."

I'd like to think if I did, I'd do what I could to protect them. At least, that was what I thought family was supposed to do. A family was made to make you feel safe, loved, accepted. The definition was concrete, but sometimes I struggled to remember not everything was so black and white. Gray Area. Two words that made the world stranger and even more difficult to navigate in my

45

day to day. My parents were a perfect example of said gray area. They didn't love *me*, or keep me safe, they only protected my talent. If they could bleed music from my veins, they would.

Royal turned his head, bringing his gaze to the nonexistent horizon. Thoughtful, he whispered, "You kind of remind me of her."

My lips fought to rise at the corners. "I do?"

"She doesn't talk too much, and neither do you... I talk too much."

"You do."

His laugh was deep, like a bow stretching across the strings of a cello. "Adding honesty to your list of qualities."

"You're making a list?" I asked.

"Yup."

I chanced another look in his direction and was rewarded with blush-dusted cheeks that pulled into a dimple on the left side. It seemed perfect that Royal's teeth were slightly crooked. That asymmetric smile lit my stomach. The flame it created hollowed me out. The dormant thing, the thing I'd been warned to keep quiet, to keep still, since I was sixteen years old, awoke with a vengeance. Royal had made it impossible for me to silence everything I'd been told. *Don't look at him like that. He's not for you. It's sick. It's wrong. You're wrong. It's perverse.* But, looking at Royal changed the way I heard their words. The moment I'd seen him from behind the small crack in my bedroom door, something inside me finally began to breathe again. Every toxic insult my parents once spewed had soured. Fallen flat as it passed my lips in a long exhale, and all I wanted, after that first sip of air was to keep breathing. Even if it meant torturing myself.

I hadn't intended to go to the library at all today. I had no reason to be there. I could've lied to myself. Made excuses. Any college student, on any given day, could stop by the library to study, grab a book, steal a bit of needed quiet. These all seemed like reasonable justifications, but I wasn't one to indulge in magical thinking. I'd gone there because of him. Once I'd found Royal sitting a few steps away from the front desk, everything I'd tried to manipulate myself into believing had seemed childish. I'd decided in those five seconds, when I'd thought the girl sitting across from him was his girlfriend, and despite the nauseous feeling that had crept its way up my throat, not knowing him was worse than knowing him.

"What's on the list so far?"

He shook his head, the tan of his cheeks deepening into red. The bright smile he'd slipped on morphed into a shy grin. "You're quiet... a piano *genius*..." He emphasized the word and I laughed.

Royal paused, the rhythmic pace he'd kept stumbled and he stared at my mouth. Blood thundered its way to my heart as his light eyes lingered over my smile.

He cleared his throat, the open feel of his irises darkened, and he continued, "Piano genius. Quiet... sarcastic."

"I've never really understood the need for sarcasm."

"Blunt." He chuckled again, and the urge to bump my shoulder into his became unbearable.

The late afternoon sun glared off the glass windows of Garrison Hall as we approached, and the sharp light pulled me back to reality. I gripped the straps of my backpack, Royal's laughter on a loop inside my head as I opened the first set of doors to the dormitory. He followed behind, but before I could pull my key, a couple of guys barreled through the second set of doors. One of them high-fived Royal, the other frowned at him. They both ignored me.

"Kai making you go over all the rules, too?" the dark-haired one asked.

I didn't wait for Royal's answer, assuming he'd follow behind me at some point, I moved through the overwhelmingly tight space of the antechamber and headed toward my suite. There was always a wall. Me and them. It had been that way since I could remember. I'd never understood my peers, not even as a little boy. My first real memory was the day I'd started kindergarten. All the boys had been covered in Kool-Aid grins, and rolled their R's. I'd hated textures and loud noises. They'd wanted to pick up crickets at recess. I'd wanted to sit under a tree alone and listen to the way the wind howled as it blew through the tunnel of the slide on the playground.

Back then, my parents celebrated my diversity.

I was different.

I was special.

I was talented.

Praise, over time, turned to expectation, and after I'd asked my mom why I preferred boys to girls, pride turned to embarrassment. It hadn't been a real coming out, more of a need for information. After that summer, I never spoke of it again, and my parents, they barely spoke to me.

"Wait up." Royal's request echoed down the long hall, but I ignored it.

I didn't turn to see how close he was as I walked inside the suite, leaving the door open behind me.

"So, we're just leaving the door wide open now?" Kai asked as I walked by the couch.

He sat up and ran his hand through his hair, scowling like the archetypal old man who yells at small children, "Get off my lawn." I could feel his glare burning my back as I made my way into my room. Once the door was shut behind me, I exhaled a shaky breath.

Too much. Today was too much.

I scrubbed my palm down my face and took stock of my appearance in the small mirror hanging on the wall. I was still me. Tall. Dark hair. Greenish eyes. Fair skin. Flesh and bone. Body and mind. Holding my hands out in front of me, I marveled at how they shook.

Definitely too much.

He's not made for you.

My eyes eventually found their way home to the keyboard against the wall. My feet pulled me there in three easy steps. My hands, with a mind of their own, switched it on. My fingers, plagued by the need to touch something, pressed down onto the ivory. I closed my eyes and ran a few scales before falling into one of my favorite songs. I hadn't been playing more than five minutes when two soft knocks sounded against my door.

The room went silent except for the loud thud-thud of my heart.

"Kai ordered enough food to feed the entirety of Garrison." Royal's voice held humor, and I permitted myself a smile, picturing how his full lips might have formed into a lopsided grin behind the confines of my bedroom door.

The wall, it was always present.

It protected me. My bedroom door was no different.

"Leave it, dude," Kai clipped. "Once he's in there, he'll never come out."

Kai's accusation created a drumroll under my skin and I turned toward the keyboard again. I raised my fingers to the keys, but the dare in my pulse made it difficult for me to hear all the reasons why I shouldn't want to have dinner with them. Turning off my keyboard, I made a choice.

The fried, salty smell of takeout surrounded me as I opened the door.

Royal's hair, without the natural light, darkened into a resonant caramel. The sun-bleached tips fell over his forehead, long enough that they touched his brows as he raised them.

His smirk was triumphant as he spoke. "The list keeps getting longer."

"What list?"

"Your list."

Something like a smile crept across my face.

"You're surprising."

"Surprising?"

He nodded, and I liked the smug set of his shoulders.

"I'm the exact opposite of surprising."

"I'll agree to disagree."

Royal was a pickpocket, stealing another laugh from me and smiling like he'd finally found what he'd been looking for.

"You like Chinese?" he asked.

"Not really."

"Good. Me either." He chuckled as he turned toward Kai and the stack of Styrofoam boxes towering on the coffee table. "I always order sweet and sour chicken. It's the safest thing on the menu."

Kai stared at us like he was witnessing the Second Coming, looting the privacy from the moment. The smile on my face disappeared, but I followed Royal anyway.

Royal

When I was little, about four or five years old, I used to do whatever I could to make my family laugh. I was pretty sure I'd run through the loft naked on more than one occasion. But as I matured, my antics for attention had simmered. I could remember spending most of my afternoons on the floor of my family's art studio, rehashing my day, basking in my father's laughter. He'd gotten a kick out of the way I'd complained about the girls in my class, and I'd learned to capitalize on the stupid jokes I'd acquired from my friends. But my favorite thing had been when my dad smiled for my mom. My father expressed emotion through paint, touch, and kisses on the forehead. His happiness was serene, reserved—quiet. His smiles meant something, and when he laughed, my mom would glow—come alive. Few people in this world really meant what they said. Everything was condensed into fake, witty little narratives placed on the Internet for the whole world to believe. My parents' love was the real thing, and it's all I'd ever wanted. As freaking crazy as it was, when Camden smiled today, something inside me burned, too. Radiant. I'd actually felt the definition of the word as it flamed my cheeks and chest.

Camden's smiles were effervescent. His laugh was hesitant, shy and husky. The rare sound of it had vibrated and stirred inside my stomach. A hidden excitement I never knew existed. I found myself wondering what I was willing to do to hear it. I stole a glance across the coffee table as I stood and reached for one of the to-go containers. Camden's hands were in his pockets, bunching his biceps under the short sleeves of his t-shirt as he stood stiff and unmoving. Our eyes met and his Adam's apple bobbed. Could he feel the thick, palpable air between us? That dizzying, heady static made me nervous, and yet I couldn't deny how much I liked that he was looking at me.

"The sweet and sour chicken is mine, dude." Kai spoke, picking up the half-gallon sized Styrofoam container I'd reached for, and I tore my gaze from Camden's.

I planted a smile on my face, letting an uneasy laugh escape. "Sharing is caring."

"You sound like my mom." Kai handed me the container, and out of the corner of my eye I saw Camden move.

"I can sit on the floor," I offered with a grin. "Or Kai can."

Camden's lips twitched, an elusive smile was right below the surface.

"Sit down, O'Connell." Kai glared as he threw a plastic fork at me, laughing when I fumbled it to the floor. "Good thing you don't play football."

"Never wanted to," I argued as I sat back on the couch.

"Thank God. We need you on the swim team." Kai pushed a container toward Camden. "Help yourself, but apparently the sweet and sour chicken is only for this princess." He punched me in the shoulder and I laughed, hoping Camden would, too. He didn't. "You can have whatever you want of mine."

"I'm not hungry." Camden cleared his throat, pulling his legs almost to his chest, stopping halfway to rest his forearms on the tops of his knees. "I mean, thank you, but I..." His eyes found mine for a split second before he brought them to the table top. "I'm not hungry."

"O-kay." The word slowly drawled from Kai's mouth, and my chest ached as I watched Camden's eyes narrow.

"Don't be an asshole." The edge in my voice was the same tone I reserved for people who talked shit about my sister in high school.

"He can't help it." Camden's deadpan delivery made Kai choke on his laugh.

"I really can't." Kai's smile was broad and proud as he raised his fork to his mouth, pausing he said, "I might've misjudged you, Cam."

"Camden," he corrected and Kai rolled his eyes.

"*Camden...*" Kai pronounced his name with more melodrama than I thought was necessary, but Camden's lips broke into a small smile and my pulse spiked.

That damn smile was a sunrise. Slow moving and brimming over with warmth and color. A smile you'd stay up all night for, waiting to catch a glimpse. I wanted to reach out and touch his face, touch my thumb to his bottom lip, feel the curve of it, taste it in some private moment I'd only ever be able to imagine. If he was a girl, I'd ask him out, burgers and a movie, hold his hand, and hope for a kiss when I dropped him off, but I was lost on some uncharted continent of *what the fuck*. I didn't understand what I was feeling, or why, beyond this deep need to open him up. Physically, he was built like most of the guys on my team. Long, lean muscle, nothing out of the ordinary. Nothing I ever would have noticed before.

Before.

Before his music had become a thief, stealing my damn sanity.

Before his gray-green eyes and all the secrets they held.

Before his mouth and the way he formed his words on full lips.

"Now that we have successfully extracted you from your room, you realize I'm going to ask you every question I've been harboring since move-in day?"

Kai sat his dinner on the table, rubbing his hands together like he was preparing to cross-exam a witness when I cut in, "I thought we were supposed to go over the details of next week's swim meet."

Camden's posture stiffened, his hard gaze raking over my face. "I should practice." He stood, nodding his head toward the bedroom door.

"I can't promise there'll be any food left over," Kai warned, garbling his words over the forkful of noodles he'd popped into his mouth.

Camden shrugged and offered me one more cursory glance before disappearing behind his bedroom door. I stared at the barrier, wondering if the distance would afford me a moment of clarity. This afternoon had been like running through one of those old carnival fun houses. All the mirrors on the walls distorted your image, confused you—made you lose your direction. Camden handing me that pencil, feeling that spark as his skin touched mine, that attraction pulled my eyes to his whenever I had a chance to look. I was stuck in that hallway of mirrors, staring at some unrecognizable version of myself, and as the sad notes of his piano seeped beyond his door, I realized I didn't really mind the reflection.

Camden Morgan had been raised in Astoria, Oregon, by doctor parents who coached and encouraged their son's natural-born talent to play the piano. After an hour of thorough internet searching, this was the only information I'd been able to find. Camden had no social media, not even a damn email address. Why I was stalking my newly acquired friend online at eleven-thirty at night wasn't really the point. The point was that Camden's mystery was addictive, and maybe I'd been looking for some way to contact him. A quick text via Facebook letting him know he should have breakfast with me and my sister tomorrow, or a "hey, it was nice to finally 'meet' you." Definitely not a text message stating anything resembling a "so I find myself thinking about you and this weird attraction I have for you, maybe we should get together over breakfast and delve into why the hell I can't stop thinking about your mouth."

I squinted at the screen of my laptop and clicked on the messaging app.

Me: Stop by on your way home?

I stretched my legs across my bed with a groan and looked at the clock again. Indie should be finished at the studio by now. Thankfully, though, I didn't have to wait long for her response.

Indie: Walking by Warren House now.

Me: Sweet. See you soon.

Indie: Perks of being your sister, access to the jock dorms.

I laughed.

Me: Because jocks are your favorite?

She didn't reply and after a few minutes, there was a quiet knock on my door. I hopped off the bed and unlocked it.

"I like jocks."

"You like me."

"You're my brother, I have to like you."

She pushed past me and I shut the door with a smile. I turned and watched her silent gaze flit across my room. Her fingers were crusted with blue and yellow paint.

"Blue, this place is a mess. It smells like dirty socks." She wrinkled her nose as she flopped down onto the bed.

"I'm doing laundry tomorrow, it's not that bad."

Her light blue eyes widened. "It's that bad."

I pulled the drawstring on the laundry sack in the corner near my desk. "Better?" I asked.

"Thanks." She yawned through her smile. "How was Kai's?"

"Good," I said with little conviction.

She met my gaze. "Want to talk about it?"

I exhaled as I sat backwards in my desk chair, resting my arms across the back.

"I'm not sure."

"That's okay."

Indie was a master at waiting me out and turned her attention to the screen of my laptop. I'd left it open and was well aware of what she was looking at. There was the message I'd sent her and another window opened. My Google search for a certain boy named Camden Morgan.

"He's quiet in class. I can tell it's loud for him, all the murmuring, and the side conversations, it makes him tense. I can see it in his shoulders. He stands out, even when he wishes he didn't. Like me. The silent ones always stand out." Indie closed my laptop before she faced me again. "I think he likes you."

I raised an eyebrow. "Likes me?"

"He doesn't talk to anyone in class, let alone look at anyone besides the professor. He *looked* at you, Royal."

"I barely know him."

"Maybe he needs a friend." Her smile was soft and made me think of our mom. Sometimes Indie looked just like her, and today I'd never needed her to look like her more, never needed that accepting smile more than I did right now.

"I..." My eyes found the floor as I picked at the seam along the back of the chair. "I think I like him, Pink."

"Good."

I brought my gaze to hers. "No, I mean, I think I *like* him." She bit back a smile. "I'm attracted to him, that's freaking weird, right?"

She shook her head. "I don't think so."

I gulped down the growing lump in my throat. "It's weird. I've never... I mean, there's only ever been Nat."

"Dad told me you can't help who you love. That love sinks its teeth into your heart and you'll do anything to be its victim." Her smile stretched across her face, and the ache in my throat pinched as her eyes met mine. "You've always been able to see people beyond their borders, it's what makes you... you."

"Nah... That's you, Pink."

"That's us."

"You really think he likes me like... *that*?"

"I don't know, but I could tell he wants to know you."

I chuckled. "Or you. Maybe he came over to our table to talk to you."

Indie crinkled her nose like she'd smelled my dirty socks again. "He has all of art history to talk to me, look at me, and he doesn't. Not like he looked at you this afternoon. Maybe he wants a friend, maybe he's attracted to you. Explore it, see what happens."

I was in the middle of a post-adolescent crisis and she wanted me to *see what happens*. I wish it was that easy.

"I wanted to invite him to breakfast."

"That's a start." She stood and crossed the room, standing in front of me. "Hey." She'd lowered her voice and I looked up at her. "You're not crazy."

"I—"

"You were thinking it."

"I'm a little crazy." I grinned.

"Text him, be his friend, see where it goes from there... isn't that what you did with Nat?"

"Yeah, but—"

"Text him."

"I don't know his number."

"Student directory will probably be more helpful than the Internet," she suggested with a placating smile.

"You've always been the smarter one."

She leaned down and kissed the top of my head. "I know."

Camden

G arrison Hall was louder than usual tonight as I made
my way up the stairs to my suite. It was easy for me
to get lost inside my head, inside the sounds of the world.
Its orchestra was loud enough to distract anyone if they
truly listened. All I ever did was listen. I heard the steps
people took, each count. I heard the way the chairs scraped
against the floor of the lecture halls. The way that guy in
my calculus class had laughed when he was nervous. The
girl who sat next to him was out-of-his-league pretty. I
could tell you how Kai's voice rumbled and broke when
he yelled at his dad over the phone this morning. How
he'd taken six deep breaths after he'd ended the call, and
how, afterward, there'd been the percussion of his fists,
not muted enough by the pillow he'd placed against the
wall. The world was loud and I liked that I wasn't the one
composing the notes.

Days would go by and I'd forget the sound of my own
voice, never adding to the melody around me, at least,

that was how I'd always wanted it to be. But I'd opened up a little, for him, for Royal, and I'd spoken more, given more of myself in our short interactions than I had since... since I couldn't remember. But that was a few days ago, and my tongue was thirsty for the words I hadn't said. He'd given me the opportunity to be normal, to sit and eat dinner. I'd messed it up, and I hadn't seen him since. I'd purposely forgotten the way to the library and hid in my room most afternoons practicing. Come to think of it, I hadn't seen Kai until last night. He was so drunk he couldn't figure out how to unlock the front door, and I'd been forced awake by the colorful tantrum he'd thrown from the hallway.

"Thanks for letting me in, dude," he'd said and ruffled my hair, pausing outside his bedroom door. He'd gawked, his dark eyes glassy, either from booze, or some emotion I hadn't been able to decipher when he whispered, "Don't take it for granted."

"Take what for granted?" I'd asked.

"Life." One syllable before he'd slammed the door behind him.

Proof that the world spun on without me, creating new songs I'd never know. Messes. Drama. Pulse. Humanity. Things I'd become accustomed to living without. Until Royal's blue eyes turned up the volume, drowning out the miserable, sophomoric music I'd been listening to for years.

It's an affliction.

An affliction no pills or therapy would ever cure. I stopped short as I rounded the corner into the hallway leading to my suite. He was sitting on the ground outside my door with his backpack at his side. The noise of Garrison became an imperceptible purr. Royal's beach-blond hair was damp and curled around ears hidden by the headphones he wore. His long legs were extended with a lazy ease of confidence. My temptation sat resting with eyes closed, his head against the wood of the frame.

The steady thrum of my heart became unbearable, robbing me of each breath as I took a step forward. He affected me and it felt good.

It's unnatural. It's a choice. Change it.

Propaganda was a snare drum that never stopped beating.

For five seconds I watched. The rise and fall of his chest, the way his top lip was fuller than his bottom, and how the stubble on his chin made my fingers itch to touch it. Five seconds was all I'd been granted before his straw-colored lashes fluttered open, and that smile, slow and beautiful, fixed on me.

Royal lifted his headphones from his ears and let them settle around his neck as he stood.

Like the social pariah I was, I muttered, "I need to get inside."

The backpack he'd been sitting next to toppled over, and he fumbled his words as he said, "Sure thing, I was just waiting for Kai."

Kai.

"It's Friday."

"I know." He chuckled and ran his hand through his hair. I noticed he smelled like soap and chlorine as

I made my way to the door. It was an effort not to inhale deeper. "I figured he'd be back by now. Practice ended twenty minutes ago, said he was heading home."

"Not on a Friday," I argued as I opened the door.

"What do you mean?" he asked as he followed behind me.

"Kai is never here on the weekends."

Royal laughed and the hearty sound of it stuck to his ribs.

"I should've known." His words fell false from his lips. Why was he pretending like he didn't know Kai's schedule as well as his own?

His smile was too wide—off. His upper lip gently trembled as he pushed his hands into his pockets. Nervous energy poured between us and I hated it. Hated that I couldn't formulate a response, that I couldn't just be normal.

"I tried to look you up in the directory last week." His blue eyes darted around the room before finally resting on mine.

"Why?"

His hand escaped the confines of his pocket and raked through his blond hair. No, not blond, blond was a gross misinterpretation. It was sun, and caramel, and this amazing light brown that melted into one color I had no name for. My eyes tracked the movement of his fingers through the strands, wishing my hand could take the place of his.

He shrugged. "I don't know... does there need to be a reason?" I didn't have an answer. "Kai said you don't get out much, and..." Creases formed along the top of his brows. "You seem like a solid guy, figured we could all hang out, grab a drink."

I wasn't a go-out-grab-a-drink kind of person, and the look on my face must have expressed as much, because he laughed softly. The corner of my lips twitched as I suppressed my smile.

"A drink?"

"Or maybe breakfast?" he asked, staring at me with blue irises that seemed to lighten as he awaited an answer. "I've had a hard time making friends here besides Kai. I'm not really into the whole party lifestyle, and Kai doesn't give me grief, but he *is* into all that shit."

"And I'm not." I surmised.

"I like that."

The smoky tone of his voice charged the room. Everything around me was static and my face heated. I'd never had friends before, never had anyone go out of their way to be close to me, and in truth, I'd never cared. But I wanted to be friends with him. To have breakfast, to *hang out,* but I was afraid I didn't know how.

"Breakfast," I mused.

"What are you doing right now?" he asked.

"I have calculus homework."

"Me, too."

"You have calculus homework?" I asked, eyeing the bag he'd set down at his feet. The words a bit more accusatory than I meant for them to be.

"Pre-calc. I was hoping Kai could help me with it."

A few grueling seconds went by as I warred with myself. Being alone was simple. Being one person inside a bubble had always been my way, but Royal was trying to break through, and all the things I shouldn't desire opened my mouth, spilling out an invitation I wasn't sure he wanted.

"I can help you."

The right corner of his lip lifted into a crooked smile. "Yeah?"

I nodded, keeping my gaze neutral, unaffected, stoic as always.

"Thanks. I have to keep my averages up or I'll lose my scholarship. I don't know how Kai does it. I struggle working two nights a week at the library."

"He drinks too much."

"He works too much."

"I didn't know drinking was considered a job."

Royal laughed as he fell casually into the cushions of the sofa.

"I guess working at Stacks isn't far from partying there, but he trains every morning, and still maintains an almost 4.0 average." Royal's textbook smacked against the coffee table. He whispered, something like embarrassment coloring his tone, as he looked forward and not at me, "Kai's a scholarship kid like me."

"I'm on a scholarship." I didn't need the money, though, and he turned a doubtful gaze in my direction.

"Aren't both your parents doctors?"

"Yes." But no one here knew that, no one at this school asked about my life, who I was, or where I was from, not even my roommate. "How do you know that?"

Flushed, he opened his mouth as if to say something, closed it, and then groaned. He groaned and it seated itself inside my chest.

"I..." Royal stuttered on a laugh, resting his head against the back of the couch. "Shit... this is kind of embarrassing."

It was out of my comfort zone, but I made myself take the last few steps toward the couch. He bit the corner of his mouth and I couldn't stop myself from staring. Couldn't stop myself from sitting down, from allowing my gaze to linger longer than I knew was socially acceptable.

He swallowed, and I watched his throat work, holding my breath as he continued, "I should've just stopped by or something, but I tried, like I said, to find a way to contact you, and the Internet wasn't as resourceful as I'd hoped, but it did pull up a few things about you being a piano *genius*." His smile was repentant and I exhaled. "And maybe a few things about your family."

Family. I've never had one of those.

"The *doting parents*. That article is still around?"

He cringed with an empathetic smile. "Unfortunately, they say if it's out there, it's out there forever. My uncle always tells me to keep the nudity strictly to the bedroom." I laughed and Royal's grin grew magnificent, spreading gradually across his lips. "What? I'm serious, I knew this one guy and... well, let's just say my whole high school knows about the weird birthmark he has on his junk."

Heat flooded my cheeks as I choked on another laugh. "His junk?"

Royal beamed, and when our eyes met, we both exploded with laughter. I could've ruined the moment by acknowledging to myself this was the first time, at least, the first time I could remember, ever feeling this open. This normal. But I chose to focus on the way his shoulders shook with amusement, the way our voices blended together, fitting seamless, side by side. I permitted myself a few seconds to absorb what had just happened, to be a guy in a dorm room, joking around like everyone else. There was nothing immoral about that, nothing scandalous. But then he exhaled a long breath, gathering himself as he sank deeper into the sofa, he turned his head to look at me and the energy shifted. The energy demanded to be noticed, to be heard. It roared and raged inside the storm of his eyes, and for a moment, I thought he'd heard it, too.

"I didn't mean to invade your privacy by looking you up online. I figured I'd message you on Facebook or something." The serious look on his face curled into a lopsided grin. "I mean, who doesn't have some form of a social media account?"

"Me."

"I'm aware." He sat up, leaning over his knees, and flipped open his text book.

"What's the point... it's all for show anyway." And I have nothing to show.

His eyes on the pages of his math book, he spoke quietly. "I think it's cool you're not all about that stuff. That you don't need it like the rest of the world."

I wasn't as indifferent as he assumed. My need just shaped itself in different ways than most people's.

Most people sought each other out, needing attention, and validation. My need for acceptance wasn't from the world, it was from myself. When your parents won't even look at you—privacy—*solitude*—it's survival.

I could've said all of those things, maybe told him the article he'd found online was from a time I wasn't sure existed, a family that was a well-written piece of fiction, but instead, I shrugged. "I don't have time for social media. My parents may be doctors, but I earned my spot at this college."

"And I earned mine." Royal lifted his gaze and pride flashed across his eyes. His crooked grin, like the classic song *Simple Gifts* I'd learned when I was six, was marked with grace. "We're not so unlike, you and me."

It was a friendly thing to say, light-hearted, even, but it was the way he said it, like he'd hoped it was true, that made me wish for it, too.

Royal

U tterly.
Rattled.

Being this close to Camden, smelling the spiced scent of his detergent and soap, feeling the weight of his body next to me as he sank into the cushion of the couch, it shouldn't have felt this... right. To say I was confused wouldn't be an accurate enough explanation. I was thrown.

Fully.

Completely.

Why him? Why was he the first guy I'd ever been attracted to? I didn't understand why his eyes made it almost impossible to breathe sometimes, like my heart was trying with all its might to punch its way through my chest. They dissected every one of my movements, and I was curious what he was mapping out inside his head.

Did he like what he saw when he looked at me? Or was I just another person, another guy. I had no idea why I was drawn to that peppery scent, when before him, I'd always been drawn to sweet and floral. Being this close, breathing him in, it made my entire body hot. There was no rhyme or reason. No explanation. And the only thing that made sense to me anymore was the philosophy I'd been raised by.

Trust yourself.

Indie and I were thirteen when our parents sat us down in separate rooms and gave us the "sex talk." I remember the explanation hadn't been neatly boxed into the societal norm. There was a certain amount of this goes here and this is why, but my parents had used this discussion as a way to teach us about the emotion of love instead of just the mechanics. They'd told us about their own history and how they'd once split up when they were younger. My mom had married another man because she hadn't trusted her heart, and it hadn't been until she'd divorced and found Dad again, that she realized how much of herself had lived inside of him. Dad had said they wasted so much time living with regret and mistakes, and that if he could, he'd reverse the hands on the clock and fix it all. Save the time they'd missed out on. Their story had resonated, and I promised myself I wouldn't miss out on something amazing because I didn't understand my own heart. I trusted myself, and the way I felt compelled to learn, ascertain, every single one of Camden's thoughts. All I wanted was to pursue this feeling. Like everything I did in life, everything I'd been taught, I never wanted to second-guess my heart. Even when it was confusing the shit out of me.

Love sinks its teeth into your heart.

I hoped so.

Camden leaned in, dropping his gaze to my textbook and asked, "What did you need help with?"

Without looking at the page, I'd opened the book and said, "Tangents."

Math was one of my better subjects, thanks to my mother, and I hated that I'd lied to him. Kai worked at Stacks every Friday night, and I was well aware of his schedule. But when I'd opened my eyes and saw Camden standing in the hallway earlier, his eyes more gray than green, his broad shoulders imposing and strong, my plan had dissolved into my threaded pulse. Originally, I'd thought it'd be no big deal to stop by, invite him to hang out, maybe go grab some food, like I would with any of my friends, but Camden wasn't just anyone. And the minute I saw him again, staring at me like I was an equation he was trying to solve, I'd lost my confidence.

Camden's dark brows furrowed as he scanned the textbook. His lips moved silently as he read the page, and I took in the structured arch of his cheek bones. For someone who didn't "fit in" as Kai would like to say, Camden was a traditionally good-looking guy. He was sharp angles, and decently built for someone who was less athletic and more of an introverted nerdish type. His shirt stretched across his chest and fit tight around defined biceps. His muscle was natural, softly cut. Touchable. Not like the sinewy bands of muscle some of the guys on my team had after spending too much time at the gym.

When Camden finally brought his eyes to mine, he hesitated, and for a long heartbeat, I worried he'd caught me staring, or worse, had seen right through me. Seen right through my lie.

"Tangents?" he asked in a gruff voice that scratched my spine.

I held his stare and nodded. A nod was all I was capable of. My mouth was too dry for words.

Camden edged in a few inches and pushed the textbook to the side. "Do you have your notebook?"

"Um..." His close proximity, the heat pouring off his body, I'd almost forgotten the question. "In my bag, one sec."

I quickly rummaged through my backpack, pulling out a notebook and setting it on the coffee table. A second too late, I realized I'd grabbed my sociology binder, but I was too far into this charade to pull out now. Opening it, I flipped past several pages of lecture notes before, thank you, God, I found a blank page.

"There," I said on an exhale, and was surprised to find Camden smirking when I glanced back at him.

He was smirking.

"Pencil?"

My gaze ran a fast track along the curve of his lips first, finding its way up the perfect slope of his nose to his eyes, noting the easy way the corners crinkled. He raised his brows, and I forced myself to look away, digging through my bag again.

"Here." I set the pencil onto the notebook, not wanting to risk touching him.

If the sensation was anything like the first time that afternoon in the library, I'd want more. It didn't matter if I was hunky-dory with the feelings I'd started to develop. Camden most likely wouldn't be.

"See," he said as his steady fingers sketched a drawing in the middle of the page. "This is a basic concept." He tapped the tip of the pencil on the page, and I stared at his perfect depiction of the familiar diagram. "Objects that touch without intersecting share one similar point." He traced the lead of the pencil over the circle, and then the line he'd placed above it, pausing where the two drawings barely touched. "That is the tangent."

I thought about the meaning of the word tangent in relation to how we were positioned. He'd moved to the edge of the sofa to have better access to the notebook, his knee close enough it brushed mine. Camden was serious again as he measured my understanding. He watched me, waiting, but all I could think about was the way his knee touched me. The way the goosebumps marched their way up my limbs, his warmth invading my skin, and if he was a girl, I wouldn't have hesitated to turn my head, and catch his lips with a kiss.

But that couldn't happen. I swallowed, turning my attention to the drawing, dragging myself out of the heat-soaked bubble I'd created in my head and said, "That makes sense."

"You sure?" he asked with a doubtful expression.

I took the hit to my ego like a man. It was my fault he thought I was struggling in the first place.

"Yeah. Clear as mud," I joked and it earned me a small smile.

He flicked his gaze to the textbook, his voice even. "It might help if you actually turn to the correct page." Camden chuckled, my stupidity, apparently the most entertaining thing in the world. "This stuff..." He turned a few of the pages. "Is more advanced, usually planned for later in the semester. Maybe you got the assignment number wrong?" He shrugged.

I shut the book without looking Camden in the eye. I was a terrible liar. "Shit... maybe I did." I gave him a smile and rubbed the back of my neck. "I'll check the syllabus online when I get back to my dorm."

The silence that descended wasn't awkward. It was catastrophic. Embarrassment wouldn't allow me to meet his eyes. Afraid he'd figured it out. I didn't want him to notice the way my cheeks had flushed, hear the way my heart was thrumming, see the way my pulse pounded in the crook of my neck. I couldn't risk him realizing I'd made it all up just to have these thirty, strange minutes, to see if what I was feeling was legit. His knee was still touching mine and I liked it. This was real, and the evidence made itself known as all the blood in my body drained south.

I stood abruptly almost, knocking over my notebook, and swore. I spun away from him, grabbing my things, and shoved them haphazardly into my backpack, not daring to glance in his direction until I had control over myself, my body. It wasn't some fluke or a confusion of chemicals. I wanted Camden. The declaration was a punch to the gut, a sinking feeling, a ninety-degree drop, because there was no obvious way to proceed. I knew I couldn't stand here silent much longer, but facing him, with all the questions I had, after my body's reaction to his, my confliction had me wanting to walk out the door with a, "thanks for the help, man," and a wave over my shoulder. The universe had other plans, and a wash of relief ran down my spine when my phone alerted in my pocket. Not a way out, but a second of distraction. An anchor.

Indie: Going to be late to the dining hall.

I tapped out a fast response.

Me: Still at the studio?

Indie: Yeah, I'm really into this project.

Camden cleared his throat behind me, and I immediately felt rude and ungrateful. I stood with my back to him, in *his* dorm room, texting like a dick. I gathered the air around me like it was a security blanket and pulled it into my lungs as I turned. Camden's eyes were fixed to the television and its darkened screen. The long line of his neck shifted. His hands at his sides, balled into fists. His posture defeated, his jaw clenched. My chest felt heavy. He looked nervous, maybe, like me, a little scared. Even so, he was still a picture of perfection, and I thought to myself, if he'd only open up, he'd be the type of guy who had a thousand friends. Probably a few thousand girls chasing him. He lifted his chin and threw the full weight of his stare onto me like a pile of bricks. His eyes, wide gray pools, and if they could speak, I thought, or maybe hoped, they'd be shouting, "take a chance on me."

"Do you like art?" I asked.

The tip of his tongue swept the length of his bottom lip and I swallowed.

"It depends." His husky voice sounded too loud for the small space between us.

"On what?"

"The artist." He stared through me, his features morphing into a mask of cool disinterest. "I find most people think they can paint, or sing, or write, but in reality, it's just a means to an end."

"How do you mean?" I asked.

"It's a way for them to get attention, gain a spotlight, regardless of talent. True talent..." Camden's façade cracked, his cheeks turning a slight shade of pink as he raised his eyes to mine. "It's hard to find."

His dark gaze held mine, and I told myself it was his lack of social prowess that had him staring at me longer than what would be considered polite. The alternative, that he might be attracted to me, as well, was just wishful thinking. "My sister's pretty damn talented, I'm meeting her at the studio on campus, and then we're going to grab some dinner. You should come."

His fingers relaxed, his broad shoulders expanding as he stood to his full height. "I can't." He tipped his head to his room. "I've got to work on my recital piece."

"It's Friday. And you have to eat, right?"

I was rewarded with an unsure smile and what sounded more like a question than an answer. "I should eat."

"Then, let's go."

Camden

I f I was a cage, then Royal was the key. I wasn't used to being looked at the way he'd looked at me. With such interest. Honest-to-God interest. Earlier he'd been graceless and awkward and with every flush of his cheeks, I'd started to entertain ideas. Part of me wondered if he'd really even needed help with his homework. Wondered if he'd come here to see me and not Kai, after all. Ideas turned into dangerous thoughts. Thoughts about kissing and how it would feel to have his breath on my lips. How peaceful it would be to listen to his heartbeat as my ear rested against his chest. Even if he had been looking at me, carving me back into existence with blue eyes that read me like a sheet of music, pulling my strings, it was just a look. It would never mean what I wanted it to mean. I could never allow it to mean more.

I raised my eyes to the muted gray sky as we stepped outside, letting all my thoughts evaporate into the late evening air. The pine trees' branches brushed against each other in the breeze, the soft sound contrasting with the disarming laughter of the students nearby. The weather had become cooler, drier in the evenings. The college's courtyard lent its sprawling grass to more people with every drop of a degree. It made me crave the quiet fall nights back home, and the driftwood bonfires my dad used to build sometimes when I was younger. I wanted the smell of toasted marshmallows mixed with salt and sea. A time when my father had treated me like I was his instead of a stranger he was afraid to know. Those nights had become forgotten memories. The ache in my throat swelled, and I searched for something to redirect my focus. Royal's rhythmic pace matched my breathing, and in a few steps, I was back in the present, walking next to the handsome boy who wouldn't leave me alone. A small smile formed on my lips and he noticed.

"Something funny?" he asked, not breaking his stride.

I met his perpetually inquisitive gaze and shook my head. "No."

The group of students and their laughter grew closer as we proceeded down the sidewalk toward the art building. A few called out to Royal with friendly smiles, and he nodded his head, waving in recognition. His attention fixing on one of the girls, her red hair like fire in the dusky sky as the wind whipped through the strands. She was small and fragile-looking with pale, porcelain skin. Feminine curves touched her hips, and her smile was almost feline as she waved back to him. An emptiness filled my stomach as I watched Royal's cheeks fill with the same pink I'd allowed myself to admire not but ten minutes ago.

"She's pretty," I said before I thought better of it.

"Laney?" He chuckled. "She's on a mission to bang the entire swim team."

His laissez-faire use of the word "bang" made me wonder if he'd already been with her. The thought had the knots in my stomach twisting tighter. I didn't want to care. I shouldn't care. Royal was a friend. An unusual and improbable fate. A person who went out of his way to include me. I couldn't afford to care who he did or didn't do things with.

I exhaled and said the most normal thing I could think of, "At least she has goals."

Royal barked out a laugh, and as his shoulders shook I found myself laughing, too.

"That's a positive way to look at it, I guess," he said with a wry smile. "I'm not into girls like that."

He was into girls. Just not girls like that...

"Girls like what?" I asked, trying to hide the disappointment in my tone.

He shrugged and rubbed the back of his neck with the palm of his hand. "Girls who throw themselves at you. I don't take her too seriously." He tilted his head back, his eyes lifted to the sky as if searching for the right words to say inside the thick blanket of clouds. "It makes me sad. She must not think much of herself, you know?" Royal's mouth tipped up into a boyish grin as he turned his head. His eyes on mine, he said, "I'd rather spend my time earning the right to know a person."

Those crystal blue eyes flickered down to my mouth for the briefest of seconds before he looked away. As if a heavy curtain had fallen around us, the outside noise that usually staved off my anxiety was gone. It was me and him and the rest of the world's clamor faded into the only sound I could hear—the erratic beat of my own heart. I couldn't find my voice to agree or disagree with him, and neither one of us spoke again as we made our way to meet his sister. The stillness only interrupted by the whispers of our breathing and the occasional bird in the distance. For most people, this would feel odd, walking side by side without some type of exchange. But I'd made friends with the awkward silences of my life a long time ago.

"Who's that?" Royal's question broke through the quiet like a knife and I lifted my gaze.

His sister walked toward us, her quiet appraisal on me, with another girl at her side. Indie's friend was tall and willowy in skin-tight jeans and a long-sleeved, fitted t-shirt. The front of the tee had the iconic Andy Warhol soup picture plastered on it. Her black hair cut short, dark to Indie's light, and I noticed, as she raised a flask to her mouth, that her bottom lip was pierced.

"Hey, Pink." Royal pulled his sister into a hug, his eyes never leaving the stranger's as he asked, "Who's your friend?"

"Pink?" the girl in question interrupted, licking the silver hoop with her tongue.

Indie laughed as she explained, "Royal and I have called each other Pink and Blue longer than I can remember."

"No real reason," he added.

"Except maybe to make Mom and Dad mad."

"But they loved it." Royal's face lit up. "Go figure."

"Our family has a thing for the color blue." Indie shrugged as she looked at the girl. "It all started with our mother's eyes."

"How romantic," the girl crooned, but it didn't sound like she thought it was very romantic at all. To make her point more clear she made a gagging motion with her finger, and Royal laughed even harder.

"She's honest... I like it, what's your name?" he asked, holding out his hand.

"Daphne." She took his hand and a weird feeling fluttered in my stomach.

I was staring at the connection when Indie spoke. "Daphne, Royal, Royal, Daphne, and this is Royal's friend, Camden."

Royal dropped her hand, his smile dimming as Daphne's dark brown eyes considered me.

"A cute brother and a cute friend, shit, Indie, how'd you get so lucky?"

Royal sputtered out another laugh, and Indie rolled her eyes as Daphne sipped from her flask again.

"You better eat before you drink anymore." Indie attempted to take the flask from her friend's hand, but with a playful scowl, Daphne screwed on the cap.

She placed the flask inside her back pocket as she whined, "Can we please go somewhere besides the dining hall? I'm so bored of tacos and salad bars."

"I want pizza." Indie clapped her paint-stained palms together.

Royal chuckled as he said, "I was hoping to get a peek at what you've been working on, next time, then?" Indie nodded with a smile. "We could go to Stacks. Kai's working tonight, discount pizza," he suggested, confirming my suspicion that he knew Kai wasn't going to be home tonight.

I didn't have a chance to think about what that meant, or if it meant anything at all. Daphne nearly squealed. "And beer. I like this plan."

"Who said you were invited?" Indie gave her friend a teasing smile.

The three of them were standing in a semi-circle, laughing and joking. I was on the outside looking in, picking and pulling apart their notes. Listening. Royal was a cello, deep and smooth, and it was his melody that played the loudest. I wasn't the only one who heard him and it was hard not to notice Daphne noticing him. If I could, I'd have taken two steps back, repeating the motion until I was home, in my dorm, behind closed doors, thinking dangerous thoughts about a boy who liked girls. A boy who wanted to earn the right to know a person. A person who wasn't me. I didn't belong in these social compilations. I belonged behind the keys of my piano, creating something that would always belong to me.

"Does that sound okay to you?" Royal asked, and I found his light eyes watching me. His brows dipped into a worried crease. He leaned in, his voice low as he spoke. "I know you said Stacks isn't your scene, but it's early enough it shouldn't be too crazy." His lips parted into a warm, heart-stopping smile. "Besides, who can say no to free pizza?"

I could say no.

But I didn't.

I'd go for that smile alone, and all the inspiration it would give me later tonight when I worked on my recital piece.

The bar had about ten people inside when we'd arrived five minutes ago. Mostly college kids and a noisy, overhead speaker that blared terrible music while the television behind the bar played a muted football game. The place was bigger than I thought it would be, but small, just the same. I imagined as the night wore on the tables would be teeming with kids looking to get drunk or laid. Or probably both. I wasn't so sheltered I didn't understand the typical appetites of people my age. I'd just made amends with the fact I was never going to have what others did.

You're sick. Perverse.

My mother's insults didn't stick to my bones as much inside this place. Even if I hadn't uttered one word since I'd agreed to come, I felt more normal than I had in a long time.

Royal and I found a table while the girls ventured into the back hall looking for the bathroom. He settled on a high-top with four stools close to a couple of pool tables. I let him pick a seat before I decided on mine, choosing to sit across from him. From this vantage point I was able to maintain a healthy distance, but still admire his long limbs and smoky laughter.

"Holy shit." Kai dragged the two words out in dramatic syllables. "Camden… look at you."

"Look at me." My smile was sardonic and Kai's eyes danced with humor.

"I'm speechless."

Royal laughed, and I fell into the sound of it as he quipped, "For once."

"Fuck off." He punched Royal in the shoulder. "Or I'll charge you this time."

"Charge us?" Daphne's electric voice rose above the din of the bar.

Kai's expression darkened as he turned his attention to Indie and her friend. His posture straight as he purposefully moved out of the way, letting the girls pass him. He shot Royal a glare and he furrowed his brow.

"What's that look for?" Royal asked.

"Nothing," Kai grunted as Daphne took the seat next to Royal.

She drawled in a tooth-achingly sweet, fake southern accent, "Kai Carter, always the moody bastard. Didn't your momma ever teach you manners?" Her long, inky lashes fluttered and he grinned.

"Sure did, should I show you sometime?"

She stuck out her tongue and he chuckled. "You wish, Carter. Now, be a dear and bring us a pitcher."

"Got ID?" he asked, the challenge in his voice made me smile internally.

"You guys know each other?" Royal asked, his eyes fixed on Daphne.

"In the Biblical sense, no—"

"Thank fuck." Kai grinned and Daphne shoved his shoulder.

"Don't act like you never tried," she said, pulling her flask from her pocket.

"Don't act like you never wanted to."

Daphne's dark eyes twinkled with mischief, while Kai looked at her with boredom.

"I've known you since grade school, just like I know you're drinking Jameson in that flask, and I know you have a thing for swimmers." He pointed his gaze at Royal. "Watch out for this one."

"Ha-ha." Daphne's mock laugh drew a grin on Royal's lips, and a twinge of jealousy squeezed my chest. "Can we order our dinner now, barmaid?" Her wide-set mouth was out of place on her pixie-like face. And if it wasn't for all the metal in her ears, and the hoop in her lip, she'd almost look angelic.

Kai's eyes lifted to the ceiling as he exhaled a sigh.

"Can we get a large..." Royal paused, and looked at me when he asked, "Pepperoni okay with you?" I nodded, ignoring the cartwheels happening inside my stomach. "Large pepperoni and a pitcher of that local beer you talk about all the time."

"Got it." Kai's eyes avoided my side of the table, and I felt Indie shift in her seat as he asked, "How many glasses should I bring?"

"I'm not drinking," Indie and I said in unison.

"One beer," Daphne pleaded to Indie, and Royal shook his head.

"I can't." Indie's voice was almost a whisper. "You know that, Daph."

"Fine, you're drinking then." Daphne's attention, unwanted, fixated on me. She held up three fingers. "Three glasses."

I didn't argue, letting Kai leave the table with our order, and wondering why Indie wouldn't, or better yet, couldn't drink.

"He doesn't have to drink." Royal came to my defense.

"It's fine." I made a show of nonchalance as I lifted my shoulders. "One drink."

He shouldn't have known me well enough to see through the lie, to hear the nervous edge to my voice, but I couldn't say it bothered me when he asked, "Are you sure?"

"He's totally sure." Daphne stepped down from her barstool, pulling Royal along with her. "Let's play pool while we wait."

He didn't put up a fight, and it might've been the way I slumped in my seat that gave me away, but Indie keyed in to my discomfort.

"Don't worry, she's not his type."

Heat engulfed my cheeks, but I kept my eyes forward, watching him as his head fell back in laughter at something Daphne had said.

"You don't think so?"

Out of the corner of my eye I saw her shake her head.

"Royal's never really had a type." I heard the smile in her voice as she continued, "But if I had to pick one, I'd say he's more into the strong-and-silent type."

My head nearly snapped as I turned to gape at her. What she was suggesting... it would be stupid to hope.

She had her bottom lip pinned between her teeth, but it escaped as she smiled up at me. "Give him some time."

Time.

Time for what?

To figure out his type?

Whether or not he liked guys?

Whether or not he liked me?

He laughed again and it sounded like a Debussy piece. Warm and lazy as it drifted around the room and through the chaos in my head. Indie stared at her brother, and I followed her gaze. He was watching us, too. Something glimmered across his pale eyes as he set the pool stick down and walked back to the table.

"You guys want to play?" he asked.

Indie didn't answer, but hopped down from her stool and headed to the pool table. I had no idea how to play pool, but like earlier, his smile reeled me in, and I had no other answer for him besides, "Yes."

Camden

"She's manic," I muttered to myself, hoping the loud music filtering through the overhead speakers would drown out my assessment.

Indie laughed and it tinkled, delicate, like the sound rain made as it burst from the sky, dropping onto the cool metal of a car roof or your bicycle handlebars. She stared at me, her eyes that ghostly blue like her brother's. Indie was beautiful, too. Her head crowned in pale shades of blonde with a hint of honey. Elegant, unlike her friend who snorted with laughter at everything Royal said.

Understanding simmered under the surface of her irises, and her lips parted into a smile. "Daphne can be... lively."

If I was the sort of person who snorted, I would have. Lively was too nice of an adjective. Obnoxious. Overbearing. Pushy. She'd been draped over Royal all night, sipping from her flask and ordering shots for the both of them, drinking more than I thought possible for a girl her size. She was thin—wiry. Her clothes wore her. Daphne's skin hung from her bones, and you'd think, with the way she'd barely nibbled at her pizza earlier, she'd be formal, peaceful. She was a bull horn, steeped in beer and whiskey, or whatever she'd stowed away in her flask.

Leaning against the wall, farthest from the pool table, I took a sip from the pint of beer I'd been nursing all night. The bitter drink had warmed. Its musky taste coated my tongue and throat, heating my belly. I'd waited for that feeling everyone went on about, the buzz, but I supposed I needed to drink more than one beer for that to happen. I almost wished for some intoxicating effect to take over. It would've made it easier to deal with Daphne's *lively* personality. I didn't go out, or drink from flasks, or hope over boys I had no business hoping for, but it would've been nice to know what it felt like to relax.

"She's drunk," Indie qualified. "She's not normally so—"

"Aggressive?"

Indie laughed that musical laugh again as she turned her eyes back to the pool table.

She let her hand fall to her side, her fingers brushing mine. "We should stop being wallflowers." Mischief turned her blue eyes bright. "Come on."

The heat of Indie's hand surprised me as she laced our fingers together. It was such a knee-jerk reaction, the need to pull away. I couldn't remember the last time someone had touched me. Actually touched me with purpose. The noisy background of the bar had become a distant hum with every step we took. Indie and I, hand in hand, was awkward, and uncomfortable, and I prayed, to no one in particular, that my palms wouldn't sweat. Our connection wasn't romantic, more of a *stick with me and all will be okay*, but when you've lived the last four or so years of your life in a self-imposed solitude, the little social details were the last things you worried about. Sweaty hands, however, had to be a faux pas of some sort. But as my anxiety reached its crescendo, Indie smiled at me.

This girl with her halo hair, and eyes that made me wish she was her brother, smirked as she said in a low conspiratorial whisper, "I'll distract her."

"I'm getting tired. Should we go?" Indie's question was directed toward Daphne, but she'd set her focus on her brother.

Royal's gaze landed on our tangled fingers and she dropped my hand.

"Now?" Daphne swayed, gripping the pool table. She whined, "I swear, we just got here."

Indie shook her head with a quiet and motherly smile. "It's getting late."

"I can walk you guys home." Royal attempted to move around the pool table and stumbled.

"I think you're the one who needs help getting home, should I—"

"I'll walk him," I offered, immediately regretting the decision to torture myself.

"Are you sure you can handle him?" Indie asked.

"Love you, too, Pink." Royal chuckled, setting his pool stick down onto the aged green felt of the table. "I may be buzzed, but I'm not an asshole. No way am I letting you two walk back on your own." Again, he tripped over his feet.

"We can all walk back together. I'll get this one back to our dorm." Indie pointed her thumb at Daphne, who in turn stuck out her tongue like a child. "And you'll make sure my brother finds himself back to his dorm, all right?"

Indie leaned up onto her toes and whispered something into her brother's ear. My stomach flipped. I hadn't admitted anything to her, but what if she'd decided to tell him about her assumptions?

He shook his head, his eyes on me as he said, "Don't worry, I'll live."

He'll live?

I wished I'd been born with the ability to mind read. Being a piano prodigy was a useless superpower.

Royal threw some cash, way too much, even with a tip included for our ten-dollar tab, on our table as we passed by. I picked it up as he walked in front of me and handed it all to his sister, knowing she'd give him the money back when his male pride hadn't ingested too much alcohol. She bumped her hip into mine and mouthed the words, "thank you." If I wasn't me, I would have smiled back. Maybe said you're welcome, or teased her and playfully pulled a piece of her hair. But instead, I watched as they walked outside before I approached the bar.

I took two twenties from my wallet. "This should cover everything."

Kai tore his gaze from the front door, his lips setting into a flat line.

"What was that?" he asked as I handed him the money.

"I'm not sure what you mean."

"That little hip check? You better stay away from Indie." Kai's shoulders seemed broader, set in challenge as he opened the till.

"Indie?"

He slammed the register shut. "Yeah, asshole, Indie O'Connell. That's his sister and I'm sure he'd fuck you up for even thinking—"

"I don't like his sister."

"You don't?" he asked, his tone laden with irritated disbelief. "You were holding her hand, standing next to her all night."

"She's nice."

His jaw tightened as he leaned across the counter, resting the knuckles of his fist on the faded wood of the bar top, he dropped his voice into a threat. "Stay away from her."

I wasn't sure if this was some brotherly warning, some chivalrous attempt to protect his best friend's sister, or something else, but if he knew the truth, he'd think it was all some big, disgusting joke.

"It's not like that. She's nice. That's it. I'm not into girls…" I slipped on my words, his icy stare making it impossible to think. "Girls like her."

He flashed a wide tiger's grin in my direction as he knocked twice on the bar top and stood to his full six-feet-three-or-so-inches.

"Good." He grabbed a rag from under the counter. "Jesus, you're sweating. I'm not that scary."

I wiped the back of my hand over my brow with a nervous laugh. I wasn't afraid of him. I was afraid of myself. Of what I wanted. Of Kai figuring out my secrets.

"It would appear that you are." His smile was crooked.

"Maybe a little."

He lifted his chin toward the door. "Make sure they all get home alive."

True to her word, Indie had distracted Daphne. They walked ahead of us the entire way back to campus, Daphne hiccupping and singing weird versions of eighties' songs, until I'd made sure they were safe behind the doors of Vigrus Hall.

"She likes you." Royal's lips parted into a smile. "I mean... I think she likes you. Who holds hands unless they like a person?" His smile faded as his head tipped back, his eyes on the sky. The stars were hidden under a blanket of clouds, but he stared anyway. "I just want Indie to be happy."

"Indie doesn't like me."

His sad regard dulled the shine around his irises. "She's never had a boyfriend."

"Does she need a boyfriend to be happy?"

The graveled path crunched under our feet for six, seven, eight long seconds.

"Nobody wants to be alone."

I did. And I didn't. I didn't know how to be anything but alone. But I wanted to know, even if it couldn't happen, even if it couldn't be.

"Are you alone?"

He shook his head, turning left toward his dormitory. "I have her. And now you do, too."

"We're friends."

His laugh buried itself inside my chest, below my heart and stitched inside my lungs. The full feeling worked its way to my limbs. Warm and heavy, down to my fingertips.

"You're stuck with us."

The stuck sounded more like shuck. I was fixated on that drunken sound, and the way it undermined what he'd said, so much so that I hadn't noticed how close he'd stepped in beside me. His arm brushed my bicep as it swung, sending a wave of goosebumps over my skin. I was about to rub them away, embarrassed by my reaction to that singular touch, when he gently took my hand in his. It was completely natural, the way Royal's hand found mine. He linked our fingers, his posture at ease, facing forward like this was something we did all the time. As if the implication of the gesture hadn't made my heart stop, or caused my lungs to forget how to breathe. Like the feel of his skin, hot and a little damp against my own, hadn't sent a jolt up my arm, causing permanent damage to the wall I'd so carefully constructed years ago. His touch was different than Indie's. Bigger somehow. Soft and hard at the same time. His grip was firm, yielding, molding.

We walked like that, his hand claiming mine. A silence so thick it mixed with the smell of his breath, sweet, with a hint of beer as he exhaled. There was no other sound around that could compete for my affection. This duet was stunning in its simplicity, every one of his breaths in sync with my own.

I let myself feel the pulse thudding inside the pad of his thumb as it rested against the top of my hand. I counted each beat as we walked, trying to understand how this was happening, or if this was just something drunk guys did?

Who holds hands unless they like a person?

Or maybe the O'Connells were touchy-feely people. Maybe this was the new normal, and I was the messed-up one, with messed-up parents, and a personal bubble the size of the Great Wall of China. Though, I seriously doubted Kai would be holding my hand right now.

Royal squeezed my hand before he released it. The cold air swept through my fingers, reminding me of the distance I needed to keep. "This is me," he said with his hand now in his pocket, tumbling over the first step in front of Warren House.

He caught his footing and laughed. His laugh was careless, the total opposite of the way I felt. Tight and scared, and wishing his hand was still in mine.

"Shit," he said. His cheeks were red almost to his ears as he punched his access code into the keypad a few times.

Finally, he unlocked the door and I followed him inside, making sure he didn't fall asleep in the common room, or worse, in the hall. Under the fluorescent lights of the dormitory, Royal's gait slowed, swayed more than I'd noticed earlier. By the time we'd made it up to his room, he'd dropped his keys four times, this time he'd left them on the floor of his bedroom, and flopped down, face first onto his full-sized mattress. The room was small for a single, the bed taking up most of the space, leaving only enough room for a small table, desk, and a chair.

"Will you be okay in here on your own?"

Visions of him lying in his own vomit assaulted me.

He grumbled what sounded like a yes and rolled over onto his back. His hair was tousled in soft, unmanaged waves I wanted to rake my fingers through. Royal's lips were full and split into a small smile as he stared at me with his hand resting on the hard plane of his stomach.

"Thanks."

I nodded my head, not sure what he was thanking me for. I bent down, picked up his keys, and placed them on his desk before I moved toward the dorm door.

"Hey," he called out, and I turned to face him, my heart making its way up my throat. If he asked me to stay, I wasn't sure I could convince myself to say no.

Royal propped his hand under his head. The movement pulled his t-shirt up, exposing a small slice of tan skin on his stomach above the waist band of his jeans. I exhaled, forcing my eyes to focus on his breathing, to the rhythmic rise and fall of his chest. The color returned to his cheeks, his eyes glossy and beautiful as he licked his lips. It stung a little, knowing he most likely wouldn't remember tonight. Remember the way the air in this room crackled and thrummed.

The shape of his face was made up of shadows and stark angles, serious, as he whispered, "You're kind of perfect."

Royal

Sandpaper, or maybe it felt more like a sponge, either way, my tongue was stuck to the roof of my mouth and it tasted like salt and death. My damp hair fell over my forehead as I rolled to my side. The angle my arm had been in all night, twisted under my body, caused my palm to tingle as all the blood rushed back to my fingers. The sensation, a flash of heat, itched its way up my skin and my eyes popped opened.

I remembered.

You're sort of perfect.

"No," I half-moaned as I tried to sit up. The thunder in my head rumbled louder than I could handle. "Did I really say that?" I asked myself as I scrubbed my eyes with the heels of my palms.

His hand in mine. Warm. And... sort of perfect.

"Shit." I fell back into the pillow, my head splitting open with another roll of thunder.

I closed my eyes, trying to piece my night together. How the hell did I get so drunk? I never drink that much, never.

"Daphne." Again, I groaned. The bitter taste of the morning, mixed with last night's whiskey and beer, flooded my mouth.

Nerves had made me sip from her flask, let her hang all over me. It was easier that way, watching him at a distance, and he seemed to appreciate the space and time to get to know my sister. But his words whispered in my head, reminding me he'd said that they were only friends. He'd walked me home, held my hand and... I turned to face the door to my dorm, his silhouette between the frame, a small smile on his lips, and then...

I couldn't remember.

Had he said something to me before he left? Or had I freaked him out. Was the smile a good thing or had he been laughing at me? Something Indie had said to me last night rustled around inside my head. She'd told me something about always being right, and to make sure I was safe, or maybe to get home safe. Another groan slipped past my lips as I pulled my phone from my pocket. The light of the screen hurt my eyes as I typed out a quick text letting Indie know I, in fact, lived through the night. I didn't wait for a reply, and without sitting up, I tossed my phone onto the bed. What did she mean when she said she was always right? I didn't get a chance to really perseverate, ruminate—wade in my own thoughts for too long. Three sharp knocks rattled my door, and before I could ask who it was, I heard his familiar laugh.

"Come on, Casanova, open up."

Casanova?

I gradually moved into a sitting position, letting the blood rush in slowly this time. My legs, like sacks of flour, fell over the side of my bed. Kai started to knock his incessant knocks again, and I was faced with two options: Shout, telling him to wait a damn second, which would most likely make my headache soar to DEFCON 5 of all headaches, or get to the door as quickly as possible without tripping over myself. I wasn't sure if I was capable of option two, but it was the only choice that lowered my chances of throwing up on the floor.

"Why are you here?" I asked.

Kai's face was out of focus. The light from the hall was an evil bastard.

His lips tugged up at the corners, and he handed me a cup of coffee. "I thought we were swimming today?"

Kai brushed past me and I stood in the doorway a little confused. It was the only Saturday this month we didn't have to be at the gym. I had to take a moment to find my bearings as I shut the door.

He chuckled. "Don't look so freaked. It's not mandatory, I figured I'd come up here, assess the damage, and see if you were up for it." His gaze lingered over my face. "And. Obviously you are not."

I took a sip from the cup and the heat of the coffee singed my taste buds. "Thanks for this," I said as I sat, more like plunked, down into my desk chair.

"Anytime, Casanova."

I rolled my eyes. "What's with the nickname?"

He was smug. "I don't know, you tell me."

The small sip of coffee turned to lead inside my gut. Did he know? Had he seen me with him?

"You both seemed pretty cozy is all I'm saying." Kai held my gaze as he drank from his own cup. A long silence, or maybe it only felt long to me, stretched between us. And to my surprise, he laughed. "You should see your face right now. You look like I'm about to arrest you or some shit. Dude. You do you. It's not my business who you're fu—"

"I only held his hand, it's not like that," I blurted, the idea of Kai thinking I was... I couldn't even process the word, and words were my thing.

"His?" Kai's brows sank into deep creases. "Who are you talking about?"

My heart was like a hummingbird trapped inside a glass box. Confusion and paranoia at war for my attention.

"Who are *you* talking about?" I countered.

He stared at me like the answer was obvious. "Daphne."

Daphne. It all clicked into place. She had been by my side, hanging all over me, all night at the bar. I guess from an outsider's perspective it might've seemed like we'd hit it off. But she was the last person on my mind. My hangover haze had stolen my deduction skills.

"He walked you home," Kai mused to himself in a whisper, scrutinizing me like I was a puzzle he was trying to put together. When his eyes widened, my stomach took a nosedive. He swallowed and kept his eyes on mine. "Camden." It was a statement, not a question.

I didn't know what to say so I nodded. It wasn't an admission. Or a denial. Camden had technically walked me home.

"He told me you all walked back together. That you were wasted last night. That I should check on you. I argued, figuring you'd be shacked up here with Daphne, but he'd said you'd both dropped the girls at Vigrus." Kai was doing that thing people do. Where they plot out their own thoughts in words. A verb and noun map of what they're trying to find, but can't quite see the way. "Camden?" he asked, and I stood up, the coffee I'd drank threatening to find its way up my throat.

"I need to use the bathroom," I mumbled and he reached for my forearm. His grip the only thing between me and my escape.

And I wanted to escape. Escape this unwanted, overwhelming surge, wash—wave of emotion. Escape my own uncertainty.

"Royal." He sighed and dropped my arm. "I don't care about that kind of stuff, man." I couldn't look at him, but I stayed rooted in place. "My cousin is gay, you don't have to hide that shit from—"

"I'm not gay." I mean... was I?

"Royal." Kai's tone was this strange blend of warmth and sternness. Maybe it was the leftover alcohol in my system, but my eyes pricked at the corners, this unsolicited onslaught of emotion choked me. "You like him? Like him. It's not my business," he repeated. "Or anyone else's business."

I took a wobbly step backward and sank into the desk chair. I let my face fall into my hands, and even though I wasn't full-on crying, tears tickled the tips of my fingers. It was easy telling Indie my feelings. She knew me like she knew herself. Like we were one person, two halves floating in this giant world together. Admitting something to her was like admitting something to my own brain, and I was never good at hiding from my own thoughts or feelings. Kai was an outsider. A friend. But a stranger, nonetheless. His acceptance didn't mean more than my own had, but it made my realization that much bigger.

I liked Camden. I *liked* Camden.

A boy.

I'd held his hand. I wanted so much more.

"I've never..." I sucked in a breath and wiped surreptitious fingers under my eyes as I faced him. "He's the first... guy. He's the first guy I've ever liked... like that."

"No shit?"

"No shit." I couldn't help it, but I laughed. "And he's not even gay. I probably freaked him out when I held his hand last night."

"You could always blame the booze." Kai shrugged. "But it wouldn't surprise me if he was into dudes. Honestly, I think he's an alien." I kicked his shin and he swore, laughing as he said, "He's odd, you have to admit that."

"Maybe that's why I like him."

"You've been with chicks, though, right?" He rubbed his shin with a slight frown on his face.

"Chick," I corrected. "Nat... Natalie, this girl I was with in high school, but that was different. We only fooled around, never had..." I felt my face heat. "We never slept together. She was my best friend, and... she was pretty and cool and it was like I was supposed to be with her. I didn't hate it... being with her, but it wasn't... more."

"More?"

"Yeah. More. Indie says she's waiting for more."

Kai's brows furrowed, creating dark shadows above his eyes. "More what?"

"I don't know really. It's a feeling, I guess, something *more* than normal. More than every day. Something that matters."

His lips pulled into a smirk. "And you're just now figuring out you're gay?"

"Shut up."

His held fell back as he laughed. "I'm kidding." He dragged out the word as he caught his breath. "I think that's cool... More." He rubbed his chin as if it was the greatest concept in the world. I thought it was. "I'm into more. Blondes, brunettes..."

"Ha-ha." I stood again, feeling lighter than I had since I'd touched Camden's thumb in the library that day. "Give me a couple minutes to get ready, maybe the pool is exactly what I need this morning. Let the water drown out the alcohol in my system."

"Hell, no. You'll drown and then our team will have to solely rely on me to win every damn thing. I was fucking with you about the pool, we're going to play Ultimate Frisbee." He pulled his phone from his pocket and started tapping away with his thumb.

"Frisbee what?"

His eyes were trained on the screen. "Take a shower, drink your coffee, I'll explain on the way." He glanced up at me. "Maybe I'll invite the roommate."

"That's a terrible plan."

"I think it's a great plan."

I glared at him. "Don't."

He set his phone in his lap, a shit-eating grin on his face. "Too late, Casanova."

Twenty minutes later, after I'd showered, convinced myself Kai was a liar, and even if he wasn't, Camden wasn't a guy who'd play Frisbee anyway, I was standing on the lawn behind Garrison Hall, feeling overheated and nauseous. Camden wasn't anywhere to be seen and I sighed in relief. I'd had too much heavy for one morning, and seeing him, after what had happened last night, I wasn't sure I'd know how to act, or what I'd say to him.

Kai glanced down at his watch. "Everyone is supposed to meet here in a few minutes, then we'll head over to the soccer field, but it's supposed to rain." He grinned. "Which means it's gonna get messy."

"Who's coming?" I asked, looking over his shoulder, spotting Corbin and Max making their way down the slope of wet grass.

"Just a few guys from the team."

Corbin called out a "hello" and Kai turned around.

"This is it? No one else could drag their asses out of bed?" Kai asked.

Kai offered up his fist and Max bumped it as he answered, "Yeah, everyone else wanted to sleep in. Last free Saturday of the season, and standing in the cold-ass rain is not how most want to spend their last free weekend until Thanksgiving."

"Dev and Sherman said they'd meet us at the field, said they'd ask a few guys they knew if they were down to play." Corbin lifted his chin in the direction of the soccer field.

"I invited my roommate, he just texted me, said he'd be here in a minute, then we can head over."

"Are you serious?" I asked and Kai gave me a knowing smile.

"I thought you said that kid was a freak." Max laughed.

Kai shrugged. "He's quiet, but kind of cool once he gets to know you. I was wrong, I guess."

"Usually are." Corbin snickered and I wanted to laugh, too.

I wanted to relax into my usual confidence, relax with my friends. But I was too busy listening to the beat of my own heart, hoping that when Camden came around the corner I'd be able to keep my cool.

I'd held his hand

His hand.

I shook my arm at my side trying to rid the feel of him from my skin. Not that I wanted to, but because it was the only way I could survive this day. He was a friend, I told myself, nothing more. That smile in the doorway last night was probably just a dream. And as if I'd summoned him with the thought, he appeared at the top of the hill with damp, disheveled hair, in blue jeans, and a fitted, maroon and navy blue, St. Peter's long-sleeve t-shirt. He was better than any dream I could have conjured up.

I could feel Kai's eyes watching me, watching me watch Camden, and the funny thing was, I didn't care. My lips broke into a cheek-numbing smile, and my heart nearly grew wings when Camden smiled back.

Camden

The morning sun was dying behind gray clouds, the breeze falling to an almost uncomfortable temperature, and I couldn't wipe the small smile off my face. I knew Royal was drunk last night, and anything he'd said or done shouldn't be held against him. But how could anyone quell their own desperate hope when another person looked at you like he was looking at me right now. With wide, big blue eyes, tugging me forward, and a smile that I wanted to imagine was meant only for me. I didn't dare glance around at his friends. Was this a normal reaction to seeing a friend? I let the corners of my smile dim and absorbed the realties around me. The air stood still in a way I'd never noticed before, it crackled with the anticipation of the rain, with the anticipation of us. It was like I was in his doorway again, watching as his eyes finally closed, and his breathing had turned soft and sleepy, and I'd wished I could recreate the sound somehow inside a song.

Royal looked tired today, though, his coloring paler than his usual sun kissed, but I liked that, too. He was a symphony of change, his smile making it harder and harder to walk away. Change was a sound I could run with, a sound my fingers could chase across the keys, even if the notes were foreign. Standing on this hill, looking down at him, at his friends, I wanted to be a part of them. A part of something. A part of him. Loneliness was a baritone beat, sinking its teeth into my skin, always rooting me in place.

"You ready?" Kai called up to me.

I headed down to where they had gathered along the path that led to the soccer field, and most likely to my embarrassment.

Sports were never my thing. I hated watching, playing, even talking about them. When I was five, my father had signed me up to play hockey. It was one of the only times he'd ever stood up to my mother. He'd wanted a more *well-rounded* son. Much to his dissatisfaction, my first day at the rink, I'd refused to put on the skates he'd bought. We'd gone back one more time, and I'd cried the entire way there. I've never stepped foot inside another rink. He hadn't given up, hoping he'd find something I'd like. He'd tried tee ball and soccer. Both had resulted in a terrible display of hysterics on my part. Red-faced, kicking and screaming in the grass. It'd been my mother who'd put an end to his hopes for a normal son. Or maybe the last grenade had been the day I'd told him I was curious about boys in ways that would cause him more shame than a son who sucked at sports. Regardless, both of my parents had put all their eggs in my musical basket. For a pathetic moment, I allowed myself to think *if he could see me now*. I had no idea what I was getting into when Kai texted me, and I'd almost told him no, but the walls of my room had narrowed knowing Royal would be waiting right outside my building.

"Frisbee?" Royal asked, his smile still firmly in place.

I shrugged. "Sure."

I shoved my hands in my pockets as Kai made a round of introductions, my eyes not quite meeting everyone else's. The moment with Royal dissolved into the awkward silence that followed me everywhere I went. It would've been easy to lose myself inside the sound of the wind, or the leaves like I always did, but I was here for him. Only him.

"I'm glad you're here." Royal smiled and stayed behind to fall in stride next to me as we moved toward the soccer field. "And thanks for taking care of my sister." He lowered his eyes to the concrete. "And for making sure I didn't end up passed out in the middle of the road last night."

I nodded, keeping my face forward, watching the guys in front of us push and shove each other. Their laughter was effortless. If only I could figure out their secret. It should've been easy to offer him a lighthearted knock to the shoulder with a fist, or laugh it off, tell him last night was a crazy good time, or spew some bullshit college kid cliché. Effortless was a waltz I'd never master. There were too many things I wanted to say all at once. Ask him why he'd held my hand. Why he even cared?

Why he was glad I was here? I felt it when he finally lifted his gaze, and my cheeks heated with the knowledge of what happened last night. Did he remember?

I heard him swallow before he asked, "Have you ever played Ultimate Frisbee?"

He didn't remember.

"No."

He exhaled what sounded like a breath of relief. I turned to look at him and he gave me a shy smile. "Me either."

"Hurry up, love birds, I want to get started before it starts raining," Corbin called to us over his shoulder, and the guys snickered.

Royal's smile fell into an irritated scowl and he gave Corbin the finger. He glanced at me and shook his head. "Ignore anything these idiots say today."

"Only today?" I asked and it made Royal laugh.

I wasn't sure why he thought what I said was funny. It was an honest question. But I smiled because hearing him laugh was better than hearing any of my favorite songs.

"They can get pretty competitive. It's just shit talk. Nothing personal."

The first drops of rain freed themselves from the thickening mass of silver-lined clouds, and Royal's lips parted into a wide-reaching smile. He tipped his head back, soaking up each drop. I watched as the water dripped down his cheek and he closed his eyes.

Nothing personal.

Everything about this day, about this moment, was personal.

At least, it was for me.

"Shit!" Dev threw the Frisbee wide of the goal and it flew out of bounds.

"Suck it, Dev, you throw like a fucking girl." Ellis, the goalie, grinned.

"You're an asshole." Dev planted his palms into Ellis's chest and Kai groaned behind me.

"Ellis, stop being a dick. Come on, Dev, let it go." Kai shivered and as he spoke, his breath condensed into a gray-white fog that quickly dissolved into thin air.

We were all soaked from head to toe, the rain hadn't stopped, and the weather had gotten worse the longer we played. If Dev wasn't so riled up about missing his shot, I figured he'd be shivering like the rest of us. Kai gave Dev's arm a friendly slap and he shrugged it off.

"You're a punk, Ellis, and one day that mouth of yours is going to get you in trouble." Dev shoved him one more time and started to walk away.

"Yeah, why don't you stop thinking about my mouth and play the game."

Ellis snickered but Dev ignored him. "Camden, grab the disc, let's end this shit show."

Caked in mud and grass clippings, I ran for the small white disc. I had no idea what I was doing, but I'd gotten pretty good at faking it. The game, according to Kai when he'd explained it, worked kind of like soccer. Both teams tried to score points by getting the Frisbee into the goal, a set of trees Kai had designated as goal posts. My team was down by two, and as much as I would've liked to have Royal on my team, it seemed the grind of the game had begun to take its toll on him. His hangover from last night most likely the culprit. Every attempt he'd made to catch the Frisbee ended with him face down, eating dirt. The game wasn't supposed to be a contact sport, but our guys were "accidentally" running into their guys a lot more as the game turned south for us. Royal had become their main target, and Dev and Sherman had picked up on his slow and sloppy play.

Even covered in mud, his blond more brown mixed with earth and rain, Royal was the best-looking guy on the field. Now and then I'd risked a glance at the way his wet shirt molded to the ridges of muscle underneath. A few of the guys, who showed up to play, I recognized from last year, all of them tall and built. But Royal stood out. He wasn't a carbon copy. His muscles were long and sculpted. Graceful, like he'd been formed by talented hands. His features were kind and strong, warm despite the fact he'd been getting hammered for the majority of the game. I stole another glance as I bent down to grab the Frisbee, but quickly averted my gaze when I realized he was looking in my direction.

I threw the disc to Dev and he thanked me, giving Ellis a death glare, he promised, "You bitches are going down."

For the majority of the game, I'd tried to stay out of the way, taking up a position by our goalie, protecting him, and attempting to grab any passes I could. Running down field, toward my safe spot, I heard the whoosh of the Frisbee and the sound of feet on the cold, hard ground. I didn't have a chance to turn, to get out of the way. The player's steps were too fast, too close. Stone against stone, back to back we tumbled. I was able to rotate enough to save myself from touching down face first, and the ground met my shoulder.

I absorbed all the weight of his impact. Even in the rain he smelled like sunshine.

Royal swore, the heat of his body like a blanket, he panted, "Are you okay?"

I realized I'd closed my eyes, and when I opened them, I found him hovering over me. Our chests heaved in synchronized breaths. Both of his hands on either side of my body, he'd caged me in. It didn't matter that the earth beneath me was frigid, or that every piece of fabric on my body was soaked through, blood pumped and pooled low in my stomach, heating me all the way to the base of my spine. I felt every inch of contact like an electric pulse. His knee touching my leg, the pressure of his chest, his hip brushing mine. I made a move to roll over onto my back and he lowered himself down alongside of me onto his elbow. The rain was pouring over his forehead, tracing his cheekbones and nose. I stared at the rivulets that caressed his lips with a bone-aching thirst.

"Shit, Camden, I couldn't stop. I tried, but it's too damn slippery." He laughed, laying his back onto the wet grass. "This game sucks."

I choked out a laugh of my own, and he turned his head at the same time I did. Our eyes met and his laughter faded. I didn't want to look at his tempting mouth, or give in to the silence that was making it difficult to breathe. I wanted to stay right here, inside the center of this crescendo, hyperaware of how close our limbs were to one another. If I reached out an inch, or two, I could touch his hand with mine. Distant voices, the pitter patter of rain, the thud, thud, thud of my heart, I shut it out. He stared at me. Just stared as the sky opened up and washed us clean.

"I held your hand," he whispered.

"You remember?"

"I do." He pulled his bottom lip through his teeth and I held my breath for three, maybe four seconds until he spoke again. "I hope I didn't..." He exhaled and stuttered on a nervous chuckle. "I don't want you to think..." Royal was the first to break eye contact, pulling his eyes to the sky, leaving me alone as he tripped over his words. "I mean... I don't want you to freak out."

"Come on, ladies!" Ellis shouted, interrupting, and we both sat up slowly, remembering that we were not alone.

I rested my arms on my knees, ignoring the way my shoulder ached. Royal wouldn't look at me, preferring to keep his head tipped down. The guys were at the other end of the field, most of them huddled in discussion, waiting for us to get up and continue the game. The only one really paying us any mind was Kai, but he didn't seem concerned. After all, most of the guys had ended up on the ground at least once today. I glanced over my shoulder at our goalie, he was farther away than I'd thought. I hadn't made it all the way down field before Royal had crashed into me.

No one was close enough to hear our conversation, and when Royal made a move to stand, I stopped him. "Why?"

He looked at me again, his brows dipped.

"Why did you hold my hand?"

He stared at me, his face serious, contemplative, and I could see the pulse in the slope of his neck, each rapid beat getting faster as every second stretched.

"I'm not sure," he finally answered in a whisper more for himself than for me.

I was lightheaded, my empty stomach filling with uncertainty and dread. I wanted to throw up. I shouldn't have asked. I should have left it alone. He'd had too much to drink. That's why. That's the only reason it could be. More than anything, I was scared he'd figure out that I'd liked it, that I wanted him to hold my hand again, that I wanted to do all the things I'd been told I could never, should never, want. I'd made a friend and I was going to ruin it.

"Are we cool?" he asked, his own anxiety making it sound like a plea.

I nodded, turned my gaze down field, and let him off the hook.

"Yeah, we're cool."

Royal

Lie.

The word was on repeat for the rest of the morning, stretching out into synonyms as the day progressed.

Fabrication.

Deceit.

Dishonest.

Soggy and frozen to the bone, the only thing I thought about as the game ended, and as I watched Camden run his fingers through his soaked hair, was how much I wanted to feel those fingers laced through mine again. I'd told him I wasn't sure why I'd held his hand. I was too much of a coward to tell him the truth. To tell him I liked him in a way I didn't fully understand. That I wanted to hold his hand, maybe even feel his lips on mine. That I couldn't stop my eyes from tracing every single line of muscle that had revealed itself under the clinging dampness of his t-shirt. The dips and valleys of his stomach drawing my attention in ways I never would have thought possible.

I felt high.

Sick with something I couldn't put a finger on.

An itch I wanted to scratch until it bled.

I'd liked having him underneath me. For that split second, when our bodies had collided and aligned, everything had felt right. Clicked. I liked guys. Or maybe just *guy*. I hadn't explored any other options because my head was always spinning his name over and over. He was a piece of thread I kept unraveling, and the more I pulled him apart, the more I wanted to keep going. Maybe I did like guys, but had never noticed because no one had ever piqued my interest. I'd always had Nat, and now...

I let my eyes roam the field, looking at each one of my friends and, without a doubt, I knew I wasn't into any one of them. My eyes caught Camden's. *He* was staring at *me*.

What was that?

I chewed the side of my cheek, biting back a smile, when Kai sent me a smirk from behind Camden's shoulder. I was overthinking all of this. Being straight didn't mean I would be attracted to every single female. And if I was gay, it didn't mean I'd be attracted to every dude, either. Attraction didn't work like that. It was discriminant. It favored what the body wanted. It was all chemical, and something about Camden, maybe it was his music, and maybe it was because he was odd, or maybe it was because he smelled like spice and soap, and so perfectly masculine, that it made me feel like I was walking toward something I've always known. He made me feel nostalgic for something I'd never had.

"Fuck, I'm hungry," Kai grumbled as he stalked up to me and shoved the Frisbee into my chest. I shoved it right back. "Let me guess, you're going to have lunch with your sister."

Rain rivulets trickled down his nose, the sky hadn't stopped its torment. It didn't usually rain this heavy. More like mist and a light, perpetual shower. Today it was torrential. "Come have lunch with us. We're halfway through this semester and you barely know her. It's weird. She's my sister, dude, and you're my best friend. You guys should be plotting against me."

He leaned in. "I figured you'd want to talk to her, about..." He cleared his throat. "You know, everything."

The guys were heading toward us. Camden was with them, off to the side in his own bubble as they all laughed and talked crap to each other. Ellis, unfortunately, had shown up to play and had been the worst shit talker of them all. It appeared he had something to prove every time he was around me. It didn't help I'd kicked his ass every swim practice. My times consistently outpaced his by at least fifteen seconds. I wondered how he'd even gotten on the team, to be honest.

"I mean, you need to process, right? You don't want me around for all the hearts and squeals." He chuckled.

"You're such a dick. I don't even know why I'm friends with you."

"It's because you secretly think I'm hot."

"You're going to say stupid crap like that all the time now, aren't you?" He nodded, his lips tugging up at the corners as I whispered, "I don't even know why I like him, Kai. I mean, I do, but—"

"Food. STAT," Corbin interrupted, and the group echoed his sentiment in grunts.

"I'm pretty sure I'm gonna need Bethy to blow me so I can get my balls to crawl back out. I'm fucking cold." Ellis made a big show of shivering and grabbing his junk.

Kai rolled his eyes. "If she can find your dick."

"Why don't you blow me?" Ellis sneered. "Oh, that's right, that's what Royal's for."

A few of the guys laughed, but the others, the older swimmers, looked to Kai for his reaction. Kai was all smiles, but I'd learned his tells. His shoulders were hard and his spine was straight as he flicked a murderous gaze in Ellis's direction. "Screw you, Ellis. Maybe next time he blows me, you'd like to watch?"

Everyone was laughing now, even Dev who was more serious than the rest of the guys on most things. I laughed, but it bubbled out more like a nervous giggle as I caught the reaction on Camden's face. Despite the freezing rain, his cheeks were bright red, his eyes down and his hands shoved into his wet pockets. He swallowed and shifted awkwardly on his feet. My smile faltered.

"I don't know how long you guys are gonna talk about your love lives, but I'm going to Annie's. I need some fucking pancakes." Sherman gave Camden a friendly shove. "You coming?"

Camden lifted his head, his eyes on mine when he answered, "No. I have to practice."

Ellis snorted, and before he could make another lewd comment, I blurted, "I can't go either. I'm meeting Indie at Beckett. I'll walk back with you."

Camden didn't respond, but he didn't walk away, either.

"Seriously, you're pulling the sister card again." Dev gave me a smirk. "Or are you pissed because we ended up winning?"

I laughed and it eased the tension that had begun to build in my shoulders. It was all smack talk. Stuff I should be used to. But Ellis had rubbed me the wrong way since the first day I'd met him, and something in my gut told me if he ever got wind of the feelings I was developing for Camden, my life here at St. Peter's would become a total disaster.

"No, man. I promised her I'd meet up with her. You guys have fun, though."

"I work tonight, if you want—"

I cut Kai off, "Nah, I've got a lot of homework."

"Yeah." He held up his fist and I bumped it with my own. "Don't I know it. It only gets worse, dude." Kai gave me a smile before he glanced over to his suitemate. "At least you have a single, no moody neighbor playing music all night." Kai spoke in a teasing tone, and to my surprise, Camden's lips twitched into an almost smile. "I'm glad you decided to live a little... thanks for coming out."

Camden lifted his chin. "Thanks for the invitation."

"You played hard, fool." Dev's smile crinkled around his eyes as he gave Camden a slap on the back. I had to bite back a laugh at the stricken look on Camden's face.

After a few more goodbyes, the group split and the guys headed to Annie's, leaving me and Camden standing side by side in a thick silence. The alcohol had been officially worked out of my system, my hangover overshadowed by the emptiness in my gut and the chill in my bones. Pancakes at the local greasy spoon sounded perfect right about now, but I needed to talk to my sister, needed her to help sort the mess inside my head. Bonus, a few more minutes with Camden, alone. I had to work through this nervousness. Figure out if he was something I could even pursue, and that was definitely worth missing out on hot coffee and a powdered sugar utopia.

"Ready?" I asked and he nodded.

Perhaps there was something there for him, too. He'd let me hold his hand, hadn't he? We started up the hill toward Garrison Hall, the previous night playing in my head on repeat. I'd held his hand, he'd curled his fingers through mine, he'd made sure I'd gotten home safely and... The vision of him in my doorway, that small smile on his lips flashed inside my head all over again.

"You stayed," I whispered, and we both stopped at the top of the hill a little out of breath. "Last night, until I fell asleep."

He toed at the wet earth with the tip of his sneaker, his head down, he admitted, "I was worried. I didn't know if you were going to puke or not. Didn't want you to choke."

I bumped my shoulder with his and he raised his gaze. His big eyes swallowed me whole, and I stuttered over my words. "That... That was really cool of you."

"Isn't that what friends do?" he asked, his brow furrowed deeply, his head tilting an inch to the side.

He wasn't asking in a way that suggested "duh, that's what friends are for." He was literally asking, *isn't that what friends are supposed to do*, like maybe he didn't know. Like he'd never had a friend before. I'd looked at this all wrong. He didn't like me like *that*. He was really that socially out of it. Was I his first-ever real friend? He hadn't left his room much, at least not since I'd started hanging out with Kai every afternoon. I knew he was a loner. Knew being a word I used loosely because I had a feeling no one truly *knew* who Camden Morgan really was. He wanted to be my friend, a friend who he had no idea what to do with. And I wanted him, a feeling I had no idea what to do with.

I couldn't help it, but I laughed.

His smile was tentative as he asked, "What?"

"Nothing." I shook my head, my smile spreading far across my face. "Yeah, Camden, it's what friends do."

His full lips lifted, smiling all the way to his eyes, and my chuckle stopped short at the sheer beauty of it. I hadn't seen this smile yet, and I felt pretty damn privileged to witness it. His hair dripped, heavy with the rain, and fell into his eyes, skimming his black lashes. I had the urge to push the strands to the side. But, that would have been creepy as hell, since friends aren't technically supposed to touch each other like that. I ran my antsy fingers through my own hair instead.

Feeling awkward, I asked, "Do you want to have lunch with me... I mean... not just me... my sister will be there."

Jesus, I was an idiot.

That smile, though. I'd deal with my embarrassment and lack of proper word use any day to get to see it more often.

"I've got to work on my recital piece, it's on the tenth of this month and I haven't mastered it."

"I doubt that. You're a *genius*. Remember? Go clean up and meet us at Beckett."

He turned his gaze to the dorms, and I regretted pushing so hard.

"Only if you want to," I added, my voice as easy-breezy as I could muster.

"I want to." The words tumbled from his mouth. Camden raised his head, his stormy eyes scanning my face. "But I have to practice."

My smile was half-hearted, but I hoped he hadn't noticed as I assured him, "Next time, then."

He nodded. "Next time."

"I think you should text him, he gave you his number, right?" Indie fell on my bed with a grunt.

"He did, before I left to meet you." I playfully pushed her hip. "Move it, Pink."

She grunted again, her hands holding her stomach. "I shouldn't have eaten so much."

I narrowed my eyes as she slowly scooted over, granting me a little space on the mattress. "You had a half of a sandwich. That hardly counts as 'eating so much.'"

I lay down next to her, the end of her side braid tickling my cheek. "I also ate two pieces of cake, and don't change the subject. Text him, go see him tonight."

I'd given Indie the complete run down of my night and morning over lunch. She hadn't seemed fazed by any of it, as if I'd told her about a girl, like there was no difference at all, like it wasn't some earth-shattering thing that her brother might be bi-sexual. Bi-sexual had been the term she'd thrown around so easily over lunch, but I guess if things were reversed, I'd be the same way. She supported me, and I'd always supported her, it didn't mean we didn't worry about the other getting hurt. We just made sure we were the net the other could fall into if need be.

"I saw him already once today. It would be weird."

She exhaled and elbowed me in the rib.

"Shit." I groaned. "What the hell?"

My entire body felt like I'd been hit by a bus, run over twice, and then stomped into the ground by a stampede of elephants. I hadn't had a chance to shower since Ultimate Frisbee, and my injuries had started to make themselves known. It also didn't help that my jeans were still a little damp, and my entire level of comfort was about a negative five.

Indie giggled. "Sorry. But sometimes you can be as stubborn as Uncle Liam."

"So, you resort to violence?"

I couldn't see her face but I swear I heard her eyes rolling. "You like him?"

"Yes."

I felt her shrug. "Then text him. What's the problem?"

She was over-simplifying. I could list at least three problems. So, I did. "One. He said he wanted to practice. Two. I'm not sure that liking him is all that healthy. And Three. There's no guarantee he feels that way about me."

She sat up, her icy blue eyes resting on my face, worry creasing her brows, as she asked, "What do you mean it's not healthy?"

My throat was scratchy when I spoke, the words like gravel as they left my lips. "Let's say Kai was right, and Camden is..."

"Gay."

"Gay," I said the word and it fell between us with a tangible, profound—substantial weight. "What if we started something and... what would..." I paused, letting the idea sink in. "What would our family say, Pink?"

"Mom and Dad love us no matter what, Blue. You know that. They wouldn't even bat an eyelash."

My heart was a thunderstorm inside my chest. It swelled, taking up too much space. I could hardly breathe.

"And Liam... he's... old school. He'd probably think I was sick for even thinking—"

"Stop." She shook her head. "You don't know that and—"

"Oh God, and Uncle Kieran." I slammed my eyes shut. "Mom said he was almost a priest before he met Aunt Mel. And what about our cousins? What if Ava and Quinn weren't allowed to hang out with me anymore."

The list of why nots kept getting longer and longer. My team, my coach—shit—Ellis. This was a Catholic private college, I'd get thrown out. *Wouldn't I?*

"Okay." The matter-of-fact word had my eyes popping open. "You're clearly in panic mode, and I'm not going to tell you that you're wrong. Yes..." She spoke like she was talking to a frightened dog, using her low—everything was going to be alright—quiet tone. "The world can be close-minded, hateful—intolerant. You can't make choices based on what others might do or say or think. What if Mom never left her first husband because she was scared about what her family would think? You know they hated Dad, but she left because she wanted a better life for herself, because she knew Dad was it for her. We wouldn't be here..." Her voice thinned, and she tugged on the sleeve of my shirt. "Our family was built on love, Blue, and if Uncle Liam or anyone has anything to say, they don't deserve to see your happiness, to be a part of your life." I blinked away the burn in my eyes, and she gave me a sad smile. "I've never wanted anyone, never had a boyfriend, and watching you talk about Camden, you get so bright, you bleed out all the shades of blue and turn to gold, and that's what I want, too. So, text him, damn it. I want to live vicariously through you." She sniffled and coughed out a laugh.

I sat up and pulled her into a hug. I'd always thought she was the small and fragile one, but she'd proved today she was definitely the stronger of us both. I chuckled and kissed the top of her head.

"I'm so glad I have you to talk to. I don't know how I would have gotten through all of this."

"It's cool Kai's on board." She pulled away and wiped her eyes. "He seems... like a nice guy." She let her eyes fall to the bedspread, and her cheeks turned a pale shade of pink.

"A nice guy, huh?" I teased, and she shot me an annoyed look.

Standing, she grabbed my phone from my desk and tossed it to me. "Text. Him."

"What should I say?" I stared at the black screen.

"Tell him he needs someone to listen to his recital piece... um... to make sure it sounds okay."

"I think that might actually work." I glanced up from my phone, the grin on Indie's face gave me confidence.

After all, friends helped each other with all sorts of things. Camden had helped me get home safe, made sure I hadn't aspirated on my own puke, and had "helped" me with my math homework.

"It will. I have a good feeling."

"You say that about everything," I said with a crooked smile.

She kissed my forehead. "And everything always turns out like it should."

Royal

M*e: Hey, it's Royal.*
I pressed send and waited.

Nothing.

Two minutes.

Nothing.

Another five.

I fell back onto my bed with a sigh, thinking Indie might have been wrong about texting him in the first place.

I held my phone over my face and typed again.

Me: Kai's friend.

My hand hovered over the send button and I rolled my eyes. *Kai's friend?* No shit. I hit the backspace. I was about to give in to the grumblings of my stomach and just eat dinner with Indie like I'd planned, when the screen lit.

Camden: Hey.

My cheeks actually hurt from the giant, dumb, smile that broke across my face.

Me: Still practicing?

Luckily, I didn't have to wait as long this time. His response was immediate.

Camden: Always.

I blew out a breath and debated on what I wanted to ask first. Did he want to hang out? Was he hungry? As I vacillated, he sent another text.

Camden: Why?

Straight to the point. I figured I'd offer him the same courtesy.

Me: Want company?

That sounded weird. Didn't it?

Me: Maybe you need a second opinion. On your recital piece?

Camden: And you're qualified?

I laughed out loud, and like an idiot, I looked around my empty room to see if anyone noticed.

Me: Yes. In fact. I am. Many years of listening to classical piano while doing homework gives me all the credentials I need.

Me: And I'm bored and hungry and really just wanted to hang out.

I pulled the pin and pressed send on the last thing I'd typed. My pulse pounded behind my temples as I awaited his response. It was completely ridiculous that my mouth felt dry, and that my hands were sweating. I rubbed one over my jean-clad thigh. Yup. Sweaty. Camden had me tied in knots. I remembered the story my father had told me about the time Mom had spoken to him for the first time and I didn't feel quite so lame. He'd said he'd never been so amped. He'd told me Mom's voice alone had made him feel crazier than any of the whispering voices he'd learned to deal with over the years. I was a little crazy right now. Electric in my own skin, but at least I knew what *this* felt like. This. I wouldn't settle for less.

The phone vibrated and I almost dropped it.

Camden: I could use a second opinion.

I sat up, the smile on my face more gregarious than it had any right to be.

Royal: Any dinner ideas?

Camden: Anything but Chinese.

By the time I'd made it to Camden's front door, the entire bottom of the to-go bag had saturated with grease. The grease from the hot ham and Swiss subs I'd grabbed from Beckett had spread faster than I could make it across campus. The flimsy, white paper bag had the potential to fall apart at any moment. Avoiding disaster, I'd chosen to support the bottom of the bag with both hands and was forced to knock, not so gently, with my foot. I tried not to bite the side of my cheek as I waited. More keyed up than I'd ever been in my entire life, I shifted my weight from my left foot to my right, and relaxed a little when I heard the metallic scrape of the bolt lock.

Camden stood framed by the door with flushed cheeks and bright eyes. He stared like he was eager to see me, too, and when he smiled, my stomach flopped like a suffocating fish on the sand.

"Come in." He stood to the side, and I passed him, telling myself to be casual.

Act cool.

Steady.

We were friends. Everything else would have to wait.

"I brought subs from the dining hall. Hope that's okay?" I asked as I set the bag on the small coffee table.

"It's fine," he said in a tone that made me wonder if it really was. He seemed nervous. Fidgety. He shoved his hands in his pockets. "I have a couple of sodas in my mini fridge."

"That'd be great." I gave him a soft smile as I sat on the couch. "Thanks."

He left me alone in the living room and I pulled the two subs from the bag. This was just like hanging out with Kai. There was no need to be nervous. It wasn't like a date or anything. For all I knew, Camden was as straight as an arrow. I lifted my gaze and caught him standing in the doorway of his bedroom. With two Cokes in his hands, he watched me in a way that had me doubting *my straight as an arrow* defense. A quiet gasp, a stuttered breath, escaped his throat as I met his almost heated gaze. I hadn't imagined that dark look, or how I'd felt it all the way to my toes. He blinked and dropped his head as he moved toward the couch.

His voice was rough when he said, "Thanks for bringing dinner."

He set the two cans of soda on the table and sat on the couch, not close enough that our knees or shoulders would touch, but closer than Kai usually sat next to me. I was thinking too much and a small chuckle escaped.

I held up the grease-soiled napkins as a decoy for my anxious laughter. "Got any more of these?"

After he grabbed a few paper towels from a cabinet in their *pantry*—the coat closet where Kai stored all his ramen and protein powder—we ate in a not-so-comfortable silence. A few minutes passed and I started second-guessing myself all over again.

I was spiraling, thinking of something to say, when he spoke first. "I'm not good at this."

I swallowed my bite, nearly choking, when I asked, "Eating dinner?"

He waved his hand. "This. Socialization." He smiled and it broke through the seemingly impenetrable wall between us.

"You don't give yourself enough credit. I'm here. You invited me over."

"You invited yourself."

I laughed openly. "I'm pushy."

When I want something.

"Kai's pushy. You're..." He turned away from me and I wished for the end of that sentence. "It's hard for me to make friends."

"Did you have more friends back home?"

He shook his head.

"No siblings, right?"

"No... I don't think my parents wanted children. I was a surprise, which is ironic because my father is an obstetrician."

"What type of doctor is your mom?"

"A psychiatrist." He set his half-eaten sub back on its open wrapper. "My parents were very strict. School. Piano. School. Piano. The roles were always set, always clear. My parents are doctors and I will be a composer."

It seemed so permanent, like a sentence he'd been given. The sadness in his voice was expertly hidden, but I'd heard it anyway.

"You can be whatever you want be." He looked at me, and his eyes filled with so many questions. "At least, that's what my parents have been telling me for years."

"What do your parents do?"

"They're artists. Painters. They own a gallery a mile from our apartment in Salt Lake."

He swallowed, and a smile hinted at the corners of his lips. "What was that like? Growing up with artists for parents?"

I leaned back into the cushions of the couch, my sandwich forgotten on its wrapper, and shrugged. "Kind of cool. Kind of dysfunctional." I cringed. Camden came from propriety and money and me... well... "My dad's also a tattoo artist. He and his two brothers own a tattoo shop together."

"Like skulls and roses?" he asked, his gray eyes finding that small spark of green. The interest lighting him up from the inside out.

I nodded and raised my brows. "We sound like hippies, right?"

"It sounds fun, actually." Camden exhaled. "Diversity was never celebrated in the Morgan household."

He should have been celebrated. From what I had heard of his talent so far, his parents should have celebrated him every damn day.

"But you love playing the piano?"

"I do." Again, his eyes searched the room. "Silence gives me anxiety." He chuckled and the sound of it nestled its way under my skin. "That's really fucking crazy, right?"

I coughed out a laugh. "I don't think so, and I'm well versed in crazy. Not too weird. I promise."

He faced me, a question forming itself inside the creases around his eyes. "How are you well versed in crazy?"

I hadn't mentioned to anyone, not even Kai, about my dad or my sister's mental illness. It wasn't that I was ashamed of who they were. It'd felt wrong offering up their privacy to people. But Camden was offering up his shattered fragments. I had broken pieces, too, and I wanted him to know broken didn't always mean bad.

"Ever heard of schizoaffective disorder?"

"No."

"My sister and my dad struggle with moods. Up and down. Depression and periods of mania. They control their symptoms with therapy and meds, but they always hear voices in their head. And some days are darker than others."

"It's why they paint? Isn't it?"

I nodded. "Silence gives you anxiety. But they would give anything for a few moments of silence." My smile was small. "Though, my sister says without the voices she'd probably suck at painting. My dad says the same thing. But I call bullshit." I laughed. "My mom doesn't hear voices and she's the most talented one in the family." I whispered, "Don't tell Indie I said that."

"I won't," he answered, his voice serious.

"I'm joking."

He smiled. "Oh."

I leaned over and took a sip from my can of soda.

"Do you paint?" he asked, and I set the can back onto the table.

"I don't. Swimming is my thing."

"And you're good at it?"

My laugh came easy. "I'd like to think so. You should come to the meet this week. Even if we all suck, it would be cool to have you there."

"I'll try. I have to—"

"Practice."

We both smiled.

"That's why I'm here, right. To tell you whether your recital piece is worthy?"

His lips parted into another heart-stopping grin. "It's worthy. I'm just a perfectionist."

"You think?" I gave him a friendly shove with my elbow. "Show me what you got."

We wrapped up the leftover sandwiches and he placed them inside the mini fridge under his desk. His room was more cluttered than I would have imagined, despite the barren walls and solid gray comforter, it felt warm—lived in. His desk had scattered sheets of music strewn across it. Most of which were riddled with pencil smudges where I figured he'd changed his compilations of notes. I didn't know the first thing about reading music, but I wished I would have learned at some point. It would've been nice to speak his language.

"If you want, you can sit on the bed." His desk chair was occupied with a leaning tower of books, crowned with his laptop and backpack. "Sorry about the mess."

He pushed his hands in his pockets and his cheeks colored. A few stray strands of his brown hair fell across his forehead. The strands looked clean and soft and I wondered if his spiced scent originated from his shampoo or soap. It wasn't heavy like a cologne, and when he turned toward his keyboard, I had an impulse to bury my nose in the hair at his nape. The thought made the tips of my fingers tingle, and I felt myself harden inside the confines of my blue jeans. Grateful he was faced in the opposite direction, I sat down on the foot of the bed, trying to think about anything but the blood pumping in my veins. I recited the alphabet in my head, and when that didn't work, I thought about the summer I'd fallen off my uncle's parked motorcycle and skinned my knee behind Avenues Ink. I'd barely turned five years old and Liam had yelled at me for leaving the shop without permission. My uncle could be scary when he wanted to be. The memory did the trick, and I kept my eyes on the ceiling until the quiet notes began to fill the air. I didn't look at him at first. I only listened. I let his music fill all the cracks in my confidence, all my questions drifting away with the haunting notes.

When I finally allowed my eyes a taste, Camden's head was down, his fingers gliding across the keys. His shoulders were broad and solid under the washed-out gray cotton of his tee. I watched as the muscles in his back stretched with each deep breath he took while he played. He didn't make one mistake. Or, if he did, I hadn't noticed. Like the first day I'd heard him play that August afternoon, and every afternoon since, I was lost to the song. To the man playing it. Listening, now, so close, it was more real. It was easy to picture him alone in a room somewhere, cold and white color surrounding him. Inside a house that could only ever pretend to be home. I could hear his lonely adolescence as the notes fell, and at the end, when the melody trickled into tight, sharp steps, I could hear his anger.

The room had become utterly silent, the last note no longer hanging between us as he turned toward me. He leaned against the keyboard and asked, "What's your assessment?"

It took me a second to answer, to catch my breath. From where I sat on his bed, he towered over me with full lips and a tight jaw. Stunned, I spoke in a whisper. "Complicated and beautiful."

"Yeah?" His lips twitched and I thought he might smile.

I nodded, and if I wasn't terrified by what his response would've been, I might've added, "Like you."

Camden

The music had proven to be a poor distraction. I looked over my shoulder at my empty bed, and the lie I'd been telling myself these past four days rang false inside my head. Out of tune. I played a new sequence of notes and let them hang in the air. If I could, I would pluck each one of them down, swallow them, and hope they'd help me remember what the hell I was doing. I gave up and fell backward onto my bed, closed my eyes, and exhaled a long breath. I couldn't practice anymore. The song was hollow. *I didn't need him here.* The lie had become hollow, too.

Like usual, Royal had been in my dorm suite every afternoon, but instead of hanging out on the couch, feeding into Kai's addiction to Chinese food, he'd made his way to my room. He'd bide his time, eat his dinner, then nine steps later there'd be a knock on my door, followed by a handsome boy laid out across my bed. He'd work on his math and sometimes we'd talk. Most of the time he'd just stare at me. I could feel it when he stared at me. The heat of his eyes on my back as I played. He never seemed to mind that I'd practice the same song over and over. I liked playing for him. I liked playing for him too much. I'd told myself I had to adapt. I didn't want to accept that my focus had begun to shift because he'd been there.

I'd always had music. Sound. It had been my only companion for so long I'd forgotten how good it could feel to share it with someone. I'd had a friend once when I was in elementary school. A girl who my mother would invite over from time to time because her talent had rivaled mine. Penny would sit on the couch and listen to me play, and I remembered smiling when she'd clapped like crazy for me. But when she had played, the stark white silence of my house had shattered with staccato bursts of warmth. Penny had stopped coming over after she won the Beth Ann Deville Youth Composition Award that year. I'd placed second. The house never sounded the same again.

I'd learned I couldn't depend on anything, on anyone but myself. I always had to be the best. But he was everywhere now. I could smell him on my sheets at night when I'd try to fall asleep. His scent of summer influenced my choice of notes as I lay in bed thinking of half steps, tonal systems, and pitch. I had less than a week left to perfect my recital piece, but I'd struggled to find the melody all afternoon.

Royal was the difference.

Those four words needled their way through my thoughts and the lie was obliterated.

His first race was this afternoon.

I should be there.

I should be there.

The sentence banged around inside my brain. Loud and annoying. My eyes opened and fixed onto the ceiling. I counted the three cracks near the left side of the wall and sat up abruptly. This room was a tomb.

I grabbed my phone and my wallet from my desk, not thinking too hard about my heart and how it pumped too quickly. The tight feeling inside my chest didn't subside until I was shutting the front door of Garrison behind me. The cool evening air clung to the light layer of sweat on my forehead as my feet hit the pavement. I'd chosen to move toward something instead of laying stagnant.

Royal had invited me, had given me something to look forward to. And that was a good thing. Having friends was normal. Going out on a weeknight was normal. I was tired of sabotaging myself.

I could be normal.

The Aquatic Center was humid, the smell of chlorine smacking me in the face as I pulled open the doors. The front desk was abandoned, but I followed the noisy cheers and splashes until I found the stairwell that led me to the set of bleachers that sat above the pool. I found an empty row at the top and took a seat. The setting sun illuminated the pool through a huge floor-to-ceiling glass wall. Shades of gold and pink and orange danced over the water, only interrupted by small, white-crested waves formed by the swimmers cutting through the pool like blades.

I found myself leaning closer, on the edge of my seat as I searched for him in the chaos. It took me only a few seconds, and if I hadn't already memorized his gait, I might've missed him. He strode with confidence, his tan skin wet and shimmering, to the edge of the pool. Royal's body was sculpted, defined with sharp valleys that dripped into a perfect V. He wore nothing but his small, tight, swimming trunks, goggles, and a St. Peter's cap. My breath stuttered as he lowered himself into position. The crowd went quiet, and when the whistle blew, and he sliced through the surface, I heard it. The moment when the sun broke past the horizon and kissed his body as he parted through the water.

Brilliant and bold.

An orchestra with each stroke. I couldn't take my eyes off him as he manipulated the elements. Using air as fuel, bending water to his will. He was fast, faster than humanly possible, and each kick of his foot mimicked the galloping beat of my heart.

"Win," I heard myself whisper.

Win.

Win.

Win.

The crowd roared when he touched the wall, and every hair on my arm stood at attention. His pride shined brighter than the dying sun, and when he pulled himself from the pool, I realized there was no going back. There was no way I could turn it off. This thing he'd lit inside of me. It burned too hot and I no longer cared for the world's definition of normal. There was nothing normal in the way my cheeks heated simply because I got to watch him walk across that room. His eyes were on the crowd and there was nothing normal in the way I sat taller, hoping he would see me. And when his eyes finally found mine, there was definitely nothing normal about the way his face split into a million facets of light.

Royal was a beacon, and I was hopelessly drawn to him. He ran his hand down his wet arm, and I didn't avert my eyes. There was no point. I was sunk. I wanted to want him, admitting to myself I needed him in any capacity. Being alone was exhausting. I made myself hold his stare, hold on to that thinly woven shred of hope. Our friendship. I even allowed my lips to lift into a smile as I nodded my chin in his direction. An atta-boy that earned me a wave.

A few rows down, a blonde head turned, and his sister greeted me with a wide smile of her own. Part of me paled at the thought of her sitting next to me. Would she read my body language, my thoughts? But as she stood, and I watched her make her way down her row and up the stairs, I relaxed a little. After all, she was the one who'd hinted I might have a chance with Royal, that I might be his *type*.

"Mind if I join you?" she asked, making herself comfortable at my side.

"I've come to the conclusion that you and your brother only ask to do things because you think you're being polite."

She giggled. It was soft and gauzy. "And in reality?"

"You just do what you want without hearing the answer."

She laughed and her head tilted to the side. "Would you have said no?"

"I want your company. I don't mind if you sit next to me."

Her lips were glossy and pink and they parted as she exhaled. "But..." she prompted.

"But it isn't truly polite unless you actually wait for an answer to the inquiry."

"Noted." She wrinkled her nose and played with the stray piece of straw-colored hair that had escaped from her braid. "I bet he's dying a little inside right now."

"Who? Royal?" I asked.

"Who else? It's why you're here."

"He invited me, but if you think I should leave I could—"

She placed her hand on my forearm. "No, that's not what I meant. He told me today he didn't think you'd come. He wants you here." Her gaze was understanding. "He likes you, Camden."

I dropped my eyes to where her hand touched the skin of my arm. She'd hinted at something I wanted more than I should, but could she actually mean that he *liked* me. I wanted to ask her what he'd said about me. Was it friendly or was she making something more out of it than she should? But I'd just lectured her about being polite, and wheedling her for information about her brother was anything but.

I settled for the truth and I'd let her make of it what she would. "I like him, too. I don't have many friends." Or any, for that matter.

Indie squeezed my arm and let go. "Well, now you have two more." She truly was a beautiful girl, especially when she smiled.

She had a sad way about her, but under the surface she was just as radiant as Royal. Indie and her brother were two of the most striking people I'd ever met. It made me wonder even more what their parents were like. My parents weren't anything special. Carbon copies of everyone on our street. Suits and monochromatic dresses. Dull brown hair and tight faces. My mother could be considered pretty, if she actually smiled, and maybe my dad was handsome, but it was hard to judge when they felt like strangers. The surface was always a lie, you had to know a person to see their beauty.

"Will you be at all the meets?" I asked.

She nodded. "Most of them. I'll miss a few because of projects I'm working on, but I'll try my best to be there if I can. Blue was kind of sad today. This will be the first swim meet our dad has missed."

We both looked out over the pool, searching for that same streak of gold skin.

"From what Royal's told me, your parents seem like good people."

"They are. They've always been there for us, not every kid is so lucky." She startled and sucked in a breath, bumping my shoulder with hers and pointed. "He's up. Let's embarrass the hell out of him?"

"Why—"

I didn't get a chance to finish my question. She stood, tugging the sleeve of my t-shirt, essentially dragging me to me feet. She was stronger than she appeared for someone as tiny as she was. Indie cupped her palms around her mouth, projecting her voice to a volume I wouldn't think her capable as she yelled, "Let's go, O'Connell!" She knocked her hip into mine and stepped up onto the bleacher. "Come on, don't leave me hanging."

Her cheeks were as red as a tomato, so I did what I had to do. I couldn't let her make a fool out of herself. At least, that was what I'd tell Royal later. If I got to see him later. I hoped I did. I stepped up next to her, feeling like a sore thumb. Everyone here had cheered, but we were making a spectacle. I raised my fingers, placing them on my wet lips and whistled. The high pitch made her whoop even louder and she jumped up and down. My entire face heated, and I was sure I'd blushed all the way to my hairline.

"God, I wish I'd made a sign," she said. "He's going to kill me." Indie giggled, flailing her hands back and forth above her head, hollering until he looked up from his position on the mark with a shy and goofy, lopsided smile that struck me in the stomach.

Despite everything, my nerves, my questions, I laughed. I actually laughed, and whistled, and acted like a complete idiot. My heart was like a cymbal, clashing and clanging. My cheeks were on fire, and I loved it.

I loved it.

Royal

I t felt fantastic to win. Hearing nothing but the beat of your heart inside your ears, flying through the water, and in the end, being the one holding the trophy. You and your team. Perfection. But tonight was more. That elusive *more* I'd always searched for, I'd gotten a glimpse of it when I'd stood on the mark for my second race of the night. Indie and Camden screaming like lunatics, it had been embarrassing... and everything... at the same time. I'd only wished they had been sitting closer, sitting on that bottom bleacher. It would have been nice to see the blush that I had no doubt colored Camden's cheeks. Indie was a miracle worker. I had no idea how she got him to cheer like that, but I planned on giving her the biggest damn hug as soon as I was finished getting dressed.

"Hell yeah," Ellis shouted as he walked through the locker room. "We killed it tonight."

"Home field advantage. Next meet won't be as easy." Kai pulled up his jeans and flopped down next to me on the bench. "You swam well tonight," he said, eyeing Ellis. "But you were slow off the mark. Do that shit in Bayview and you'll lose every race."

Ellis snorted, and I grabbed my shirt from my locker, ignoring the pissing contest about to commence. Kai was our captain, and he would always tell us straight what we needed to work on. But Ellis never wanted to hear anything that Kai had to say. I'd get Kai to fess up, eventually. There had to be a reason Ellis hated him so much.

"Royal was slow off the mark on his second round. His little pep squad distracted him." Ellis's smile was more like a sneer as I turned to face him.

I stuffed my goggles and cap in my duffel and zipped it. "Don't drag me into this. I bested my practice times by one-point-two seconds."

"I bet your sister and your boyfriend bring pom-poms next time."

Kai stood and took a step toward Ellis. I placed my hand on his shoulder. "Hey, cool it. We won, right?" I wouldn't let Ellis's comment ruin my night, even if his boyfriend jab had hit a little too close to home. He didn't know that.

Kai grabbed my hand and pulled me into a side hug. "Yeah, we won because you're a badass." When he pulled away, he ruffled my wet hair. "You deserve a blow job."

I coughed, and he winked with a smirk.

"You guys are disgusting." Ellis shouldered his bag.

"Aw, don't be jealous, baby." Kai made kissing noises and Ellis narrowed his eyes.

"Screw you, Kai."

"Are you offering?"

Ellis gave him the middle finger.

Kai and I both laughed as Ellis stalked out of the locker room. Once I caught my breath, I asked, "Tell me why he hates you so much again. It can't only be because you're a scholarship kid."

Kai tugged his shirt over his head and leaned down to zip up his duffel. "We went to the same high school."

"In Rockport?" I asked, and he nodded. Rockport was about forty minutes west from Pines Hollow, toward the coast.

"Yeah, I lived on the outskirts, though. Rockport is where all the rich kids live. I was lucky enough to live on the dividing county line." His tone hadn't suggested he'd felt lucky at all. "My dad was always traveling, mechanic turned car parts salesman. My mom stayed home and raised me. She wanted me to get a better education, so she made me go to the Rockport County schools. I had to earn my keep. I had to be the best in everything I did. I had to prove I belonged there."

"He hates you because you don't come from money?" My eyes widened. "That makes no sense."

He shrugged. "I might've had a thing with his girlfriend once." His smile was sly, and I shook my head with a laugh. "Hey, it was retribution. I was a grade older than that asshat, but he and his snob friends made my life hell for a long time. Once I made the swim team, I proved I was more than some poor kid playing dress up for the rich assholes. They treated me like I was shit on their shoes. Still do. But I'm out of there now. The past is the past. He's the only ghost that still follows me."

"I bet you were pissed when he showed up here?"

"Nah, I knew he would. He likes to call me a townie, but he is, too. Ellis wouldn't stray too far from the silver spoon that feeds him." He raised his chin toward the door. "Come on, I'm meeting Brie at Stacks. I'll buy you a congratulatory beer."

I lifted my eyebrow. "Brie?"

"Yeah, she's cool."

We headed toward the exit. "She's the blonde I saw you with at lunch today?"

"One and the same." He pushed open the door and I followed behind him.

"You like her enough to keep her around?" I asked, trying to hide the humor in my voice. Kai was a player. He was the definition, the quintessential.

"We'll see."

It was cooler outside than I had anticipated, and I shivered as we made our way to the front of the building. The crowd had dispersed, and I figured Indie would be waiting for me, so I was surprised, pleasantly so, to see Camden waiting with her.

"Aw," Kai crooned. "He waited."

"I will totally punch you in the dick."

Kai chuckled. "I'd like to see you try." He held up his fist and I bumped it with mine. "I'm gonna head to Stacks."

"Wait, let me see if they want—"

"He won't want to go to Stacks, Royal." Kai rolled his eyes and made a beeline in the opposite direction from where my sister and Camden stood.

"You think you know everything," I shouted, my lips spreading into a wide smile as he waved over his shoulder.

Kai was right. Camden wouldn't want to go to Stacks at this time of night, but it would've been nice having other people around as a buffer. I was freaking awkward otherwise. I'd spent a lot of time this week stretched out on Camden's bed thinking thoughts I shouldn't while listening to the most beautiful music I'd ever heard. And at times, when he'd looked at me, I thought for sure he'd felt it, too. The heat, that spark, but then he'd close down, drift off to some hidden place inside his head, and I'd call it a night. I'd go home with a million more questions and an ache I had no cure for.

I took a steadying breath and walked the last twenty or so yards to where they waited. He smiled, his face lit in moonlight as I approached. He seemed more relaxed than I'd ever seen him. His hands were tucked away inside the pockets of his faded jeans, and I ignored my sister's knowing smirk as my eyes scanned the tight fit of his t-shirt.

"Where did Kai go?" Camden asked, his voice infused with a warmth that tickled at the hairs on my neck.

He was happy tonight. Different. Open.

"He has a date."

"You were phenomenal." My sister nearly toppled me with a hug. I held her tightly against me until she squeaked. "As always," she whispered as I let her go.

"That was quite the pep squad."

Camden's smile dimmed. "Your sister is very pushy. Almost as pushy as Kai."

"I am not." Indie tugged on his shirt sleeve, and I was jealous of their intimacy. I knew it was only friendly, but I couldn't touch him like that and probably never would.

"Honestly, I thought it was cool. My own cheering section." I met Camden's eyes, and the blush I'd craved all day returned to his cheeks.

"I figured if you won, you wouldn't be too pissed, Blue." Indie giggled and pulled her braid loose from its tie. Her long hair fell in waves over her shoulder, and I noticed Camden watching the strands float in the faint breeze. "In Camden's defense, I did force him with threats of bodily harm."

"She did." He smiled again, and I began to think his change of mood was for her.

I cleared my throat and they both looked at me. "Some of the guys are going to Stacks, and—"

"I have stuff to work on at the studio. Daphne is bringing dinner." She reached up and hugged me again. "I better get going, actually. You guys have fun." She squeezed Camden's shoulder. "It was fun having a partner in crime."

"The word partner implies willingness," he muttered under his breath, but I saw the smile on his lips.

"We'll see how willing you are next time. You're a pushover." She gave me a pointed look. "I'll call *you* later, okay? Make sure you call Mom and Dad at some point, they'll want to hear about the meet."

She kissed my cheek, and I'd usually offer to walk her to the studio since it was dark, but it was just around the corner from the pool. I promised to call our parents and gave her another hug before she left.

"You're going to Stacks?" Camden asked, his disappointment palpable.

"I don't have to." I put away my earlier jealousy. Indie was a force. I'd challenge anyone to hang out with her and not be in a good mood. Besides, he was all cute and nervous again. His hands in his pockets, his bottom lip slightly pinned between his teeth. "You feel like hanging out?"

His eyes focused on the dorms across campus. I was ready for him to say no. To tell me he had to practice, so I was kind of shocked when he said, "Sure. What did you have in mind?"

I unzipped my bag and grabbed the two hoodies I had inside of it. One was a Pioneer Lake High sweatshirt I always kept with me, and the other was the St. Peter's hoodie Coach had given me today for our warm-up. I closed the bag and threw my old high school sweatshirt to Camden. He caught it and gave me a curious look before putting it on. A slow smile crept across my face. I liked that he was wearing something of mine. Some basic, primitive satisfaction settled over me as I stared at him.

"Let's grab some shitty gas station food and go to the lake?" I suggested, slipping my sweatshirt over my head.

He smiled. "You didn't swim enough tonight?"

"I don't want to swim." My chest was light, my heart in a free fall as my pulse quickened. The rise and fall of his chest matched the fast pace of my own as I said, "Walk with me."

Two orders of cheese-stuffed tater-tots, a large bag of plain ruffled chips, two, thirty-two ounce, purple Gatorade drinks, a bag of Reese's Pieces for me, and a box of Junior Mints for Camden. Our dinner menu might've lacked class, but it covered all the courses, including dessert. We'd walked the short distance to my car, driven to the nearest gas station, grabbed some snacks, and headed to the lake about twenty miles east of campus. Even with the chill of the night, we'd driven with the windows halfway down, snacking on our choices, while I played Camden my favorite classical playlist. Occasionally, he'd remark about certain technical parts of the songs, but most of the time he'd stayed quiet. Listening. In his element.

When we pulled up the dirt road leading to the lake, he commented, "I've never been here before."

"You don't go off campus much?"

"No need. Unless I'm scheduled to play somewhere, I hardly use my car."

"Indie and I found this place on the map the first week of school. We drove out here once, but I've never had time to come back."

Pines Hollow was nothing more than a college town surrounded by wilderness. The closest real town was Rockport. Everything else was either state-owned parks or forests. You couldn't really commute to the school.

Everyone who went there depended on the campus and the small businesses that were scattered around it.

"I wish I'd come here sooner," he whispered as the tree-lined path thinned and we pulled into a small clearing.

I parked the car and turned off the engine. The large fir trees loomed around the lake's edges. The black glass surface was calm, even with the light wind rustling through the trees. As we stepped out of the car, the bows of the branches creaked and groaned.

"It's kind of creepy out here," I said as I shut the door.

I walked toward the beach, and I could hear Camden's door click softly, his footsteps right behind me. The sky stretched out in midnight blue with glittered points of light that seemed to wriggle and dance. I blew out a breath, and a cloud of moisture hung in the air. It was much colder here than it was at St. Peter's.

"It smells like fall." Camden's deep voice made me jump and he laughed softly. "Sorry. Didn't mean to scare you."

"Fall is my favorite time of year."

My eyes were trained on the still water of the lake when he asked, "Because swim season starts?"

I shook my head. "No, it's when everything changes. It's colorful. And you can actually feel it happening. It's like static."

"It's the only time death is pretty." I turned my head and admired his profile as he spoke. "The leaves are dying. It's why they change color."

"I never thought of it like that before."

He faced me, his breath hanging in the air, mixing with mine as he said, "Fall is my favorite season, too."

He had to hear it. The way my heart was thundering. Anxiety welled up inside my stomach, my muscles screaming, my head hazy with so much want I couldn't stand it anymore.

"I held your hand that night because I wanted to." I sputtered my admission, blurting what I'd been wanting to tell him since the day he asked. His eyes were silver, tinged with sage under the darkness of the moon. "I-I wanted to know what it would feel like."

"How did it feel?" he whispered.

I swallowed and shored up all of my courage. Looking down at his hand, I reached for his fingers. When he didn't pull away, I laced them together with my own.

"Different... good... really good."

His breath caught and I raised my eyes. Camden's lips were wet and parted and I wanted to reach up, push the mop of brown hair from his brow, and kiss him. But his eyes were cautious, maybe even a little scared. I squeezed his hand gently and asked, "Is this alright with you?"

He nodded once, turning to look toward the lake. We stood there, his hand in mine, his heat a promise I wanted to hold on to. "I'm not sure if it's right, but I don't want you to let go."

So, I didn't.

Royal

He held onto the silence, and my palms began to sweat, my grip a little less sure as my confidence faded into the soft sound of the lake and the water lapping against its shore.

I heard him swallow before he spoke. "You make the quiet more bearable."

I turned to face him, studying the line of his jaw and the way the muscle flexed under the surface of his skin as he clenched his teeth. I wanted to touch his cheek, but I wasn't sure if I should.

"When I asked my parents why I liked boys the way some guys like girls, my whole world went quiet." He coughed out a bitter laugh and leaned his head back to look at the dark sky. An ache began to form in my chest as the moonlight revealed the grief forming in the deep lines of his brow. "Not that my parents were ever the warm and cozy type. We've never really hugged much. Emotion was reserved for music, not for real life. But after I told them I might be gay, instead of being the boy they were proud of, the boy they could brag to their friends about, I became a dirty secret."

"Camden, I—"

"It's interesting, though," he continued. "I've never done anything to embarrass them, anything to cause them worry that I ever would. I've always done what was asked of me, lived on their terms. I opened up to them when I was sixteen because I was curious. I was young and confused, and I hoped they would help me understand the feelings I was having. But they shut me down, told me it was a perversion, a sick way to think. I've never allowed myself to..." He dropped his eyes to our linked hands. "To feel anything... for anyone."

The burden of his story, the trust he offered me by telling me all of this, it rooted me to the ground and I tightened my hold on his hand. "You've never had—"

"A boyfriend? No. I've never had a relationship." His gray eyes met mine. "No one has ever been worth the risk."

He'd been alone all this time. My throat contracted, and the anger inside me rose to a boil. "I think your parents are assholes. You can't help who you're attracted to. They should've been there for you. They should be proud of you. No matter what, their love should be unconditional." The indignant tone of my voice made me cringe. His parents might be assholes, but they were still his parents. "I'm sorry, I'm just—"

"Angry." His smile was small and shy as he tugged on my hand. "Thank you."

I exhaled a nervous laugh. "For what?"

"For being angry. I live with my mother's voice in my head, telling me I'm wrong—sick—abnormal. After a while, it starts to feel true. Deep down I know it's not, but when it's all you hear... all you've ever been reminded of and told..." He shrugged.

"Your dad is the same?" I asked.

"He doesn't talk to me much. I used to be close to him, but... everything changed." He cleared his throat and lifted our hands. "What about you? How did your parents take it when you came out?"

"I haven't. I mean, I-I'm not..." Camden held my stare. "I've never liked a boy before." My thumb gently brushed against his.

"How can you be sure about this?" he asked.

"I'm as sure as I would be if you were a girl."

"And you've had a girlfriend?"

"One. In high school. But she never made me feel like this. This feels..." I risked brushing that piece of his hair from his forehead with my other hand. When he shivered, I smiled. "I don't know." I wanted to chuckle at the irony. Me, of all people, not being able to think of a word to describe this electric pulse beating inside me. "I think about you all the time."

"I think about you more than I should," he admitted, the low timbre of his voice snaked its way around my spine, dragging me closer.

The space between us dwindled as we both leaned in, feeling that irrefutable attraction. Camden's breathing accelerated as I closed the distance, dropping his hand only to lift my own to the back of his neck. His skin was softer than I imagined. The fine strands of his hair like a coarse silk against my fingertips.

"This isn't wrong," I whispered, daring to take another inch. "This isn't sick."

Somewhere, faraway, I could hear that melody playing from behind his bedroom door. The same song I'd been listening to over and over again. Our eyes locked, our bodies no more than an inch apart. The lake, the trees, the chilled breeze whipping its way around us, everything but him, it all disappeared as I pressed my mouth to the corner of his. He tilted his head, the smallest of invitations as I began to pull away, and our lips met in a sweet, slow collision. His lips, warm and dry, and the heat of his breath soaked its way into my bones as he let himself fall deeper into the kiss. Camden's fingers ran through my hair, pulling me even closer. His tongue dipped into my mouth, and we both groaned at the same time. A low rumble echoed inside our chests. He was solid, built. The hard pressure of our bodies aligned, foreign and unbelievably perfect. Framing his face with my hands, I eased our hungry kiss. Lazy and measured, we tasted each other's lips as I tried to calm my wild pulse.

Camden was the first to pull away, his eyes alive as they searched mine. His gray irises were hooded, filled with lust, and had sprouted with bright specks of green. I was so mesmerized by the color, I almost forgot to let him go. The heat of his skin against my palms felt good—felt right—as I traced a line with the pad of my thumb across his jaw. I finally lowered my hands, linking our fingers together as he took a step back.

"Everything okay?" I asked a bit dazed, worried reality would set in, and he'd regret what we'd done.

His Adam's apple moved smoothly as he spoke. "Yeah, everything is... okay."

Camden's smile tiptoed across his face. Kissing him was unlike anything I'd ever experienced. I wanted to do it again.

And again.

And again.

His taste lingered, sweet and salty. Firm lips that had become butter soft. Both of us were steel, composed of different elements that fit together, nonetheless. I liked that his fingertips had been heavy in my hair, that his control had matched mine. There'd been an equal surrender.

Taking a ragged breath, I rubbed the back of my neck with my free hand. "I don't know what happens next." I huffed out a laugh.

Camden let his gaze drift back to the lake, letting several, long seconds tick by before he whispered, "I don't want to be an experiment."

"That's not what this is." He kept his eyes toward the lake. "Hey, look at me."

Reluctant eyes found mine.

"I... I was being serious when I said I think about you all the time. Camden, I can't get you out of my head. You're always in there, your music, the way you chew your lip when you're concentrating on getting the notes right, or how you hum to yourself when you think I'm not paying attention. And now, this... this kiss. This isn't an experiment for me." I could admit that I was scared, nervous about how to proceed. But he needed to understand, despite my lack of experience, I was sure about one thing. I was falling for him. "I may not know what I'm doing, but I know I want you."

"I don't know what I'm doing either..." Camden's eyes fell to my mouth. "There's a part of me that wants to kiss you again." He released my hand, stepping toward the lake and away from me. "But there's this other part of me... it's deeper, Royal, ingrained. I'm not sure I'm ready. What if my parents found out, or your friends, we could lose... everything."

I wanted to believe he was wrong. Tell him about Kai, and how he'd purposely invited him to Frisbee for me. Not all people were as close-minded as his parents, but I knew better. Ellis alone would use Camden, our relationship, as a way to torture me for the entirety of my time at St. Peter's. And if I was honest with myself, it wasn't just Ellis. I wondered how many guys on my team would freak out about having a gay kid sharing the locker room with them. Not to mention, I had no idea what the administration's stance was when it came to diversity on campus. For all I knew, we'd both lose our scholarships. Camden didn't need the money like I did, but his parents probably wouldn't hesitate to enroll him in another school, uprooting him to save face.

That one kiss.

That one incredible, life-changing kiss had the potential to destroy us both.

I pushed my hands into my pockets and sidled in next to him by the shore.

"I can't go back to the silence, back to being alone." I didn't miss the way his words wavered.

"You don't have to. I'm right here." We kept our eyes on the fog that had rolled in over the pitch-black lake. "No one has to know right now, let's keep it simple."

"How do we do that?"

I smiled, trying to bring him back to that bubble we'd created. That happy, finite bubble after we'd kissed, when his eyes had shined brighter than any of the stars in this granite-colored sky. "For starters, you can invite me to your recital."

Camden turned, his full lips pulling into a lopsided grin. "You're not sick of that song yet?"

"Completely." I made an attempt to playfully punch him in the shoulder, but he gently grabbed my wrist, and slid his hand into mine.

"You don't have swim practice?" he asked.

"I do, but I'll head over right after. I wouldn't miss it. I was just waiting for an invitation not to."

"Keeping it simple," he mused.

I thought about leaning over and starting where we'd left off earlier. There was no world to judge us. Just the ground under our feet and the air in our lungs. I gave in to the temptation, curling my fingers into his sweatshirt, needing him closer, and kissed him again. Deliberate and deep, not in any hurry, and like the first time, when he pulled away, we were both panting.

"I didn't think it would feel like this."

Camden placed his hands on my waist, his fingers grasping at the cotton of my sweatshirt. "Like what?" he asked.

"I never want to stop kissing you. Like this could be enough, and I'd die a happy man." I chuckled, but when he didn't respond I asked, "What about you? How do you feel?"

"The truth?"

"Yeah."

"Like I can finally breathe."

Camden

We held hands on our way back to campus, the heat of Royal's palm completely saturating mine. I didn't mind that his hand was a little damp. If anything, it grounded me, knowing this was all new for him, too. He navigated the car smoothly with one hand, while I got lost in the shadowed blur of trees as we passed them, feeling more alive than I ever had before. Breathing in the soft, electronic music as it played through his speakers, stealing its beats to mute the percussion of my own heart. I wanted to hear him breathing, hear this moment. This moment where I had become something tangible, someone actually living inside the shell. My fingertips buzzed and my heart hammered, and he was the song I never wanted to stop listening to.

With the lights of the town peeking their way around the next bend, I shut my eyes and made myself catalog everything that had happened tonight. I loved that I smelled like him, his sweatshirt hugged my arms and chest, time had softened the fabric, but it was Royal who'd left his warmth inside it for me. I tasted my lips, hoping to get a trace of his mint flavor, but it was gone. I could almost feel the pressure of his lips, like the way my fingertips pressed against the keys of the piano, delicate at first. Precise until passion took over and all you had left was need. The need to pursue, to chase the feeling only music had given me.

Until Royal.

The song ended and the next began as the car slowed. I opened my eyes and realized we were almost to St. Peter's as we passed Stacks. The windows were lit and a few patrons dotted the sidewalk outside the front door of the bar. My eyes snagged on a couple, a boy and a girl, meandering down the narrow concrete path, hand in hand, and I wondered if Royal and I would ever be able to do that. He'd openly held my hand that one night, but he could have easily blamed the alcohol. Would we ever be public like that couple, and for that matter, were we even a couple? I watched him as he hummed along to the song from his playlist, and he turned to face me, a small smile growing on his lips. I really liked those lips. The first lips I'd ever kissed. I wondered then, if he had been able to tell, if he knew how special tonight had been... for me.

"I've never kissed anyone before... before you." The confession was a rush of words and nerves.

He glanced at me briefly, taking his eyes off the road. "I figured."

Embarrassment flooded through me. "That bad, huh?"

He chuckled and squeezed my hand. "Oh, God, no. I didn't mean... I just figured when you said you'd never had a boyfriend... or anything." The car rolled to a stop. The looming trees outside of Warren House gave us a small amount of privacy as he turned off the engine. His blue eyes fell to my mouth. "That was the best kiss..." Royal blushed and let go of my hand, preferring to toy with my fingers instead. "You have nothing to worry about."

My body reacted to the gruff and vulnerable sound of his voice. My pulse spiked as he leaned toward me. I was hard and mortified, but he hadn't noticed. His eyes were fixated on my mouth, and it didn't matter that we were parked in front of the dorms, or that anyone could see. I relied on the trees to be our safety net. The dimly lit lot made for a much more clandestine hideaway than I'd given it credit for, or maybe I just didn't care as his lips brushed softly against mine. I closed my eyes and forgot where I was, who I was, as Royal's teeth nipped at my bottom lip. I reached across the console, wrapping my hand behind his neck, pulling him in. His taste, the quiet and bottomless sound of his groan, the heat flushing my face, my skin, my tongue dancing with his, eager and hungry. His fingers gripped the collar of my hoodie as he pulled away enough to speak, "Come upstairs with me."

We stared at each other. Royal's blue eyes reeling me in. I wanted to say yes. Yes, I'll come upstairs. Yes, I want you to touch me. Yes, I want to touch you. But distant laughter brought me back to reality and I panicked, surveying the lawn outside the car. Far enough away—they wouldn't have seen anything—was a group of girls making their way across campus. I let out a harsh sigh and sank lower in my seat.

"It's okay," he said, his gaze tracking the same small group of girls. "I'm sorry, I got—"

"Carried away," I finished.

"I can't help it. Your mouth is..." I could see him searching for the right word, his eyes on my lips, his body stealing another inch over the center console. "Captivating... addictive." His sheepish tone made me chuckle. "When I kiss you, it's like nothing else matters. I just want more."

"We have to be careful," I reminded him.

He'd said we could keep it simple and I wanted to believe it. But he didn't know my parents were well ingrained inside the walls of this school. They'd both completed their undergraduate studies at St. Peter's. The dean and his wife were friends of my parents, had been ever since they'd all attended here together. I would have gone to a different school if I hadn't taken pleasure in the fact my mother never wanted me to attend St. Peter's. I had a full ride here, and I didn't need her money, but if anyone ever found out about Royal, about me... I shuddered to think what could happen, what they'd do.

Royal could get kicked off the team, lose his swim scholarship. This could ruin his life. I could ruin him. My parents' reputation would be destroyed, and someone would have to pay for that. They'd most likely ship me to Juilliard like they'd wanted to do in the first place, or somewhere they could put me in a glass case, wipe away all my dirty smudges, and say, "Look, he's so talented."

And Royal, his time at St. Peter's would be over, and who knows if he would be able to transfer. I'd get a new start and he'd get nothing. He'd have to leave his sister, his dream...

"Hey." He rested his hand on my thigh, the point of contact gave me chills. I wanted so much from him, but not enough that I would take him away from his sister, take away his chance to swim. Royal not swimming, not getting the chance to do the one thing he'd told me was his own, it would be like me losing the ability to use my fingers, the ability to play. He smiled, slow and reassuring, like he was afraid to spook me. "You look like you're going to be sick. Camden, we can be careful. We're keeping it simple, right?" He lifted his hand from my leg, watching me with anxious eyes.

"Is it worth it?" I asked and his smile faded. "What if you got kicked out of school? What if you couldn't swim?"

"I thought about that, but I don't think—"

"That's the problem. We didn't think. You make it hard for me to think."

"Maybe that's a good thing," he said. He smiled again, but it looked like a lie. A defense to cover his own worries. "You said it yourself, you're tired of being alone, of hiding?"

"We'll still be hiding." I stared out the window.

"Maybe we don't have to." He rested his palm on my knee and I closed my eyes. I didn't want to acknowledge how much I'd needed that simple touch. "This is different. With you," he whispered to himself or to me, I wasn't sure. I opened my eyes and turned to face him. Royal stared at me, looked right through me. "I never felt like this with Nat. Never felt like I'd come out of my skin if I didn't kiss her. It's worth it to me, kissing you, being with you, and if that means we have to be careful then we'll be careful. But if it's not worth it for you then—"

"It is."

He smiled that smile. The one with the dimple in his cheek, the one that made it difficult for me to look away, to feel unsure about anything. *I* was coming out of my skin. I'd only ever been a Me. One insignificant piece of a gigantic sheet of a music. A note inside a refrain. Every day repeating itself. Every day nothing new. Until a Me had become an Us and the boy sitting across from me came out of his skin when my lips touched his. We could be careful. We could keep it simple.

I glanced at the front doors of Warren House.

"You'll tell your sister?" More a statement than a question.

He nodded. "Kai knows, too. I told him I liked you and he's cool with it. He only knows about my feelings for you, not that you reciprocate them. But I want him to know. And my sister. That's my only condition... for this... for us. I care about them, and I don't think I could lie... not to them."

Kai knew and he didn't care. Something unlocked inside my chest, not fully, an almost inaudible click. How many more locks would I get to break? When would I be able to be totally free?

"I don't want you to lie to them."

"It shouldn't be this hard." He was inside his head again, looking through me, his brow heavy with concentration. I loved watching him think. "It sucks that a small, ignorant minority gets to tell me who I can and can't kiss. I wasn't raised like that."

"Not all of us have bohemian parents."

He laughed, his head falling back against the seat. I memorized the smooth, long line of his neck.

"Bohemian. I like that, it's a good word."

"Kai and Indie, then?" I asked and he nodded. "Okay."

He quickly scanned the lawn before raising his knuckles to my cheek. "It's going to be... challenging." He swallowed and lowered his fingers. "Not getting to hold your hand in public, not kissing you when I want—hiding behind a screen just because you're not a girl. But I get it, and I want this, so I'll be careful... for you."

Silence filled the car. Did he still want me to go inside with him? Did I tell him thanks for tonight and head home? I doubted even the most socially skilled person would've known what to do when the heat of a kiss dissipated and an invitation was left to dangle in the chilled afterwards.

Royal opened his door and made the decision for me. "Come on, come inside, it's still early. You can help me with my homework." There was nothing careful in the way he smirked or how it promised things that made my cheeks feel warm.

We walked side by side, and I missed his hand in mine as we walked through the common room. Sweat beaded along the back of my neck as a few guys passed us on the stairs. The smell of their cologne stung my nose. I wanted to lean into Royal, steal his scent, but as we made our way down the hall, and stopped in front of his room, the door behind us opened.

"What's up, O'Connell?" The husky voice made me flinch.

Royal looked over his shoulder as he opened his door. "Not much, you heading out?"

"Yeah, meeting Ari at Vigrus. That girl can't live without me." He flashed us a wolfish grin. "Congrats on the win tonight... I heard you guys nailed it."

Royal's face split into a smile. "Thanks. We earned it."

"Fuck yeah." The guy held out his fist and Royal bumped it. He gave me a cursory glance. "You a swimmer, too?"

I shook my head.

"Shit, sorry. Gus this is my friend Camden. He's roommates with Kai."

As if that explained everything, he said, "Nice to meet you." Gus nodded his chin in a silent see you later. "Ari's waiting on me. You coming to the game on Sunday?" he asked Royal as he turned to leave.

"I'll try."

"It's un-American you know, hating football."

"I never said I hated it." Royal's raised voice was drowned out by Gus's laughter as it echoed down the hall.

Royal held the door for me, and once Gus was out of sight, he placed his hand at the small of my back, leading me into his dorm room. The gesture sank itself inside my stomach and it was too soon when his hand fell away. It was easy to ignore the oppressive anxiety building below the surface when his hand was on my back. His room was muted colors and smelled liked him, soap and summer, and sweat. I could taste his mouth as I stared at his bed. Feel his hand in my hair. I could almost hear the trees by the lake, and if I looked up, maybe his ceiling would crack open. The night sky would grant us the shadows we needed to feel comfortable again, to find our way back to a moment where we were two people, not two men, just two people connected and lost inside the other.

Maybe he was good at reading people, or maybe he was just good at reading me. Royal's firm hands settled on my hips, pulling my back to his chest, the embrace putting me at ease. His measured breaths beat against the crook of my neck, quicker with every second that passed. The curve of his chest, the flat plane of his stomach, the bulge in his jeans, pressed against me as his lips fell along the arch of my neck. His thumbs slipped under the hem of my sweatshirt. Skin on skin, the tiniest of touches, and I was falling into him.

He left a path of wet kisses on my skin and goosebumps on my arms. His lips brushed my ear. "Tell me if it's too much?"

I didn't say anything. Everything was too much and not enough. He could paint those tiny circles on my skin and I'd be content to stand in this very spot until the sun came up. He could ask me to leave, and I'd hope to see him tomorrow. He could kiss me until I could no longer feel my lips and I'd ask for more. But I turned to face him and answered with a small nod.

He cupped my face in his hands, his eyes searching, asking before he leaned in and kissed me. Top lip, bottom lip, a slow study. His mouth was gentle, no aggression. His tongue honeyed. His kiss burned—ached—as I grasped his shoulders. It was torture waiting, waiting for more, and I found myself pushing—wanting—giving in. I bit his bottom lip and he moaned into my mouth. Breathless, Royal rested his forehead against mine.

"Camden," he said my name like it was an answer to a question he'd asked.

He kept his hands on my face, his hold light against my cheeks as he leaned back and opened his eyes. "How late can you stay?"

As late as you'll let me.

"I should work on my song. Maybe an hour?"

"One hour." The pad of his thumb found its way to my bottom lip, tracing the arch. "I'll take what I can get."

Royal

We'd spent the last twenty minutes kissing. Lying on my bed, both of us hard, both of us holding back. Our fingers in each other's hair, wrapped in the others' sweatshirt, everywhere except where we truly wanted them—not touching his stomach, not touching my hip, not tracing the muscles in his back, not opening the button on my jeans. We didn't explore beyond the invisible barrier we'd created by pressing our bodies together, our arms tucked away, our hands resting on a shoulder, or at the nape of the other's neck. We kissed and talked and kissed some more, and when I couldn't take it any longer, I'd push my hips into his, the friction made everything impossible. Trapped behind denim, any slight connection was a painful plea.

Touch me.

Touch me right here.

Touch my hip, unbutton my jeans.

But I was afraid. Kissing him was easy. Everything else, even though my body was begging, yelling—screaming—for more, more seemed too raw, too messy, and I couldn't bear the thought that this could be the moment he said, "Too much."

It was too much wanting and denying. How would it feel, would all this pent-up tension release, and once it was gone—the need we'd developed—would it disappear? A box checked off. I wasn't sure, but I feared it, nonetheless. What if we crossed the line, and in the end, he hated himself for it? What if I hated myself?

"Royal," he said my name, and I opened my eyes, stunned and unsteady, realizing we'd stopped kissing. Had my thoughts stolen minutes, maybe five, maybe twenty? I glanced at the clock. My hour had dwindled. Our lips almost touched when he chuckled. "Did you fall asleep?"

"No." I watched his eyes carefully. The gray color had become an almost translucent green. Touching his face with my palm, his cheek hot against my skin, I admitted, "I was thinking."

"Thinking?" he repeated as he often did. I liked the way he answered a question with another question. Milking me for my thoughts, for more.

I licked his lips, kissed his mouth, soft and open, not willing to let him inside my head. This was a beginning and I didn't want to scare him away. I didn't want to scare myself. Warm lips shaped and molded to mine one last time before he fell away, resting on his back, his eyes to the ceiling, he sighed. "This feels... surreal."

I wanted to add to his statement. The way I did, with words and definitions. Surreal, odd, strange, but this, him, it was anything but strange or odd, it felt genuine, honest, more real than anything I'd had before. Perhaps, since I was his first, he had nothing to compare it to, but I wanted to tell him this was how it should always be. I wanted him to know, that when his lips were on mine, kissing me until all I could feel was the pulse in my veins, and all I could taste was him, his breath, I'd give anything to lose myself inside his body, or let him lose himself inside mine. If it wouldn't ruin everything about this night, I'd kiss him until he realized he'd wanted the same thing all along. Until my unspoken words became a reality.

"Is that a good thing?" I kept my eyes on the ceiling, too, my head filled with all that fear, all that wanting, all those unsaid words. Fear if I pushed things, wanting to push things, wanting to see where this *thing* could go.

"It is." He turned to me. "I don't have a lot of good things, Royal."

I wanted him to have every good thing imaginable. "I want to fix that."

He closed his eyes, a smile sneaking its way across his face, and I kissed him again without any regard for my own sanity. I didn't stop kissing him until my hour turned into ninety minutes. He'd left my room with flushed cheeks, a promise to see him tomorrow, and the taste of my mouth on his swollen lips, in a sweatshirt that belonged to me but looked better on him anyway.

The next morning, on my way to breakfast, my muscles burning from the early morning workout, my head was filled with the taste of his kiss, and his skin, and the soft contour of his neck, and that small, dark spot in the hollow of his throat. A birthmark, he'd told me when my lips had stalled over the discoloration. It was my favorite thing about last night. That small patch of skin had belonged to me, I'd been the first one to kiss it, claim it as my own. I wondered now what other things I'd get to discover about Camden. How many freckles would he have on his shoulders? Did he have freckles at all? Did he prefer sleeping without noise, or did he have to fall asleep with music playing in the background, like me? A soft piano or a tinny guitar? Would he sleep with an arm around my waist or would he want me to hold him? Did he need space instead?

The questions in my head only fed my fantasies, leading me to think about other things. Like the way his eyes had turned dark when his hips had aligned with mine, how his fingers had crept into my hairline, daring me to press myself against him, and how his kisses had become desperate, growling when I'd given into his dare. I was so far gone, inside the memories from last night, my head still back on my pillow, lying next to him, I hadn't realized someone was calling my name.

"Royal," she shouted again.

"Pink," I whispered as I watched her walk across the quad. She carried her oversized bag. The same bag that she'd deemed as *her life* because it held all of her sketchbooks.

"Hey," I said as she approached.

"Good morning," she said, more like good morning? A question, not a greeting.

Her cautious eyes searched my face, looking for something, waiting me out. I didn't meet her gaze, half hoping she'd ask me how last night turned out and half dreading it. I kept quiet as she fell in step next to me, both of us resigned to keep to ourselves. I shared most everything with my sister. But Camden, I wasn't ready to share him with anyone. Last night belonged to Camden, to me. It was mine. And I wanted to hold on to the intimacy of silence. Indie was feeling my mood, and I could feel hers—curious. Shared intuition, there was little privacy in being a twin.

I gave in.

"Camden," I guessed. "What do you want to know?"

"Did... I mean, are you guys... are you okay?" She was worried.

"Better than okay."

I finally turned, meeting her inquisitive stare, her lips breaking into a smile.

"Do you want to talk about it?"

I shook my head, holding onto my secrets. "It's good, don't want to jinx it. But we're not really telling anyone."

"Who would I tell?"

"I want to make sure you understand. He's scared we'll get kicked out of school. I mean, I think I could lose my scholarship."

"That's discrimination, Royal, the school wouldn't—"

"Maybe, but where everything is new, I don't—we don't—want to risk it."

She pursed her lips, but the finality of my statement sank in.

"It's not like you to hide."

"We have to lay low for a while. I like him, Pink."

Indie paused before ascending the stairs that led into Beckett. "A beautiful thing can only stay in the shadows for so long before it starts to wilt. You're happy and I can feel it, Blue." She linked our fingers and stared at her feet. "But I know what it feels like to hide in the shadows. I live in them. The longer you linger, the harder it will be to see the happiness inside the darkness."

I tugged on her braid, and when she met my eyes, I smiled, offering her a small piece of myself. "I kissed him. I kissed him, and it was... I can still feel it, feel him..." Heat flooded my cheeks as I raised my hands to my lips. "I'm scared, Indie, scared of what could happen. Scared of losing him before we even get started. Everything's fragile. People date all the time and don't march across campus declaring their love for each other after the first date."

She giggled, and I knew I'd won, for now. "It was a date then?"

"There was food, and making out so—"

"Spare me the details."

"What about the gory ones?"

Her face sobered. "Will you tell Mom and Dad?"

"Soon." A flash of disapproval crossed her eyes, but I didn't allow it to bother me. "Can we at least have breakfast before we start that argument?"

"I'm not arguing, I'm—"

"Being just like Mom."

"I am, aren't I?"

"Yup."

"Come on." Rolling her eyes, she pulled my hand. "Let's stuff our face with carbs."

It didn't take us long to stack our trays with food and find our way to the table in the corner by the large window. The sun was warm enough, and the view, towering trees, and sprawling green lawns, and sometimes, if it was early enough, the gray morning fog lingering over the sidewalks, made this spot our absolute favorite. A few of the guys from the team, Dev and Sherman, were already sitting there. I stifled a groan when Indie's friend Daphne waved at me. She patted the seat next to her, and I pretended not to notice as I pulled out the chair across from where she sat. Indie, being the saint that she was born to be, took the seat next to her friend.

"You missed an amazing party last night." Sherman lifted his chin before shoveling a forkful of eggs into his mouth.

"Yeah, man, where did you disappear to?" Dev's grimace was comical. "I had to deal with Ellis and his fucking girlfriend all night."

Daphne rolled her eyes. "Bethy is being so dramatic. I didn't even kiss him on the mouth."

I almost spit out my orange juice. "You kissed Ellis? Why?" I couldn't hide the horror on my face.

She chewed on the stem of her grapes. "Why? Are you jealous?"

"Hardly." Kai laughed as he set his tray at the head of the table. "Ellis and his sloppy seconds, no thank you."

Daphne threw a grape across the table and it landed against his chest. His hand stilled on the back of the chair.

"Don't be an asshole."

"I'm not the one who got caught making out with Ellis."

"Jesus Christ. I kissed him on the cheek. The. Cheek. You guys are ridiculous."

Indie's soft laughter floated across the table and Kai cleared his throat, grabbing his tray. "I wish I could stay and bullshit, but some of us actually have responsibilities. See you idiots at practice tonight."

He sauntered off, like every morning, and I noticed Indie staring after him, a small frown appearing on her lips. I was about to ask her if she was okay when the chair next to me shifted.

"Hey, it's the Frisbee king," Dev said, holding out his fist.

Camden sat down, disregarding the gesture and set his tray of Cheerios and milk onto the table. Muttering, "Hello." He kept his eyes fixed on his bowl of cereal.

Dev lowered his hand with a snicker, and the conversation around the table resumed. Indie gave Camden a small wave, but no one else bothered. I, on the other hand, couldn't look away. His hair was damp and curled around his collar. My fingers itched to touch him, to slip through the wet pieces of his hair, pull his mouth to mine. He smelled like the shower, like soap and heat and I was stirring, coming alive for him, for his red cheeks and shy smile. The longer I stared, the more obvious it became, and suddenly, everything Indie said made sense. If he was my girlfriend, I'd be able to kiss him right here, in front of everyone and not one eyelash would bat. My stomach was a mass chaos of butterflies. My pulse charged, and God, I wanted to touch him.

I set my left hand under the table, palm up, resting it on my thigh. "Hey," I whispered, unable to disguise the husky need infused in the one syllable.

Camden hesitated, taking a second to look around, everyone was busy with their gossip and coffee, and to my surprise he lowered his hand, too. He wrapped a few fingers through mine, his pinky taking the most claim, and I exhaled a shaky breath. My thumb stole a touch of his skin, warm and soft, and as he leaned in, the tiniest of inches, the smell of him, the heat, it invaded me, pulled itself inside of me. Breathing him in, I whispered, "Will you sit with me every morning?"

His jaw muscle contracted beneath his smooth skin, and before letting go, his fingertip drew a slow line across the top of my hand. I shivered as goosebumps scattered up my arm. Was that his answer? It wasn't a yes and it wasn't a no. It was a let's see how today goes, let's see if we make it through this morning without combusting, without giving in, without giving anything away. It was the shadow, the place where beautiful things go to die.

Without thinking about the consequences, I guided my hand to his thigh. Camden's spine went rigid. No one could see, no one would know. I held my palm in place, letting my own heat soak through his jeans, until he finally looked at me, until his posture relaxed, until he melted under my touch, until he said, "Yes."

Camden

Quiet applause, dim lights, the auditorium was filled to capacity, and I was falling apart backstage. My ability to play music was something I'd simply been born with, but the performance had always been for my parents. I was a creator, not a performer. I created the sound and would rather listen to it be played than be the one playing it. In their absence, their love having only been tied to the spectacle, I felt useless, alone, and...

"Good luck tonight," he'd said in that husky post-kiss voice of his earlier today when we'd stolen a moment between classes to meet at my place. "I'll be there as soon as I can."

My eyes shuttered closed as I remembered. The heat of his palm on my cheek, on my thigh, his fingers linked with mine under the table at breakfast these past few mornings. The rush, the beat of my heart, of his heart, it muted the voice inside my head telling me I wasn't good enough. The memory of his indolent smile last night while he'd listened to me play for the hundredth time, his messy hair, rumpled by my fingers, these were the moments I held onto as I listened to my theory professor introduce me to the crowd. The promise of his lips, his hands, his taste, as I walked out onto the stage. The lights blotted out the audience, kept my feet moving forward until I sat at the bench. My fingers shook as I pulled at my tie. The sleek, tailored, navy blue suit I had on, was purchased by my mother last week with expedited shipping, a note placed neatly inside that read, *Earn the applause, Mom*. There had been no sincerely, no love, just her tight cursive script—the same firm lines as her lips.

I kept my eyes on the keys as I set my fingers on the ivory. With a deep breath I started, each note chasing after the next, and for a few seconds, I stopped thinking about my parents and played like I was alone in my room with him. With Royal. I played and a small smile etched its way onto my lips. My spine relaxed, and I became the song, the music. My limbs an extension, pouring out of me, my soul onto the keys. I hoped he was here. Hoped that he could feel each note inside his chest, because they belonged to him. And though it was dangerous to think so, I pretended the sound, the music, had forever belonged to him, that my parents were never the curators of my talent, that it had always been him. He was the reason I'd walked across the stage tonight, and as the song formed and breathed its own way into the air, perhaps I wanted, for once, to believe that the music I'd created belonged to me, too. It could be mine, never theirs, and I could share it with him.

The last note hung in the air and the poignant silence that followed enveloped me. Each breath I took was marked and shallow, and all I wanted was to open my eyes, be alone with him in his room. This night behind me. This thing inside me, it wanted, it begged, and there was no slowing it down. It wanted more kisses, more touches—more skin. The audience burst into applause and cheers as goosebumps spread along my skin. I stood on weak legs, half-awake and half in dreams with Royal. The adrenaline galloping inside my veins, as I took a bow, reached its climax, roaring behind my ears. Once upright, the stage lights dimmed enough I could see the entire room on their feet, clapping, smiling, eyes wide with wonderment. I celebrated, allowed them to see me smile, allowed them to know, after all, maybe I was a performer. My parents weren't here. Tonight, I had played for myself, for the people who'd sat in the red velvet seats, for him.

"Remind me, when it's time to sign up for the Winter Concert, not to follow after you," the pimpled freshman in my composition class gave me a sad smile. "Your execution was killer."

With a quiet thank you, and a nod of my chin, I found myself walking toward the back exit door left of the stage. Cold, damp air woke me as I stepped outside. My dream-like state left behind with the piano, with the crowd like a parting gift. I was out of breath, and I laughed nervously at the dense fog each exhale created. I leaned against the wood-paneled wall and looked up at the cloud-covered night sky.

I'd never played as vibrant as I had tonight, never permitted myself to feel it, to let go. Torn between believing the cause had been the possibility *he* was in the audience, or maybe the fact my parents were not. So much hope had been tied to his presence. If he hadn't actually shown up, the disappointment would be a crushing wave. He had practice, and I wouldn't hold it against him, but the venom, the one thought, that I'd never be able to find that other world again, the place where the music had become transcendent, would work its way into my brain, poisoning me, knowing I'd been alone all along. Tonight, I wore my talent with pride, and I wanted to hold onto that more than I ever had before... more than I ought to.

"Camden?" His soft whisper floated through the dense fall air, and every muscle in my body sagged with relief at the sound of it.

Royal walked toward me, his blond hair damp and disheveled, wearing a suit with a blue paisley tie that was too small. "They looked for you, someone said you were back here."

He was here, for me, only a few feet away. I chuckled, the smile on my face growing wider as he got closer, the suit jacket he wore was oversized and hung off his broad shoulders in an unnatural way.

"What are you wearing?" I asked, unable to disguise the humor in my voice.

He ran his hand through his golden hair, a lopsided grin forming on his lips as he said, "I had to improvise.

I didn't have anything formal to wear." He crowded me against the wall and I tugged on his tie. "It's Dev's." He blushed and I wanted to kiss his cheek.

"And the jacket?" I asked.

"Kai stole it from his dad." He shrugged. "I had the pants and the shirt for when we go to meets out of state." He leaned in like he did, without any regard for who could be watching. "You were fucking phenomenal."

My heart skipped, he wasn't one to use such language, and I let the tone of it wind its way around my body, pushing myself into his hips and off the wall.

I felt fucking phenomenal.

His lips brushed mine, once and then again. His tongue dipped inside my mouth for more. The smell of chlorine and cologne, his smell, surrounded me as his arms wrapped around my waist pulling me against his hard body. Tongue and fire and the distant sound of a violin drifted from the stage door I'd left cracked opened. A low moan sounded at the back of his throat as he rested his forehead against mine.

"You've never played like that for me," he whispered, and the heat of his breath tickled my lips.

Tonight was all for you. The sentence sat on the tip of my tongue, but in giving him the words, I'd be giving him the rest of me, and I was terrified by the implication, by the idea of being too interspersed, blended, one person inside the other. Without him, who was I? Without him, where did the music go? I was high, thinking in loops. My earlier fears began to surface, and as if he could read my mind, he pulled away, his blue eyes beseeching, he asked, "What's the matter?"

It could've been the question, or the way he'd asked, his voice laced with real concern. It could've been the way I felt empty all of a sudden, the energy from tonight wasted, and gone, scattered on the stage, where hope had been the driver to get me to this point. Hope that had my throat lodged with an overwhelming pour of emotion, stealing my willingness to speak the truth.

My parents didn't care about me.

I was falling in love with a man.

All this time, I might've been playing inside the shell of another person. A person who was afraid to be hopeful. A boy who was too afraid to be happy, who felt commonplace and invisible before *he* came into my life.

Royal cupped my face in his strong hands, and I liked the way his fingertips were wrinkled and pruned from the swimming pool as he skated them across my cheeks. "You know, right? That you were amazing. You brought everyone to their feet. Camden... I know your parents weren't there but—"

"Take me home," I asked, recognizing how weak I was.

Holding my face for a few more seconds, he nodded. "Sure."

Royal lowered his hands, and I linked our fingers together. Everyone was inside anyway, and I needed the connection, his heat, to keep my head on straight. I was too helpless to let go, too raw. Maybe this feeling was what my theory professor had tried to explain last Friday in class. He'd said the songs you create should be like falling in love. Heart stopping, vulnerable, beautiful, even if you were the only one who could see its beauty.

"It was for you."

Royal stopped mid-step. "What's for me?"

"Tonight. It was for you. Not for them."

"You mean your parents?"

I faced him. "They were always there, and I never understood, not until tonight, it was them holding me back. I like playing for you in my room, when it's just us, but tonight I wanted you to see me, really see me, Royal. And I think I got scared, because what if you didn't want it. What if you hadn't shown up tonight, but then... you were right there, smiling, and I guess... I was overwhelmed."

"By me?"

"And your tiny tie."

He laughed openly, and I marveled at the way his throat moved, the long expanse of it, and knew exactly what it tasted like in the dark.

"This tie is terrible." Royal's eyes raked over my body and he swallowed. "You look really good."

My face heated. "Thanks."

"Still want to go home?" he asked.

"Yeah."

He kissed my cheek. "I was hoping you'd say that."

"Will you play again? Like you did tonight." Royal asked as he shut my bedroom door behind us.

"I'm not sure I can." I avoided his eyes as I placed our last-minute dinner, pizza from Annie's, in the fridge under my desk.

"Try."

He was sitting on my bed, arms stretched behind him, palms resting on the comforter, his suit jacket and tie forgotten in the car. Royal's sleeves were rolled up to his elbows. His easy grin, confident and sexy, made me want to try. For him. I shrugged off my jacket, and pulled off my tie, laying it over the back of my desk chair. Switching on my keyboard, it always centered me, but I was too nervous. Too amped up. Something about tonight. It was different. The way he'd watched me from across the booth at the restaurant, his eyes were hungrier than usual, like tonight we were standing on the tip of a knife, and something between us was about to shift, cut us open, bare our dirtiest secrets to the other. I fumbled the first few notes, stopped, and closed my eyes. I remembered he'd been there, in the audience, and I found the courage to play for him again.

If I hadn't been lost inside the piece, I would have heard him move, heard the telltale creak of my mattress, but I'd given myself over to the performance, and like I'd played earlier, the music soared, becoming greater than anything I'd ever been capable of before. My eyes were shut when his lips touched my neck, when his hands gripped my hips from behind, like clay, I molded to his touch. My fingertips shivered against the keys, silent.

"Don't stop." His voice wavered, pleading, and I tried to continue.

Hot kisses on my neck, hands at my belt buckle. I had no idea what I was even playing anymore. All I could feel was his chest at my back, his heat soaking through the fine fabric of my shirt, and his body, awake against me. He easily unclasped my belt—the button, and his hand, hesitated at my zipper.

"Can I touch you?"

"Yes." I didn't breathe.

He turned me toward him, the piano a third wheel, and his mouth found mine, open and deep as his hand slipped an inch below my waist band. Like a spark against a bed of dried pine needles, we exploded. His fingers tore at the buttons of my shirt until he'd freed me of it completely. His warm palms flattened against my chest before trailing lower, lower. I shuddered when they found their way back to my zipper, my pants dropping to the floor. I stepped free and kicked them to the side, reaching for his shirt buttons with shaky fingers. He gently grabbed my wrist.

"Wait." Royal's kiss was soft and slow. "Not yet."

He smiled against my lips before he pulled away. He stared at me for what felt like an eternity, his blue eyes piercing, wanting, before he kneeled down in front of me.

"Royal?"

He placed his hands on my thighs, working the muscle with his fingers, looking up at me with what I figured were the same questions I had storming through my head. Was this what he wanted? Was this going to ruin us?

He leaned forward and kissed the waistband of my boxer briefs, his lips lingered against the coarse trail of hair that led below as he asked, "Are you okay?"

My fingers threaded through his hair and I nodded. He was worth it. Royal exhaled, easing my underwear down, he held my gaze the entire time. I needed his eyes on mine, in this bright room, where all my dirty secrets were spilling out and onto the floor. I couldn't hide how much I wanted him, standing here before him—bare. My arousal on display and embarrassingly hard. The grip I had on his hair tightened, and I gasped when he took me into his mouth. His lips tentative. Mumbling, I swore, letting go with one hand, and grasped the keyboard behind me. The loud notes resonated in the room as he found his pace, taking me in deeper, giving sound to the moment, and replacing my shame with need. The same disjointed notes played over and over in the background as his mouth destroyed me.

I was being deconstructed piece by piece by the heat of his wet lips, his tongue, by the vibration against my sensitive skin every time he moaned. My spine and ribs pulled at my stomach, the muscles in my jaw, my neck contracted as he dragged me toward the inevitable end. I didn't want it to stop. I wanted to feel everything, feel all the pieces set into a new pattern inside me, feel the devastating energy surge through me, creating a new me, a me who knew nothing but Royal and his mouth and that wet heat that was changing me. I wanted to be changed. I wanted to be remade under his touch. I wanted to never doubt that this was righteous and good—this was ours. The tangled knot in my gut untwisted, and a strained sound ripped from my lips, choking and desperate as I held his hair in my fist. I tried to pull away, to warn him, but he took my hips in his hands and held me up, held me while I came, while I fell, while I reassembled into something better—something that belonged only to us.

Royal

God, I was shaking.

My hands, like leaves in the wind, shook as I held Camden's hips, held on for dear life. His taste in my mouth, what we'd done, I was dazed, with him, with lust, and aching for him to touch me, too. I was nervous to meet his eyes, afraid that when I looked at him, all I'd see was the shade of confusion, or fear, or even worse, guilt.

"Royal." His gruff voice thrilled me, deep and commanding as his gentle palm cupped my chin, tilting my head back, I looked into hazy gray-green eyes.

There wasn't any shame. No *holy shit did I make a huge mistake*? Just raw and real lust clouding around his irises. Camden was trembling, too, his hands on my face, holding my stare. I'd questioned myself only once, when I'd hesitated with his zipper. I had no idea what I was doing, what I'd wanted, what he'd wanted, but I'd been overwhelmed by the heat of his body, by the soft touch of his mouth on mine, and when I touched him, when I felt him in my hand, all rational thought left my mind and instinct took over. I was his, and I'd wanted everything he could give me in that one moment. To combust or die trying. I'd never known such an urgent feeling. And in seeing the flush of his cheeks, as I'd kneeled down in front of him, it had been all the encouragement I'd needed.

"Come here," he whispered and I stood.

He stared at my mouth, his fingertip tracing my top lip, as he leaned in to kiss me. It started as a simple kiss, sweet and light, but as his tongue rushed into my mouth, fervent and thirsty for his taste, his fingers twisted into my hair, his body pressing against me, already hard again. It wasn't long before my shirt was off and hastily tossed to the floor, before I backed him against his bed, before he sat down and took in my towering form.

He gazed at my bare chest, the palm of his hands running over the ridges of my stomach, looking up at me, with wide-opened eyes, need, and awe, his face flushed with desire as he shook his head and admitted in a low, rough voice, "I'm nervous."

He dropped his hands to my waist and averted his eyes.

"Camden, don't be—"

"You're the only person... the first person. I feel naïve, like I'm going to mess this up."

"Hey." I ran my knuckles across his hot cheek.

Glassy gray eyes found mine. "You're intimidating."

"I'm intimidating?"

"Yes."

"Because I've had some experience?"

"Because you're beautiful. And not only beautiful in the way you're supposed to be. You're kind, Royal. The type of person who eats every meal with his sister so she's not alone. A guy who sees people for who they are. A guy who isn't afraid to do anything. The guy who saw me, saw beyond what everyone else couldn't. You inherited my loneliness and made it your own. You've changed me."

He pressed his lips to my stomach, below my belly button, and my knees threatened to buckle. I ran my fingers through his hair and he shivered. His loneliness was what drew me in.

"Your loneliness is what makes you beautiful. Makes you hear things no one on this planet can hear. Your loneliness, Camden, it's what sets you apart, makes you someone I'm lucky to have because you're letting me in. You've changed me, too." My voice trembled as he skimmed the tip of his nose across my skin. "There isn't a minute in the day when I can't hear your song in my head, when I'm not thinking about you, about this, about how I want you more than I want to dive into that pool every day."

His brows knitted together, something vulnerable writing its way across his face. "Do you mean that?"

I swallowed as the truth ignited inside me. "Yes."

I leaned down and kissed him, his head falling back, his lips parting and opening for me. I reached between us, touching him again, hard and velvet in my palm, he groaned. His hands worked open my belt, the zipper of my pants. There were no more obstacles between us, no going back as I shed my pants and underwear to the floor, or as the grip he held on my waist tightened and pulled me toward him. I straddled him, the dark hair on his thighs coarse and rough against my legs. I liked it. I liked the way it scratched at my skin, the way his lean body felt beneath me, the way his heat seared and branded me. Burying my face into the soft, warm crook of his neck, I inhaled. Sweat and soap and him. I stopped breathing as he lifted his hips, rocking himself against me. Chest to chest, his kiss claimed me, sipping from my mouth with long, slow sweeps of his tongue. I was light-headed, my limbs tingling and heavy as he ran his fingertips down my arms.

I held on to his broad shoulders as I pulled away from his lips. Resting my forehead on his, I closed my eyes, unable to hide the pleading tone of my voice, "Touch me."

I heard him swallow, his breathing uneven, while his fingers trailed over my chest, my stomach, and reached between us. He took me in his hand, his lips opening on a moan as I moved my hips, pushing us together.

Closer.

Closer.

I was his puppet. Willing, ready—complete. His mouth moved against mine, in rhythm with his hand, and I wanted to touch him, too. I followed his lead, taking him in my hand and he shuddered. His groan almost a silent thank you, mine a whispered, *please, let's do this together because I feel like I'm dying and I don't want to die unless you do.* My jaw clenched and we kissed, teeth, and tongues, and lips, and groans. Hard against hard until our bodies were not our own to control, until I couldn't take it, until his thighs, my thighs, started to shake, until his left hand was digging into my scalp and mine was grasping his hair so tight it had to be painful, until we didn't care about the pain, until our harsh, unsteady breathing became the only sound in the room, until our palms flooded with the heat of our relief, and we were no more than breathless kisses and satisfied, until the scent of the room was heady and intoxicating, and I never wanted to move from this spot. With him.

Our lips were deliberate, trying to wind the clock to a pace we could accept, to keep this moment a little longer, to ignore the fact we were both naked and sticky and sweating.

He smiled and his lips curved against my mouth. "You have goosebumps."

"So do you." I pulled away to find Camden's black pupils had nearly eclipsed his irises.

His cheeks were splotched with color, his hair disheveled, and I imagined I looked the same. In disarray, but shining from the inside out.

"Here." Camden grabbed a small fleece blanket that had almost fallen off the bed and cleaned my chest, my hand, and then his own body before throwing it into a hamper sitting to the right of his keyboard.

He licked his swollen lips, his left hand settling on his stomach as he lay back onto his elbows and asked, "Do you have practice tomorrow?"

Marveling at the way we were positioned, I shook my head. "Nope."

His long body stretched out below me, his stomach muscles on display, all that creamy pale skin, I was lucky. Lucky to be here. Lucky to have had this night with him. Fortune had given me a gift. Camden's features gentled as his eyes scanned my body, his palm raising and falling to my thigh, his fingers tracing circles on my leg. Did he feel it, too? The hand of fortune, tugging at our bones, reaching inside of our bodies and rearranging the elements as if to say he was made for you and you for him.

"Then you can stay a little while?"

I didn't miss the hope in his tone, or how, because I'd grown to learn his tells, his insecurity was wearing him like a blanket. I leaned my body over his, kissing him once before I repositioned, lying next to him, he rolled onto his side to face me.

We were both staring at the other, a smile playing at the corner of my mouth and I said, "I'll stay all night if that's what you want."

He held the back of my neck, drawing me less than an inch from his mouth. His eyes closed as he whispered, "Stay all night."

Royal

"Is it getting serious?" Kai raised his brow.

The smirk on his face had my palm itching to splash him. Resting my hand on the side of the pool, I glanced over my shoulder to make sure no one was in ear shot. "I think so..." Kai's grin was massive, and I felt my face heat. "Don't freaking look at me like that."

Camden and I had been together over a month and a half, and I'd been fielding these types of questions from my best friend a few times a week. We hadn't labeled anything, but I thought of him as my boyfriend. I liked him, I more than liked him. He was the first thing I thought about, always in the forefront of my mind. When I did my morning workout, I thought about how he'd felt lying next to me the night before, the soft, smooth skin of his chest, silk under my palm. In class, I thought about what he could be doing at that moment, wondered if he was playing music, wondered if he was thinking about me. In the library, I wondered about certain books, wondered if he'd like them. I thought about watching him read in his flannel pajama pants stretched out across his bed, my head on his chest. In the pool, when my skin turned cold, I thought about his hot hands, and how he'd have me sweating in less than two minutes.

Of course, I wasn't about to tell Kai any of this, he didn't need any more ammunition. He was relentless. Sometimes when I stayed the night with Camden, he'd knock on the wall and shout, "Keep it down." When in reality we hadn't made a sound. Camden had a strict no fooling around policy when Kai was home, which I argued was ridiculous since Kai always had Brie, his girlfriend, over and subjected us to his late-night marathons. I never won that argument. Instead, we stayed at my place, which unfortunately, wasn't as often as I would've liked. Swim season was in full swing, and with fall break only four days away, our coach was drilling us hard. His plan, he'd said, was to get us as fit as possible before our mothers stuffed us with turkey and sweet potato casserole for five days straight. Honestly, I think the guy just loved watching us swim, he loved the sport and this team.

Kai stared at me, waiting for more of an explanation, I diverted, "What about Brie? You guys still holding steady?"

His smile plummeted and he clenched his jaw. "That girl is draining."

"Then why stay with her?"

His lips twitched.

"I'm serious." I lowered my voice to a whisper, "Besides the sex? What's the point?"

Kai's eyes darkened. "The point... Is I don't have time for one-night-stands. Chicks wanting more and getting pissed off when they get exactly what I offered them in the first place. Drama, and Brie is... she's not so bad once you get to know her."

"That's convincing."

I chuckled, and he splashed me with a wave of pool water. "Fuck you, O'Connell. I have my reasons, you're a nosy shit."

"Says the guy who's always in my business."

"It's interesting, dude. You're a straight guy turned gay, and you're banging my roommate, it's like reality TV."

"Jesus, lower your voice." In a panic, I scanned the pool. Everyone was doing their own thing, swimming laps or doing pushups on the deck. "We're not... banging."

Again, his eyebrows raised. "Aww. You're waiting for the right moment, aren't you?"

I exhaled an annoyed breath. "You're an asshole. An immature asshole."

He laughed, and it made me laugh, too. After a moment, he ducked his head, his wet hair flopping over his forehead, his face somber as a stone. Kai's voice was almost inaudible as he asked, "Are you scared?"

I didn't know what he was asking me. "Scared about what?"

"About getting caught? Is that why he hardly stays at your place?"

"Swim season is rough—"

"Lie. I swim, work, get decent grades, and find time to fuck my girlfriend. You're scared, and after a while, hiding is going to hurt you both."

"You sound like Indie."

"Well." He shrugged.

"I want him to stay the night all the time." Kai's face broke into a smile, and I ignored it, moving on, hoping to avoid some wisecrack remark. "But he has to leave at an ungodly hour. Everyone in Warren House is an athlete. They get up early for their gym times, or whatever, and he has to sneak out before the sun comes up. I'm exhausted all day because after he leaves I feel like shit, like I've treated him like a dirty secret and can't fall back asleep."

"He's the one who said no one could know though, right? So, it's his choice."

"It's more complicated than that and you know it."

To prove my point, Ellis walked by with one of his buddies, the sneer on his face directed at either Kai or me, I couldn't tell. The guy had a chip on his shoulder the size of Alaska, always with something to prove. So far, my times at every meet this season had continued to best his by at least three seconds. It was safe to say I wasn't his favorite person. He'd use whatever he could against me to make himself look like the better person.

"It's not." Kai's jaw set in a stubborn line. "He's the one who's making a big deal, hiding. It's his choice."

"Yeah, like it's his choice he doesn't like to stay at his own place because his roommate's a jerk and teases him all the time."

Kai's brows dipped into a deep line. "Shit, really? Now I feel like a dick."

"Good."

"It's totally my fault you guys aren't having sex."

I scrubbed my wet palm over my face and raised my eyes to the ceiling, praying for patience, as I said, "Lower your voice."

Sex. The word of the day it seemed. Sex was defined in such a predictable way. The world's penetrative view. Black and white. Camden and I were multi-tonal. We had sex. It might not fit the traditional view, but we spilled ourselves open for each other every time we were together, and as much as I thought about what it would be like to be inside him, to have him share his body with me in that way, being with Camden the way we were, touching him, tasting him, feeling him let go, it was enough. It was everything.

"You know you can ask me anything." Kai smirked and my eyes narrowed. "I heard the pharmacy on Beech Street sells the best lube."

"I'm not talking to you anymore." I pushed off the wall and fell into a fast rhythm, cutting through the water, leaving Kai and his smart mouth laughing hysterically behind me.

Swim practice finished, thank God, without any more *advice* from my best friend. The guys all wanted to go to Stacks, get a beer before they headed back to their respective homes for the holiday. Kai and I both declined. Kai was heading home tonight, and after I'd suffered through an early gym session this morning, classes, and a short, four-hour shift at the library, all I wanted was to eat dinner with my sister and my boyfriend. Boyfriend. I hadn't spoken the word out loud to anyone. Maybe it was time I did, though. I was mulling over a way to bring it up to Camden as I made my way across campus in the frigid air. Thanksgiving was next Thursday, and the frost clinging to the wet strands of my hair was another sign winter wasn't far away.

A small arm wrapped itself through mine, and Indie's shivering body snuggled up next to me. "S-slow d-down. I'm f-freezing. N-need body h-heat."

"You realize it's probably snowing back home."

She groaned.

"And that we'll be heading to said *tundra* on Tuesday."

"That's still four days away, don't remind me."

Chuckling, I pulled her closer, draping my arm around her shoulders, I asked, "Feeling warmer?"

"Yes. Thank you." Indie burrowed into my side as we ascended the stairs to the cafeteria.

Once inside, the heat of the room was almost suffocating. The place was empty, most of the kids had left today to head home early for break. We could've left today, too, but I'd made the excuse to my parents and Indie that I couldn't risk missing Monday classes. I'd told them my scholarship was too important, but the truth was I wasn't ready to leave Camden.

Since the beginning of October, I'd spent almost every evening with him, and after Camden's recital, after our first time together, we tried to spend as many nights together as possible while keeping up appearances. We might not have slept in each other's bed, but we spent time together every night. I wasn't embarrassed to say I was addicted to him. His music, his voice, his lips, his hands, his skin. I was addicted to the way his fingers always traced the lines of my palms, and how when he thought I wasn't paying attention, he'd sing softly while he played his piano. Camden had become the air I needed to breathe, the pulse I needed to get through the day. Leaving him behind, with his parents, it actually made me physically ill when I thought about it.

"Where's Camden?" Indie's question cut through my reverie.

My eyes traveled across the large, open space of the dining hall, the few remaining students were settled at their tables, but our spot was vacant.

I shrugged my shoulders and pulled my phone from my pocket. "I don't know."

"I'll grab you your usual?" she asked.

"Yeah, remember I want—"

"Extra meatballs. I know." She smiled and shook her head. "And extra marinara on the side for dipping."

I leaned down and kissed her cheek. "Love you, Pink."

"Mm-hmm." She hummed and walked toward the deli as I tapped out a quick text.

Me: Hey. I'm in the cafeteria. Want me to grab you a meatball sub?

I walked slowly to our table in the corner, my eyes fixed on the swaying trees outside. The sun had set and, maybe it was the pending distance I was about to put between me and Camden, the tall firs, normally beautiful, seemed ominous—foreboding, like the dark branches of the trees could read my mood.

Camden: I'm not hungry.

I sat down and rolled my thumb over the screen until Camden's number was on display. I hit the call button and the phone barely rang once.

"What's the matter?"

He exhaled into the phone, his voice hoarse as he answered, "Not the best afternoon."

"Are you sick?"

He didn't say anything. The seconds ticked by. "Camden... talk to me."

I couldn't help how my heart started to beat faster, how worry sank inside my gut like a brick.

"My mom called me today." Shit. "They're going to Stowe for the holiday."

"Vermont?"

He cleared his throat. "Yeah."

"When will you leave?"

He laughed without humor. "I'm not. I'm not going. I wasn't invited. They're probably there by now. She called from the airport a while ago."

I hated his parents. I couldn't comprehend how any parent could be this cruel to their kid. Maybe Indie and I were lucky to have the parents we had, but Camden's mom and dad seemed to be next-level assholes.

Indie sat next to me at the table, and with a smile on her face, mouthed his name, "Camden?" I nodded, and an idea bloomed inside me. For the first time today, the looming holiday didn't seem so daunting. Thanksgiving was my favorite holiday. It was a big deal for my family, and the only reason I'd been dreading it, was because I couldn't be with Camden.

"Come with me and Indie."

"What?"

"To Salt Lake, drive home with me and my sister." Indie's eyes met mine, and without a word, she understood. A smile parted her lips, and I knew this was the right thing to do.

"That's not a good plan."

"It's a great plan."

"So you plan to come out to your parents by bringing your boyfriend home?"

My lips spread into a smile.

Without making a big deal about the fact he'd called me his boyfriend for the first time, I agreed, "Yes, people bring their boyfriends home for the holidays all the time."

"Yeah, and those people are girls. Royal, I don't want—"

"You're not a burden."

"That's not what I was going to say. What if they freak out? I don't want to be the reason your family has a shitty Thanksgiving. Fuck, my family doesn't even want me there and they're my *parents*." He'd said parents like it was a swear word.

"I want you there."

"Royal."

"Please. I promise, it will be good, and if it's not, then we'll leave together."

He didn't speak, but I heard the heavy sigh that escaped his lips. I could picture him, standing in his room, pacing. I wished I was there, I needed him to see how much I wanted this, wanted him to meet my family. I wanted him to see not all people were careless with their hearts, with their love.

I motioned to Indie that I had to leave and she handed me the paper wrapped sub with a whispered, "Good luck."

I nodded my chin, and she gave me a sad smile before I turned to leave.

The door to Beckett House closed behind me when he finally spoke. "You'd do that? You'd leave."

"If my parents didn't accept me for who I was, didn't accept you... I'd leave in a heartbeat."

"Can you come over?" His voice cracked as he whispered.

"I'm already on my way."

Camden

He never knocked anymore, and the relief I felt as I heard him move through the suite scared me. It had always been me. My parents proved as much today, another showing of their affection, leaving me behind. I'd let him in, but how long would he stay? The light from the streetlamps outside filtered through the slats of the blinds, disturbing the silence I'd always feared, cutting through the pitch and illuminating the room with dull strands of light.

My bedroom door opened and I closed my eyes. The chill of the room had permeated my skin, and I wished for the heat of his body. I wished for his mouth to make this hollow sound inside my head disappear. I told myself I was used to this, used to being left behind, but it stung more this time. It stung because I'd found someone I cared about, and I saw in him what I should have seen in my parents. Love.

I heard the creak of my mini-fridge door as it opened and shut. I heard the thud of his shoes. One. Two. My eyes stayed closed as the bed sank under his weight, as the heat of his body, his chest, pressed against my back. Royal's warm hand rested against my bare stomach and I let him melt into me.

"Hey," he whispered running his nose along the bow of my shoulder.

I exhaled as he placed a small kiss to that perfect spot under my ear. "Hey."

"What are you listening to?" he asked. His voice a gauzy cotton, subdued as he burrowed his lips into the crook of my neck.

"Erik Satie."

Royal's smile stretched across the expanse of my shoulder. "I like the French accent."

A smile found its way across my own lips. He'd only been here for a few minutes and already everything felt a little better. The music sounded better. The room and its dark silence filled with the drum of my heart, of his heart.

I rolled onto my back, opening my eyes. He adjusted his body, resting on his elbow, his gaze tracing the lines of my face, settling on the wetness that covered my cheeks.

"Tu me rends heureux. Je suis tellement content que tu sois là." I stuttered the last few words, the admiration in his eyes, the broad smile on his lips, it almost hurt to look at him.

"Is that French?" he asked, his brows plunged into serious creases as he wiped away the dampness from my cheek with the pad of his thumb.

I nodded.

"What did you say?" he asked, his touch moving from my cheeks to the strands of hair that covered my forehead. My eyes shut.

"You make me happy," I whispered. "I'm glad you're here."

He kissed my mouth. Soft. Soft. And I opened my eyes for him.

"I didn't know you could speak French."

"I have no need for it. It was my father's thing, I know a little bit of Italian, as well." Thinking of my father soured the smile I on my lips.

"I'm sorry," he said.

"For?"

"Your parents."

I swallowed past the growing lump in my throat. "I have this memory... I can't let go of it. I think I was six or seven, and I'd been playing all day... the tips of my fingers ached..." Royal took my hand in his and gently massaged my fingers. "I'd been crying. I remember my mom kissing me on the cheek. I can feel her hand on my shoulder as she said, 'Don't cry, Cam. Show Mommy how strong you can be. Play it again.'"

The memory washed over me. The sound of the room, the smell of her perfume, lilacs and something too sweet. I struggled to breathe, and Royal squeezed my hand, kissed my cheek, wet with fresh tears.

"I'd played for another hour, and my dad... he'd fought with my mom. And I knew it was about me. I couldn't hear what they were saying, but my father's voice, he was so angry, and I remember how quiet everything had become after she'd left. I still don't know where she went, she was gone all night. She'd slammed the door, and there was no sound, and I couldn't play anymore. I couldn't find the notes, and I panicked. My dad kneeled down and..." I choked on the memory and turned toward Royal, burying my face in the cotton of his t-shirt. His hand settled on the back of my head, running long, soothing strokes down my spine and up the nape of my neck. I tilted my head, wanting to see his face. His blue eyes glittered under the low light of the room. "My dad smiled at me. He smiled, Royal, and I think it might've been the last time his smile felt sincere. He took me down to the beach, and we explored the tidal pools, made a fire, and stayed until dark. I remember thinking how easy everything could be if I had been stronger. If I hadn't cried would they have fought? I always blamed myself. I always did."

"It's not your fault," he said, his voice as thick as mine.

"I used to think my mom's kindness was spent on her patients. She had nothing left for my dad, for me, by the time she got home. She doesn't care about me, and over time, I think my father forgot to care." I couldn't stop the crack in my chest from breaking open. The rush of tears falling down my face sounded like the bitter end of a song as I pushed the shaking words from my mouth. "Maybe they never cared about me."

Royal took my face in his hands. "I care about you."

He spoke with anger and conviction and that crack, my walls, they splintered and shattered. I wanted to believe him, to give him my body and my heart, to have him hold it all in his hands and hear me. Truly hear my heart, my soul. I hoped he liked the way it sounded, hoped he'd never want to stop listening. I was weary of the doubtful chorus inside my head, the echoes of my parents that had taken root. Since I'd met Royal, their notes had become almost indecipherable, and until today, I thought I might've silenced them.

I sucked in a ragged breath as he pressed his lips to my forehead. I closed my eyes and let him kiss away the tears from my lashes. The heat of his mouth on my mouth, the friction of his thumbs on my cheeks, my body sagged, my muscles tired and relieved.

I care about you, too.

I. Care. About You. Too.

I. Care. About. You. Too.

"Show me," I pleaded, my lips brushing against his.

He leaned back. His eyes searching mine. "How?"

"You know how."

He swallowed, and I watched in awe the way his throat moved, the way the pink in his cheeks traveled down his neck.

"You're upset and I want to kill your parents. I don't think—"

"I don't want to think."

He licked his lips. Nervous. "Camden. I care about you."

"You already said that."

"I don't want... I want you to want this when you're ready, not because you're trying to distract yourself from—"

"I want this. I'm ready." I curled my fingers around the hem of his t-shirt and kissed him, hard and desperate, until I started to cry again, panic taking me over, goosebumps prickling at the hairs on my neck.

Want me.

Want me.

Want me.

Royal held my face in his hands, my tears pooling on the tips of his thumbs.

"Camden, I—"

I rested my head on his shoulder, inhaling sunshine and hope. "I need this, need you. I need a new memory. I need to remember I'm good."

His breath hitched, and his hand cupped the back of my head. He was quiet and I was terrified he'd tell me no. Tell me we should wait. Tell me I wasn't good. But he didn't speak as he leaned away from me, lowering his hands from my face only to lift his shirt over his head.

"You're good," he said, his features stoic under the moonlight.

He started at the tip of my nose, his lips dusting kisses on my tear-stained lashes, my cheeks—my jaw. His hands ran along the expanse of chest, pushing me back onto the bed. He kissed the hollow of my throat, lingering like he always did on my birthmark. His blond hair teased the underside of my chin and I shivered.

"Camden." He worshipped my name. "I..." He dropped reverent kisses on my neck, my shoulders—his chest blanketing my chest, his arms holding his strong body above me.

"Open the bedside drawer." I flushed at the needy sound of my own voice.

He did as I asked, and his body stiffened enough that I noticed.

"Are you sure?" he asked, his blue eyes wide and wanting.

"You're the only thing in my life I'm sure about."

Royal stared at me, and I could almost hear him thinking it through, warring with himself, warring between desire and logic. He left the drawer, filled with the condoms Kai had placed there as a joke, open as he stood. I watched as he took one from the pile, and as he unbuttoned his jeans, he pulled away the final piece of clothing. Royal was beautiful, standing in the motes of dust swirling in the sheets of light that spilled through the blinds. Framing him, like a marble statue, etched and perfect. It was almost too much to take in all at once, like the way a song could swell, the notes overpowering and gorgeous and all consuming. I took off the rest of my clothes and waited. Shivering with need as he covered himself with the condom, trembling as the unknown spread itself around the room in a muted silence, like the way snow swallowed sound, leaving its white static in the air.

Royal sat on the bed and raised my hand to his mouth, kissing my palm, each finger, my wrist, the inside of my elbow. His body shifted, and he straddled my waist, his hard length rutting against my own. We'd been naked like this before, but tonight was different. Sadness and hope had made the air humid, had made it difficult to breathe, but I inhaled it, inhaled him as he leaned down and kissed me. Anticipation was the flavor of his tongue as it dipped into my mouth. I sat up, needing to be closer, trying to quicken the pace of his kiss, but he wouldn't relent. The control was his, and he took my fevered need and cooled it, slowed it down, his fingers making maps on my skin, remembering tiny paths to all my sensitive spots.

He leaned back, his eyes on mine, gauging how ready I was—I was simmering. The heat under my skin almost unbearable.

I wanted to taste him, too, my lips finding their way over his skin, and he let me. Let me take the lead as I took him in my mouth. The bitter taste of the condom was unfamiliar, but he gasped, and I didn't care. Royal's fingers gripped the back of my head, and I liked the way his body tensed, the way his stomach muscles contracted. He swore under his breath, and I liked that, too, that I made him feel as out of control as he made me feel. All I'd ever known was control, it was the way I got through each day of my life. On my terms. Who I let in. Who I didn't. Who I spoke to. Who received my silence. He was all I wanted.

"Camden," he whispered in a strangled voice, taking my chin between his fingers, and raising my lips to his.

This kiss was wet and uncoordinated as Royal's body unfolded over mine, pressing me down into the mattress, draping me in his scent. I wrapped my legs around his waist, offering myself to him. There was no more space, no him, no me, until he was inside me, and I gave him my last pieces of innocence.

"You..." His straw-colored lashes briefly shuttered closed. "This feels unreal." He breathed my name. "You okay?"

Incapable of words, I nodded. He moved slowly at first, his eyes holding me to the Earth, until the pain became a searing heat and we became one in a way I'd never want to forget. This moment a memory I'd have, a new defense against a past that never wanted to let me go. I'd always remember the blush of his cheeks, the hazy look in his eyes, how his lips parted as he forgot himself inside the rhythm, the beat, the pulse of our bodies—the mark he left inside me when we both gave in.

He groaned, his mouth on mine, his arms vibrating, I wanted him to collapse. I needed to feel the weight of him against me when I came. He read me like he always did, and as we fell over the cliff together, chest to chest, his weight was my weight. My breath was his breath, my pulse was his pulse. His sweat was my sweat.

He stilled and lowered his mouth to mine, kissing me long and slow, reaching for the last possible pieces of me, until he'd collected every last one and made them his.

His nose touched mine, and he smiled, sweat lingering on his brows, he said my name. I kissed his chin, nipped at the flesh with my teeth, and his smile grew wider. His hand rested on my cheek as we both caught our breath, and he placed one more kiss to my lips before letting himself fall onto his back. Our heads lolled to the side at the same time. His blue eyes were crystal clear, and I imagined I could see all the way to his heart, because I knew he was looking into mine.

Royal lifted his hand and lightly stroked his knuckles across my cheek. "You're kind of perfect," he repeated the words he'd said to me what felt like an eternity ago.

That night was a universe away.

I hadn't believed him then, and maybe I shouldn't believe him now, but for once, I let myself believe it. I let the tip of his finger trace the smile on my lips. Because even though he didn't say it, I saw it in his eyes, felt it in his touch—heard it in his voice.

You're kind of perfect.

You're mine.

I'm yours.

I love you.

I love you, too.

Royal

Heat poured from his palm as it skated across my stomach. The dark strands of his hair tickled the base of my neck as he rested his cheek against my chest, his body spread over me with contentment. I wondered if he could hear how my heart hammered as I brought my hand to his cheek, let my thumb trail lightly over his skin, and cradled him closer.

Closer.

If I could crawl inside him this moment, I would. I'd never been this close to anyone. Never had anyone let me in like Camden had tonight. Perfect. Perfect. Perfect. My mind unable to find a better synonym as I focused on the way our breaths had become one.

"I mean it," I whispered and kissed the top of his head.

"I'm not perfect, no one is," he replied, drawing tentative spirals on my ribcage.

Shivering, I wrapped my arms around his body. "You are... at least, to me you are..." I chuckled. "And anyone else who says otherwise is either wrong or crazy." He didn't speak, his fingers pausing softly on my skin. His sharp intake of breath caused my heart to skip. "Camden?"

This was new to me, new for him, maybe I should have done more, maybe I'd been too rough, or did something I wasn't supposed to?

"Hey."

No answer.

I shifted and he pressed himself against me, holding me, his arms still trembling. He'd asked this of me. I'd given in, even when I thought I shouldn't, but I wanted it, wanted him. The last bridge, we had crossed it together, but I was starting to think maybe we shouldn't have.

"Hey." Worry sank inside my stomach, made the room feel warmer, smaller somehow, and a sense of selfishness washed over me. "Camden, look at me."

He wouldn't.

"Did I hurt you?"

It certainly hadn't seemed like he'd been in pain, he'd kissed me with urgent lips, lips that had pleaded for more. *Don't stop. Please, don't stop.* But I'd never been with a man or a woman... not like that, and maybe I should've...

"No." His voice was rough and heavy and it twisted its way into my heart.

Stripped. Defenseless. Exposed.

"It was..." He exhaled and lifted his body enough I could see his face, the cold air of the room invading the space between us. Camden's gray eyes were a calm and quiet storm. Lifting his gaze to meet mine, he said, "I've never had much to say before, choosing to speak when I wanted, keeping people at a distance, it's all that was ever expected of me. It made me feel safe, staying inside my own head. But there's too much... so much I want to say now..." He rubbed his fist along the length of his sternum like it caused him actual pain to admit these things to me. "You make me want to say things... Things I'm afraid to say, things I shouldn't."

I ran my fingers through his hair and his eyelashes fluttered closed. Goosebumps broke out across my arms as he leaned down and placed a light kiss to my collar bone.

"You can say whatever you want to me."

But I knew what he meant. I had so many things I wanted to say. All the words aching to pour from my lips. *I was just inside you. Inside you.*

He let me in.

He gave me everything.

He was my something *more*.

"Anything you say..." My mouth was dry, my throat suddenly tight. "I want to know what you're thinking, Camden."

He rested his forehead to my chin, and I cupped the back of his neck. My fingers played idly with the short strands of his hair as I waited him out.

"What if I said I'm falling in love with you?" His words came out in a slow, quiet exhale—soft, to the point I actually thought I'd made up the words myself, wished them into existence.

"My dad told me he knew he was in love with my mom the first time she spoke to him."

Camden raised his head, his face so serious I wanted to smile, lean in and kiss the crease between his brows.

"He said, 'Love sinks its teeth into your heart, and you'll do anything to be its victim.'"

"Victim," he mused. "That's a dark way of looking at it."

I chuckled and held my hand to his cheek. His eyes closed briefly, as he leaned into the heat of my palm, and when they opened again, the pull between us was palpable. "It all makes sense to me now."

"It does?"

"Yeah." I nodded. "One month, two months, four years— a decade. Love is love, and the way I feel about you, Camden, isn't something I've felt before."

"What about Natalie?"

"She was just a friend, what we had, it wasn't the same as this, I never, we never... you're the only one I've... I've been with like this. Tonight was a first for me, and not just because you're a guy." I lowered my hand from his face, and an easy smile played at the corners of his lips.

"Yeah?"

"Yeah."

It was more than losing my virginity, though, more than being with just anyone. It was him. I bottled up my nerves, and made myself tell him the truth. He deserved to know, he needed to know I'd fallen for him, too.

"God, Camden, I want to protect you from your asshole parents, from the world. Spend every minute like this, naked and hot. Underneath you, above you... inside you." He bit his lip, and my heart tripped over itself, but I kept talking, somehow, my lips kept moving despite the way my hands had started to shake. "I want to know what it's like to have you inside me. All of me, Camden. All of my flaws." I smiled. "All of my imperfection. All of my body and heart and mind. It's yours. Maybe six months from now it won't feel this way, and I'll have to take what we've given each other and grow from it. What I'm feeling, this steady thud..." I took his hand and placed it above my heart. "This need, this constant deep breath stuck in my lungs, until I saw your face, heard you play, touched you, until I could breathe, too. It's love, it's *more*, and it's ours to share."

Camden held his body over mine. "Ours," he whispered and kissed me gently on the lips. "Ours," he repeated and rolled his hips against me.

He was hard and the contact sent a jolt to the base of my spine. My hands traveled down his back, along the expanse of muscle I craved, resting my fingers on his hips, I held him against me. Camden placed more open-mouth kisses along the curve of my shoulder, against my neck, nipping his teeth on my jaw and my bottom lip. His kiss was deep, his tongue sweet as it slipped into my mouth.

He pulled away, our lips brushing against each other as he murmured two words, "Love you."

I smiled against his lips, aligning our bodies, my heart frantic, flapping—flying, perfectly willing to be his victim.

Royal

"I know what you're thinking."

"Yeah? What's that?" Camden asked, his eyes fixed on Indie's retreating form as she walked through the back door of our apartment building.

I reached over the console and wrapped his hand in mine. "You're wishing I hadn't talked you into coming home with me. You're thinking my parents are going to chase you away with pitchforks the minute we walk through the door."

He paled, and I stifled my smile. He was overthinking. He was always overthinking.

He turned to look at me, his face covered with earnest shadows. "You're not scared?"

"No."

"How?"

"Because I know my parents."

"Hate hides itself until it has something to prove." He exhaled a shaky breath and turned his stony gaze to the door again.

I leaned over the center console and placed a soft kiss to his cheek. Camden's entire body froze, his breath catching inside his throat as he turned to look out his window. We were too public it seemed.

"Truthfully, there's a small part of me that's nervous, but not for the reasons you're brewing up in that sexy head of yours." His lips twitched, fighting a smile. I liked when I made him smile, made him forget that he was afraid all the time. "I think... I think I'd feel the same way if I told my parents I'd fallen in love with a girl. It doesn't matter that you're a guy, it matters because I'm telling my parents something private, something personal, and that's always a little nerve-wracking. I'm in love with you, Camden, and that's all that will matter to them. They might say this seems fast, or ask me if I'm sure, or tell me to be careful. Not because you're a man, but because they don't want me to get hurt."

He lowered his eyes to his lap. "I'd never hurt you."

My stomach did a cartwheel. I trusted those words, and I didn't care if it made me naïve or stupid. I wanted Camden here, wanted to spend time with him in real life, out, in the open. Show him there were things worth opening up for—that he was worth it all.

"Should we head in?" I asked, and he nodded, releasing my hand.

I grabbed our duffel bags from the trunk and tried to shoulder both of them.

Camden protested. "I can carry my own bag." He made an attempt to take it from my arm, but I slipped it over my right shoulder before he could.

"I'm being a gentleman."

"I should carry my own bag."

I sighed, my smile falling a degree or two. Choosing my battles, I handed him the strap to his duffel. "I take it we're not walking in holding hands?"

Camden's face paled as I opened the door. I wanted to rest the heel of my palm on his back, whisper in his ear, *I've got you*. I wondered if maybe I *should've* taken his hand. I should've linked our fingers and been done with it. There'd be no big reveal, no big deals made. Simple.

This is Camden.

Kiss on the cheek.

He's my boyfriend.

Nice to meet you, Mr. and Mrs. O'Connell

Call me Paige.

Call me Declan

Where's the pumpkin pie?

End of story.

But I could see the way his chest worked with shallow breaths, the cold, Salt Lake City air leaving his lips in nervous little puffs.

"It's going to be okay," I assured as we made our way up the stairs.

He didn't answer. I hated the idea forming in my head, but for him, to make him feel at ease I'd say whatever he wanted me to say. We paused outside my family's loft. "I don't have to say anything. I don't have to tell them. You're a friend from school. They already think your parents had to go out of town for work. They know me. I didn't want you to be alone. They'll believe it."

What I didn't say, was eventually, they'd notice the way I looked at him. The way I gravitated to his side, how he blushed if I stared at him too long. They'd know in less than twenty-four hours how crazy we were about each other.

His Adam's apple bobbed. "I can't ask that of you." His bottom lip trembled, but it parted into a small smile. "It'll be okay."

"Yeah. I think it will be."

The front door swung open and my mom, despite her tiny human status, practically knocked me over as she barreled into me. Her small arms wrapped around my midsection, her fingers curling into the fabric of my St. Peter's hoodie. I felt her shudder, and I knew she was crying.

I chuckled. "Jesus. Mom, I can't breathe."

She pulled back, her ice blue eyes glittering with tears. She wiped her cheeks with her hand and she laughed, out of breath. "Now you know how I feel. I've been holding my breath all day. I'm so glad you're home." She tugged on the strings hanging from the hood of my shirt. "I missed you." She cleared her throat. "We missed you."

"I'm glad we could make it home, even if it's only for a few days," I managed to say. Seeing her again, after so long, all that homesickness wedged itself inside my throat making it hard to speak.

She took a deep breath, her eyes landing on Camden. Her smile stretched wide as she held out her hand. "You must be Cam."

My heart hammered as the seconds ticked by. He hesitated, staring at her proffered hand a beat longer than would be deemed socially acceptable, reverting to the anti-social boy I'd met back in September.

"It's Camden. Thank you, for having me." He took her hand and I let out a relieved breath.

My mom shook his hand, her eyes curious. "Well, Camden. Come on in, we're grateful you're here."

She spoke quietly, apologizing for the mess, excusing the multiple canvases strewn about as we walked through the living room. "Dad and I were commissioned to paint a few pieces for the children's art museum down in Draper. He bought the supplies the other day, but he's been... inside his head." She glanced at me. A silent warning. I smiled, hoping I'd get to see whatever he was working on in the studio while I was here. "You know him, he gets an idea, and everything else has to wait."

Camden soaked it all in, seeing my family home for the first time. The dark art, the bright colors. The smell of burning candles, Frankincense and something that couldn't be named. The familiar smell had always made me feel safe. This was home. I watched as Camden devoured the room. The stereo played a quiet jazz playlist, competing with Indie and Dad's soft laughter from the kitchen. Camden paused, looking through the expansive floor-to-ceiling windows. I had the urge to walk up behind him, drape my hands around his waist and whisper in his ear, "It's amazing, isn't it? This could be your home, too."

But I stood at a safe distance and lowered my voice to ask, "You okay?"

One slow nod.

"Royal tells me you play the piano?" my mom asked, grabbing Camden's attention. "I'll have Declan pull the keyboard from the attic."

"You don't have—"

"It's no hardship, Royal's dad is in the attic digging out one thing or another on most days anyway. Besides, I'd be honored to hear you play." Mom's smile reached past her cheeks, lighting her features, her eyes finding mine as she pushed a strand of her light blonde hair behind her ear. "Every time I talk to Royal he says how amazing you are."

My face flushed with embarrassment when Camden leveled me with his gaze. I shrugged. "What? You're a *genius*. Remember?"

For the most part, the introductions went smoothly. Camden met my dad and made it through a tour of my parents' studio. Camden's silence, I hoped, would be perceived as reverence for their craft. His shyness often misinterpreted as unsociable and distant. My dad had always been an unobtrusive force, and it was hard not to see the similarities between him and Camden. They were both humble and unassuming, both trapped inside their own heads. I watched them as they stood in front of a massive seven-foot-tall canvas covered in deep purples, blues, splashes of crimson and gold, a smoky black streak through its center, cutting through the vibrant tones like a specter.

"It's back," I whispered to my sister, nodding to the painting and to the eerie ghost-like image it portrayed.

"Mom told me he's been down lately."

"I'm glad we came then." I took my sister's hand in mine.

"Did you see Camden's face when Dad walked out of the kitchen?" she asked, her quiet laughter just for me.

I squeezed her hand once and let go. "Yeah. He was slightly terrified."

"Now look at them."

My father was built strong, his shoulders broad, the muscles in his arms cut and covered with ink. The only thing over the years that had changed was the length and color of his beard. The salt and pepper strands were the longest I'd ever seen him grow it, hanging from his chin at least four inches. Dad turned to say something to Camden I couldn't hear, and I chuckled at the way he stared at my father. To an outsider, my father would seem the polar opposite of Camden, but I knew they both had talent and shadow in their veins.

"Royal." My dad's deep voice echoed through the open space of the studio.

Camden turned to look at me, his gray eyes warm. The butterflies in my stomach soared, and for the first time today, panic took root inside my heart, however small, it was there. I looked between my father and Camden, realizing how much I wanted this to work, how much my family's acceptance meant to me. How Camden got through each day, knowing his family didn't accept him? It was a harsh reality I wasn't ready to face. If I came out today, and my parents turned me away, as much as I'd told him I would get through it, being in the presence of my family, seeing what I could lose, it would ruin me. My heart pumped out two fragmented beats, and the ache in my sternum spread past my ribs and down to my stomach. Camden's smile was private, and I stood in awe, owning the fact I'd never be as strong as him.

"I was going to take a few appointments at the tattoo shop tonight, help Kieran close up the place so Liam can help Kelly at Irene's."

"Is tonight the benefit?" Indie asked.

Every year, my Aunt Kelly threw a Thanksgiving fundraiser at The Irene O'Connell House. The women's shelter she'd started and named after my late grandmother. The money she raised went directly to the families who needed help during the holidays. Our entire family had always donated in their own way to the cause since we usually couldn't attend. My dad and his baby brother Kieran kept the shop open, while Indie and I, in the past, had helped our cousins with the decorations.

"It is." My dad pushed his paint-stained fingers through his hair. "I shouldn't be too long. Royal, bring your friend to the shop after dinner, show him around." The creases around his eyes crinkled as he smiled.

"Maybe," I said, wanting to ask Camden first before I made a decision. Meeting my parents was one thing, but meeting my dad's brothers, all in the same day, would be sensory overload. "It was a long drive, the shop might have to wait till tomorrow."

"Either way," Dad said and walked through the studio door.

Indie bumped her hip into mine before lacing her fingers through Camden's. "Want to see the shrine my parents have for Royal?"

"What? No way, Pink... come on—"

"Yes, yes, I do."

Camden grinned, and before I could protest, Indie had pulled him down the hall to the extra bathroom my father had converted into a trophy room. Indie had the studio, and Dad had made sure I had my own space, too. It embarrassed me how my parents never threw shit away. I groaned as Indie literally skipped down the hall, and I was about to follow to my own mortification, when I heard my mom and dad talking in the kitchen. Camden glanced over his shoulder and I nodded my chin, my smile growing as he disappeared into the small, makeshift room. Those eyes, his eyes, I could be brave like him. Finding the courage I needed, I made my way to the kitchen.

"You guys have a minute?" I asked as my dad slipped on his jacket.

"What's up, honey?" My mom placed the knife she'd used to chop up the vegetables for tonight's stir-fry on the cutting board.

My dad's perceptive blue eyes started to pick me apart piece by piece, and even though I knew better, my courage wavered. That small *what-if* Camden had talked about churned inside my gut. My mouth watered and an anxious laugh bubbled past my lips.

236

"Royal?" My dad took a step toward me, and I held up my hand, hating the way my fingers trembled.

This shouldn't have felt so scary.

This was Camden and me, and everything I wanted.

The *what if* stabbed and poked at my ribs.

"Thank you for letting Camden stay, I... I... Thank you for letting him come. I know Thanksgiving is for family and—"

"Of course, he's your friend. It would be terrible to leave him behind all by himself in an empty dorm room." She let out a small sound of disapproval. "It's too bad his parents had to work."

The lie I'd told my mother slapped me in the face.

My gaze fell to the floor. "They're in Stowe... skiing."

"Skiing?" My dad's voice shifted, its blunt edges starting to show.

"I lied because I wasn't sure... they didn't invite him," I whispered and looked into my dad's eyes, trying to convey my anger without raising my voice. "They do this shit all the time, leave him behind."

"I'm glad he's here then." Mom's eyes were glassy, and she hadn't yelled at me for swearing. A good sign.

Dad's arms relaxed and he rested them at his sides. "You didn't have to lie."

"I'm sorry."

He clapped his big hand onto my shoulder. "You can tell us anything, Royal. You know that."

The corners of my eyes began to burn, my throat aching as I pushed myself to speak. "I... I have... I mean, there's..." Everything I'd thought to say, all the words, evaporated as my dad's strong grip held my shoulder, keeping me together. "He's... Camden and I... I... I'm in love with him."

The silence only lasted a second, maybe two, taking the moment into its pores. It was absorbent—permeable. It allowed my dad's smile to spread slowly to his eyes, and my mother's gentle voice to cover me. "In love with him."

She hadn't said it with malice or confusion. More like it was something she'd been thinking about for a while. Something she was happy to hear.

I started to cry.

Tears fell down my hot cheeks, and when my dad wrapped me into his bear-like embrace, I allowed myself to feel like a little kid again. Allowed his soapy scent into my lungs. Allowed the pressure to release, the tears to absorb, just like the silence, into his chest. My mom rested her cheek against my back, her arms snaking their way around my waist. I folded between them, my pulse soft, and I could have been ten years old or nineteen, but the thing that I held on to, the word I'd forgotten in that split second of fear, was acceptance.

They held me between them, my father's heartbeat steady and comforting, for longer than was probably necessary, until we heard Indie giggle. Mom was the first to let go, and when Dad finally did, I saw my mom wipe under her eyes for the second time today.

"He's a lucky kid... to have you. My special son." He placed his hand on my cheek for a brief moment before he zipped up his jacket.

Indie walked into the room, Camden behind her, and I rubbed away the tears. If they'd noticed anything, they hadn't acted like it. Indie walked past us and opened the fridge, grabbing a can of soda. She threw it toward Camden and he caught it.

She laughed and picked up the knife from the cutting board. "Give it a second before you open it."

Camden placed the can on the counter, and before he could lower his hand, or shove it into his pocket, like it had been all afternoon, I reached for him. Surprised he hadn't pulled away, I entwined our fingers, watching as his jaw clenched. I held his hand, grateful for his heat, and leaned in, brushing a quick, soft kiss across his cheek like I'd been dying to do since we'd arrived.

His eyes darted around the room, terror widening his pupils. My mom and Indie, oblivious, or acting as such, argued over whether or not to cut up one or two onions.

"I'm heading out." My dad pressed a kiss to my mom's cheek. "One onion," he said, settling the argument. Indie raised her hands in victory.

Dad turned, staring at us, a discreet smile forming, his own gaze fixed on our tangled fingers. Camden tightened his grip, inhaling a sharp breath. I wanted to tell him not to be scared, not to pull away, but I didn't have to.

Dad rested his hand on Camden's shoulder, the vibration of his usual gruff voice settling inside my bones as he spoke. "When I get back I'll grab the keyboard from the attic."

Camden

I was a c-sharp hovering, brash and uncomfortable, above the crowd—an imaginary number, complex and confused, defined by the man holding my hand, in a kitchen, a foreign space, but yet somehow a home. Royal's palm, the heat of his skin, settled me. His dad's eyes had spoken volumes, had played out like a Sergy Slavsky piece, bold, holding me in place all at once. His eyes had said stay. They'd told my heart to stop working its way through my sternum, to grip Royal's hand harder, to take a breath. The weight of his hand on my shoulder had told me I was welcome here, the soft squeeze of his fingers before letting go had made me believe it.

"I hope you're hungry?" Royal's mom asked, tapping the top of the soda can, the same one Indie had tossed to me earlier. "I think it's safe to open now." She tugged on Indie's sweater. "Can you grab me a few basil leaves?"

"Same place?" Indie asked.

"No, I put the herbs in Royal's window, his room always gets the most sunlight."

Indie left the room, and I wanted to go with her, follow her into Royal's room and close the door. Hide from the knowing, pale blue eyes staring straight through me. What had Royal said to his parents? I'd only been in the trophy room for a few minutes. Had he come out to them? His hand in my hand was the answer to my question, but had it really been that easy for him? I gulped down the sour, anxious aftertaste in my mouth.

His mom grabbed a rag off the oven door and wiped her hands. Leaning against the counter, she watched us, a spark of curiosity brightening her blue eyes, the same shade of blue as her son's. I didn't have the nerve to look at him, worried the ball was about to drop.

"So, how did you two meet? Royal told me you're his best friend's roommate..." I held my breath, despite the casual tone of her voice. "What I mean to ask, is when did you start dating?"

Dating. My spine straightened and Royal squeezed my sweaty palm. He leaned in closer, as if to say, *easy now.*

"I don't know. I don't think we ever officially started dating, it just... happened." He chuckled. "Camden's hard to know, but I'm glad I put in the effort."

He bumped a flirty shoulder into mine, and his mom's face split into a big smile. My pulse reacted, smoothing into an easier rhythm. And like I was the planet and he was the sun, I needed his heat to survive this, to remember to keep moving. Time would not stand still, and those dark hallways inside my head would see the daylight again.

Because of him. My golden light.

"I'm glad you were persistent," I said. Finding a bit of bravery, I turned to face him. The blush on his cheeks, his bright eyes welcomed me home.

Royal's gaze dipped to my mouth. I wanted to kiss him. Show myself this was okay. Everything was all right. We could do this. Here. And no one would get hurt. No one would tell us we were wrong or sick. No one would shut us out. No one would make us feel small and insignificant. This house, where the slight hint of turpentine mixed with the scent of onions sautéing on the stove, a weird blend of aromas, but one that somehow fit. It's what freedom smelled like. Freedom was a soft jazz piano playing in the background, the quiet acceptance of the stranger in the room. It looked like the boy I was in love with, tall and strong, sun-kissed hair, and tan skin.

As he leaned in, his lips brushing my cheek, he whispered in my ear, "*Leaves of Grass.*" I smiled. "I think I wanted you then, but didn't know it."

Heat bloomed inside my stomach at the memory, and without thinking about it too much, I caught his mouth with mine. Someone cleared their throat and Royal's gentle kiss turned into a smile against my lips. I quickly pulled away, my cheeks heating with embarrassment. Clarity washed the room in a wave of pinpointed sound. Jazz piano. Sizzling stir-fry. Indie's giggle. I waited for the scorn of disgust, but it never came.

Instead, his mom's mood only bloomed as she spoke with wet lashes. "This world is such a big place, and most of the time we never find the people we're looking for. People look all their lives for the one person who understands their heart. We search, and hope, and I think... it's a blessed few who find it on their first try. I'm also glad he was persistent."

Paige took a step toward me, and Royal let go of my hand. She pulled me into a hug, her small frame fitting against me, and though it only lasted for a few seconds, she gave me more acceptance, this stranger, than I ever had from my own mother. She released me, only to wrap her arms around her son. I kept myself gathered in such tight knots on most days, but today, instead of avoiding, I let the lump in my throat lodge in place, let my eyes sting, and told myself to see, to let the sounds of the room go silent and appreciate the people in it.

"Should I leave and come back in like... five minutes?" Indie offered, and Royal thumped her gently on her nose with his thumb. "Hey," she protested and threw a basil leaf at his face.

He laughed and swatted the herb to the ground. "What?"

"You made Mom cry."

"It's a good cry."

"She always cries." Royal rolled his eyes, but the smirk on his face won him another quick hug from his mom.

She shrugged. "It's cathartic." She pointed at him. "Now, go grab that keyboard from the attic so Dad doesn't have to."

At dinner, there were more questions. Have I always lived in Oregon? *Yes.* When did you start playing the piano? *I was three years old.* Why didn't you try for Juilliard? *Because that's where my mom wanted me to go.*

"Did you get in?" Royal had asked. The shock in his tone had silenced the entire table.

"Yes."

"You never told me."

"It was irrelevant."

He'd swallowed and placed his fork on his plate calmly before he'd stood and excused himself.

I waited a full five minutes.

"Which way…" I asked as I stared down the hall.

"His room, third door, on the right." Royal's mom gave me a sad smile.

"Thanks."

I passed the keyboard I'd avoided playing before dinner and headed down the hallway, looking at all the paintings and sketches on the wall, wondering which one belonged to which O'Connell. I only knew for sure none of them belonged to Royal.

I knocked once, and when he didn't give me any sort of reply, I opened the door. Royal was on his bed, staring out his window. The lights of the skyline twinkled, competing with the stars for the night's affection. Royal's phone was plugged into a docking station sitting on his dresser. The same Erik Satie album I'd had on the night we'd made love played. Heat spread over my neck and arms, my skin tingled with goosebumps as flash bulbs of memories spotted my vision. His scent. His control. His hands on my hips. The sounds he made. My hands on his skin. The way his kisses begged. The way my lips had given him everything he'd asked for, and his body had given me all I'd ever wanted.

"Did I do something… wrong?" I asked, standing still in the middle of his room.

Fidgeting with the hem of my sweater, I took a step toward him when he didn't answer. His eyes stayed fixed on the window, and I stole a glance around his room. His walls weren't covered with sports posters, or girls from swimsuit magazines like Kai's room back at St. Peter's. Royal had a series of small paintings hanging above his pinewood headboard, and when you looked at all of them together, they formed a wave that seemed to move depending on how the light hit each canvas. In fact, he only had one poster, a band I'd never heard of. Everything in his room was hand painted in spectacular shades of blue and gold, reminding me of the small painting he had on his desk back at school.

Breathless, I broke through his silence. "It's like watching you swim."

He looked at me.

"The paintings."

"My dad."

I met his gaze.

"You should've gone to Juilliard."

My jaw clenched and I shook my head. "I'm where I belong."

"You're so fucking talented, Camden."

I risked another step toward his bed. "It was her thing. I wanted to do it on my own. I wanted this scholarship."

"You could have gotten a scholarship for Juilliard."

I laughed and it caught him off guard. He gave me a small smile. "Royal, it's Juilliard, you only think I'm as good as I am because you're my boyfriend."

"You're that good."

I sat on the bed, placing my hand on his knee, I drew a timid circle with my thumb. "I wasn't offered a full scholarship. At St. Peter's I'm a prodigy, at Juilliard, I'm a middle-class citizen, nothing special in a sea of geniuses."

A gruff, almost growl sounded in his throat. "They're idiots then."

"I would have never met you if I'd gone to Juilliard."

Royal wrapped his arm around my waist. "True." He frowned, his brows plunging into frustrated lines. "Still. You belong there. I mean... imagine what you could do with a degree from the top music school in the country."

"Royal." He didn't get it. "Juilliard is what *she* wanted. I don't care if going there means I could become a famous composer. My terms for once. My plan... my goddamn life."

His eyes softened. "I don't usually think about it anymore, but I could have tried for a Division One school. I wanted to go where Indie could go, where my parents wouldn't have to pay for me, so yeah, I understand... my plan..." His lips lifted into a lopsided smile. "My goddamn life."

I held his face in my hands and kissed his forehead, his cheek. He relaxed his head, tipping it back, offering himself up to me, and I caved. His tongue slid into my mouth, and his fingers pushed into my hair on a moan. It was the first time we'd been alone all day, and I wanted to make the most of it. He turned his body, deepening our kiss. His hands fell to my shoulders, his fingers fisting the fabric of my sweater. He bit my top lip, and then licked it, soothing the slight pinch. My hands found their way under his sweatshirt, my thumb dusting the fine hairs of his happy trail. His whole body shuddered, the muscles in his stomach twitching beneath my fingertips. The blood in my veins wanted, each beat of my heart fed the need building between us. If we didn't stop soon, I didn't think either of us would be able to. I'd give myself to this man, in his childhood bed, with his mother in the other room. Maybe I really was sick after all.

"Royal." I pulled away first, catching my breath.

He wet his lips, his eyes hazy and warm, he said, "We should probably—"

"Stop."

He nodded, adjusting himself in his jeans, and I had to make myself look away, make myself scoot over a few inches.

He laughed, looking me over. "Your hair." He reached over and combed his fingers through it and my eyes closed slowly. "There." He ran his thumb down my cheek. "Way more presentable."

I opened my eyes. "For who?"

He grinned. "My uncle, I figured we'd go to the shop."

"Tonight?" I tried not to sound nervous.

"Yeah, it'll just be Kieran. Liam will be at the benefit, but you'll meet him Thursday."

Just Kieran. The same uncle he'd once told me had almost become a priest. My fingertips itched for the keyboard we'd dragged from the attic earlier, needing to dust the ivory, test the ebony, pretend I was back in my room, and hide behind the haunting melody trapped inside. But I wasn't in my dorm. Those four walls were lonely, and I'd come here, to the house that smelled and sounded like freedom.

"Sure."

"Let's go, then."

A convincing smile plastered on my face, and a stomach brimming with nerves, I took Royal's offered hand, stood when he did, and hoped that the rest of the O'Connells were as accepting as his mom and dad.

Camden

It was the persistent buzzing I noticed first as we walked through the door. My head filled with the awkward departure from Royal's family's apartment. I hadn't really noticed much of anything on our short walk to his dad's tattoo shop. Royal's mom had watched us reemerge from his bedroom, me red faced, him with a giant smile. Her nervous gaze had turned suddenly shy, and she'd averted her eyes to the table and picked up a couple of the plates. We'd only been in his room for a few minutes. I'd started clearing the table with shaking hands, worrying what she'd thought had gone on in there.

"Let me help you with that, Mrs. O'Connell," I'd offered.

"It's Paige." She'd lifted her hand and ruffled Royal's hair. "You can help, too, kiddo."

But that incessant buzzing sound, it niggled at my brain, dragging me away from my tendency to overthink, picking away until I couldn't ignore it any longer. How did people sit in here all day? I grit my teeth as the door shut behind me, a gust of cold wind sneaking in at the last minute. The rap music blaring over the speakers, nestled into the ceiling, did nothing to quell the droning beehive of a room.

Royal let go of my hand. "Kieran!"

The frigid night air evaporated and I started to sweat. Dinner unsettled itself in my stomach as Royal wrapped his arms around the large man sitting behind the desk. They clapped each other on the back, the way men do, and I struggled to hear what words were being exchanged. That ever-present hum kept bleeding into my ear drums. I swallowed and shifted on my feet as the man's light eyes found mine. He looked at me, without judgment of any kind, open, clear with crystal, sky blue eyes that said, "You can tell me anything." Even if I hadn't known about the priest thing, I would have categorized him—for his eyes alone—as a hymn.

"Uncle Kieran..." Royal turned to face me, his smile a little crooked, his eyes a little wide. "This is my boyfriend, Camden."

I almost tripped on the casual use of the word boyfriend. The buzzing in my head burrowed its way into my temples, finding the fast rhythm of my heart. Royal took a step toward me, taking my hand in his, he pulled me close to his side. It was the exact opposite of soothing. The eyes in the room, aware of our presence, fixed on the gesture. The focus barreled in on me, on him, and that buzzing finally dulled, silenced by the two boys holding hands in the front of the store. My paranoia created a melody of white noise inside my head, drowning out the hum as the edges of the room went fuzzy.

"Camden." Kieran held out his hand, his grin filling up his well-sculpted face. His high cheekbones cut into the creases around his eyes, making him appear younger than the smattering of gray in his beard would've led you to believe. "It's really good to meet you."

It was surreal, the warmth of his smile. It flowed down to his palm as I shook his hand without offering any greeting in return. Kieran's smile didn't falter at my social incompetence as he released my hand. "Declan said you were coming by tomorrow, this is a nice surprise."

"Is he in the back?" Royal craned his neck, looking beyond the partition and desk for his father.

"He's finishing up with a client." Kieran eyed me. "You want to make an appointment?"

His tone was playful, and an unexpected chuckle bubbled up my throat. "I think I'd rather die."

Royal laughed at my overdramatic statement. "You should get a music note or a treble clef on your wrist."

"You're a musician?"

"He's so much more than that." Royal's declaration made his uncle's smile stretch even wider across his lips.

He watched his nephew watching me, and the heat of the room crawled up my neck.

"What instrument do you play?"

"The piano," I answered, proud I hadn't let my voice waver.

"I'm going to make him play his recital piece on Thanksgiving. It's phenomenal."

"Can't wait." The two words rang true, and my heart found its normal pace again.

I'd survived two coming-outs and was still alive, no blood had been shed. People had gotten a glimpse, had seen me, seen the truth of what I was, and they hadn't turned away.

"I was thinking of getting a tattoo," Royal said, and I thought maybe I'd misheard him.

The shop was pulsating again, but the buzz less grating now that I wasn't as anxious.

"A tattoo?" I asked, and Royal nodded.

"Your dad know about this?" Kieran raised an eyebrow.

Would his dad care? I doubted it. I noticed Kieran had no ink on his arms, though. His long-sleeved shirt was pushed up to his elbows, exposing tan, cut muscle, but not one tattoo. I dared a quick inspection and saw a bit of ink peeking out of his collar. After seeing all of Royal's dad's tattoos, I assumed his uncles would be as heavily covered. It seemed I'd been wrong about a lot of things in regard to this trip. The stereo started to play heavy metal, and my surroundings, the ink, the pierced artists in their red and white booths, reminded me I was a long way from the disparaging eyes of my own family.

I never wanted to leave.

"Do you think he'd mind?" Royal asked, and Kieran shrugged.

"Not if you let him do it. What are you thinking of getting?"

Royal's gaze darted to mine, his cheeks turning the same shade as a tomato. "A quote." He rolled up his sleeve and gestured to the crook in his elbow. "Just below here."

I stared at the soft skin, pale in comparison to the rest of his arm. It was an intimate place, a place I'd kissed a few times, and wanted to kiss as many times as he'd let me.

"What quote?" My question came out as a whisper.

It was like Kieran had disappeared as Royal leaned in a little farther, close enough I could smell his soap and the mint gum he'd thrown away before we'd walked into the shop.

"*Do anything, but let it produce joy.*"

"Walt Whitman?"

He held my stare. "*Leaves of Grass.*"

If I wasn't a coward I would have kissed him right there in front of his uncle, in front of God, inside this hive, where I was allowed to hold his hand, allowed to love that he was sentimental. First love, it was a Schubert symphony, timeless and unforgettable. It was ink placed permanently into skin, and I couldn't wait to kiss the words once they'd healed.

"Does it still hurt?" Indie asked as she violently mashed the potatoes sitting in front of her.

"It doesn't." Royal scratched at the skin around his new tattoo. "It itches like crazy."

"Don't itch it." His dad laughed and handed me a stack of napkins. "Would you mind handing these to Paige?"

Royal's dad hadn't batted an eyelash when his son had asked him for the tattoo. If anything, he'd seemed excited, or maybe proud. His mom loved the meaning behind it, and I hadn't even gotten nervous when he'd told her about our library encounter. Being in this home, this independence, it was everything I thought I could never have. I wasn't sure how I'd be able to give it up when we got back to Pines Hollow.

"Can I set these napkins out for you?" I asked, and Paige gave me a smile.

"Sure." She was doing mental math and counting on her fingers when she said, "Eleven... there's eleven of us." She gently tapped my shoulder. "I'll go grab the plates."

Everything smelled like thyme and poultry spice, and a splash of cinnamon and nutmeg. The apartment was overheated, the large windows in the front room sweating as much as me, and as I laid out each napkin, I thought about what it would be like if I'd gone home. There'd be no bluesy Christmas music playing. No laughter in the kitchen. The room would be cold and gray, and the flavor of the day just as bland as the people who had hosted it. I liked how Royal's dad whispered to himself sometimes. Declan had demons, Royal had warned me, but he was quiet mostly, like me. Sound spoke to me wherever I went, and his voices spoke to him. The history of his life hid under his fingernails, and covered every wall in this apartment. His parents were always crusted in some color or another, it was part of them, it belonged to them, and I wanted to belong to them, too.

Paige had returned from the kitchen with a stack of plates when the doorbell rang.

"I got it," Indie shouted from the kitchen, and I heard Royal laugh as she bounded toward the door.

He was right behind her, but instead of following, he made his way around the dining table and whispered into my ear, "Don't forget to breathe."

Royal pressed soft lips to my cheek, and the apprehension that had been snaking its way around my spine melted away. I turned my head and stole what I thought would be a quick kiss, but the past few days, we'd had hardly any time to ourselves. I'd forced him to let me sleep in the guest room all week in an attempt to be respectful to his parents, and maybe I had other motives, too. Sleeping next to him every night wasn't something I should get used to. This whole loving out loud would come to an end soon, and I couldn't mourn the loss of something if I'd never had it in the first place. My reasoning was flawed in many ways. For one, I'd already had my fair share of him during this week, and going back, having to hide who he was to me, after getting the privilege of being open, would be difficult regardless of where I slept at night while I was here. Having his lips like this, tasting and tugging at my heart in ways I wasn't ready to give up, I had to draw the line somewhere, had to give myself a break before it all disappeared behind a dorm room wall at St. Peter's.

I pulled away, dazed, his blue eyes burning, he said, "You're sleeping in my room tonight, don't argue."

I didn't argue.

"No shit." A light female giggle made its way into our no-so-private moment. "Dad wasn't lying."

Royal shook his head and chuckled. "Ava, this Camden."

"Your boyfriend!" A tiny, teenage girl topped with a head full of black curls practically bounced as she stared at me with piercing hazel eyes. "Holy shit."

"Watch your language, Mija." Kieran gave me a sympathetic smile. "My daughter has never been good at holding back her feelings."

"Thank God." Royal laughed, wrapping his cousin into a tight embrace. She squeaked, kicking her feet as he lifted her off the floor. "Missed you so much."

Indie walked into the room, taking a place by my side as she watched her brother spin Ava in a circle. Warning me, she said, "So it begins. Remember, if you just nod and smile they'll think you're listening."

"Hey." A woman with salt and pepper hair impishly poked Indie in the ribs. "Don't give him the easy way out, he has to pass all the tests.

"Tests?" I swallowed, my voice dry and paper thin.

Her chin dipped and she laughed, holding out her hand. "I'm joking. Melissa, Kieran's wife. It's Camden, right?" I nodded, and she held my hand a few seconds longer than I usually preferred, her keen chocolate eyes watching me. Her tan face had honest lines. She wore scarcely any makeup, and was probably one of the most beautiful women I'd ever seen. Royal had told me his cousin and aunt were fluent in Spanish. Her accent lightly curled around each word she spoke, making everything she said sound like a song. "I apologize for Ava in advance," she said, her lips turning up into a teasing smile.

"Mom," Ava protested, drawing out the one syllable word into a whine.

Melissa shrugged. "Sabes la verdad."

"What did she say?" Royal asked me as he took my hand in his.

"Something about knowing the truth. My Spanish isn't as good as my French."

"You speak French?" Ava's jaw hung open, her brows lifted almost to her hairline.

"Yes."

"Oh my God, say something."

"Ava," Royal cautioned with a chuckle.

"On m'a tellement parlé de vous." I've heard so much about you.

Her shoulders sagged and she groaned, "I don't even care what that means. All the good ones are gay."

My breath hitched and the room went silent.

"What?" Ava held up her hands in surrender. "It's true. Royal's boyfriend is hot, *and* he can speak French, it's not fair."

Indie was the first to laugh, and when Royal tugged on my hand, I started to breathe again. It was ridiculous how one word could make my heart stop. It affected me, made every hair on my arm stand at attention, made my bones ache. I'd been referred to as Royal's boyfriend all week, and obviously I was... gay. But Ava was the first to point that finger, and maybe it was my muscle memory, my conditioning to cringe, to want to run to the closet and shut the doors, to hide behind that damn piano sitting over in the corner, but as the word hung in the air, blending with the chorus of chatter and laughter, it lost its negative connotation.

Thankfully, after a while, the attention turned to a less personal subject. Kieran's family caught up with Royal and Indie while we all helped bring the food to the table. Deals were made on how many servings of sweet potato casserole Quinn, the cousin who hadn't arrived yet, would eat this year. Melissa made small talk at first, including me, divulging one of her regrets in life was that she hadn't taken her father up on his offer to buy her piano lessons when she was little, and that she and her sister had inherited her family's Mexican restaurant after her father had passed away last year.

"I'm sorry," I said.

"It's a part of life," she said. "He was a good man."

I stared out the window, wanting to give her some space, and out of the corner of my eye, I saw her make the sign of the cross.

You're a good woman, I wanted to say, but didn't.

His uncle Liam and his wife Kelly finally showed a few minutes later. We'd already picked our seats at the table, and there was no big introduction this time. They apologized for being late, blaming Quinn and his inability to dress himself respectfully. Everyone laughed, and like Indie had suggested, I nodded and smiled not finding anything wrong with the blue button up Quinn had chosen to wear.

Liam never once made eye contact with me beyond his first hello. His face was stoic, his dark eyes unforgiving. He was the only O'Connell to make me feel uncomfortable. His black dress shirt was unbuttoned at the collar, exposing a significant amount of ink on his neck and chest. His sleeves were rolled up, and I found myself staring at the tattoos that dripped down from his elbows to his fingers. Quinn quizzed Royal about his new tattoo, asking if it had hurt, and if he planned to get more, when Liam finally looked at me again.

I dropped my eyes to the plate, embarrassed at being caught gawking.

"You're a music major?" His tone commanded my attention, and I snapped my eyes forward to meet his.

"Yes, sir."

"And what the hell do you plan to do with that?"

Royal shifted in his seat, his hand resting on my thigh under the table with a nervous laugh. "He's going to be a composer. He's really talented."

"I bet." Liam's entire face frowned and his wife sighed.

"Declan said you were going to play for us tonight." Kelly's smile was genuine. Every one of her features, indulgent—her eyes, her hair, and the line of her nose. A large scar cut down the side her face, from an accident Royal had told me, but it didn't detract from her beauty.

She even softened Liam, it seemed.

"Yeah? You'll have to show us what you got." Liam forced a smile, lifting his forkful of sweet potatoes to his mouth.

Wishing I'd never agreed to play, I nodded.

Liam's chilly reception led me to believe he'd been informed about my relationship with Royal and wasn't as laissez-faire about the gay thing as everyone else. It wasn't until after dinner, and everyone spread out in the living room to watch football with overfilled stomachs, his distaste finally showed. I was on the floor with Indie, her head in my lap, like she usually did with her brother. Royal had volunteered to help Liam clean up, and when I'd asked to help, he told me to keep Indie company. I figured he wanted time to feel out the waters, to see how much Liam hated the whole idea of his nephew being gay. Kelly and Quinn hadn't treated me any differently than the rest of the O'Connell clan, and if anything, that seemed to piss Liam off even more.

He was their leader. And he had been overthrown.

"What's taking them so long?" I asked.

Indie rolled her body, looking up at me, she said, "He's hard to know." She smiled. "Like you."

"I'm nothing like Liam."

Her laugh was delicate. "Give him some time. He's just... protective."

I hummed in agreement. "I'm going to check on him."

She sat up. "Camden, that's a bad—"

"I'll be right back," I interrupted and stood, despite the look of disapproval on her face.

No one stopped me as I made my way to the kitchen. Royal and Liam were nowhere to be found, the dishes half-finished on the counter and in the sink. I picked up a plate and was about to turn on the water, when I heard raised voices. I followed the sound down the hall, to Royal's bedroom, my heart in my stomach as I approached the opened door. It hadn't shut all the way, and I could hear everything.

"This is your fucking life! You have to know everything you've worked for will be gone if this shit gets out."

"I don't think it—"

"You'd do that... to yourself, throw away your chance at a better life because you're fucking curious?"

"Liam." Royal's voice cracked. "I love him."

Liam laughed without humor. "You've known him since when? A few months. You're nineteen, you don't even—"

"I don't need your approval. You're not my father."

"I'm not, but I raised him and Kieran. While my dad chose to drink himself to death and my mother forgot who she was, I provided. You're my family... I fucking love you... All I want...all I ever want... is the best for you. You deserve the best. The world is filled with assholes who don't understand, who will never understand. This relationship could destroy your future."

"I don't want a future without love."

Liam's laugh was tear-stained. "You sound like Declan."

My own hot tears ran down my cheeks, the anger in my chest seethed as I pushed the door open. Liam's forehead rested against Royal's, his hands gripping his shoulders. Royal's arms lay at his sides, his cheeks wet and red. Neither of them noticed I'd come into the room.

"I'd never let him destroy his future." It was a small miracle I'd maintained a steady tone. Royal pulled away from his uncle, and I kept my eyes on him. "Not for me."

"Camden." Royal shook his head.

I faced Liam, and his exhaustion wore him like a leaded vest. "I was born this way. Born to feel sick every time I look in the mirror, to hide behind my skin." I stood in the doorway, one step in and one step out. I was exhausted, too. "Born to only love in the dark." Liam's face collapsed, his stern jaw relaxed, and a knowing window opened inside his eyes. "I love Royal and all the fucking light he gives, but for him, if it was me holding him back, I'd walk away."

"You're not holding me back." Royal took nine steps, the same number he took every afternoon to my bedroom door, and stood in front of me. "You're not holding me back," he repeated in a desperate whisper. "There's no walking away, not for you and not for me." Royal's brows dipped into a furious line and he turned to face his uncle. "I've always looked up to you, Liam. Sought you out for advice, but if you can't accept this, you can't be a part of my life."

My heart cracked opened, leaking into my gut. I never wanted this for Royal. I placed my hand on his arm, ready to tell him I wasn't worth it, that he shouldn't do this, not for me, but his uncle spoke first.

"Do you mean that?" Liam asked.

"Yes," Royal answered without hesitation.

"I'm talking to Camden." Liam glared at me. "You'd walk away, to protect him?"

"I would."

Liam gripped Royal's shoulder. "I don't care if you're straight or bi or queer. I just want you to have more than we did, kid. Your dad threw away nine years of his life waiting on your mother, and Kelly, shit, she threw away way more waiting on my sorry ass."

Royal held his ground, his blue eyes shining as he said, "Dad got everything he wanted in the end, and so did you."

"Doesn't mean I want you to have to go through that battle."

"He won't have to," I promised and meant it. If our relationship threatened Royal's scholarship, his dream, I'd let him go. I could go to any school. I'd even go to Juilliard if it meant he could keep everything he'd worked for.

Liam let his hand fall to my shoulder, for what I took as a fatherly bit of affection, as his lips formed into a straight line. "I'll hold you to that."

Royal

I counted every breath he took, my cheek against his bare belly. Camden's dorm room was lit by the falling snow outside. The blinds were cracked open, and the rare white flakes caught the light streaming right across his bed. I couldn't sleep. I should've been exhausted, after driving in shit weather for over twelve hours, but my eyes wouldn't stay closed. The heat of Camden's body did little to lull me, and I was half-tempted to wake him. All I'd have to do was turn my head, press my lips to the spot just below his belly button, and he'd wake up, ready for round two. But it was four-thirty in the morning, and not even sex could dull the ache in my stomach.

I hated how I'd left things with Liam. I'd never been on rocky ground with anyone in my family before. But I'd witnessed the conviction in Camden's eyes when he declared to my uncle he'd walk away to save me. It scared me, losing him, and it was all Liam's fault. It was his stupid way of showing love, his hardline logic. Family was family, and no matter what, you took care of them before you took care of yourself. But this was my scholarship to lose, and if I lost it, the world wasn't going to end. I'd figure something out. I always had. I wouldn't allow my choice to affect my family. My school debt wouldn't be their burden, it was mine to bear. There was always a solution.

Thinking about everything was like picking at an open wound. Saying goodbye to my parents had been harder this time, watching them with Camden this week, he fit into our family with an effortless snap, and when he'd played for them, they'd felt it, too. Maybe I should've called Liam before I left to return to school, sent out an olive branch, after I'd told him he wasn't allowed to hold my boyfriend accountable for my decisions, but I'd chosen to leave well enough alone. I didn't want my dad to find out about our fight and have to take my side, causing a rift in his relationship with his brother. It was all a little melodramatic, if I was being honest with myself. No one at school would find out about my relationship with Camden, and if they did, I highly doubted we were the only gay couple at St. Peter's. After Indie's urging, I'd skimmed the code of conduct when I'd first arrived on campus and didn't remember reading anything negative about homosexuality. The document was mostly comprised of vague mentions of illicit behaviors on school grounds, morality, cheating, and plagiarism. In reality, I hadn't paid too much attention at the time. I needed to read it again, from page one. I needed evidence, some form of collateral just in case.

"You're not sleeping?" Camden asked, his voice scratchy with sleep.

He ran his fingers through my hair, and like a cat, I hummed with appreciation. "I'm almost there."

His chuckle shook his belly and my head. "No, you're not." His fingertips skated down my spine. "Come up here."

I obliged, bringing us nose to nose and he smiled. "You should call him."

"No. Not after the way he treated you."

"I've been treated worse." He lifted my hand to his lips and kissed my fingertips.

"Camden..."

"He's just trying to look out for you. My family would have thrown you to the wolves. He doesn't care that we're together, he only cares that it could mess up your education."

I closed my eyes, tense with frustration. "Let's pretend the dean knew about us... You actually think he'd throw us out?"

I opened my eyes as he sighed. "I don't know. But this school is based on its moral code, and I could see him finding some loophole to get you, get me out. He's friends with my parents, Royal. If he found out they'd be mortified. God knows what they'd do." He kissed my palm. "There's no gay student organization on campus. This is my second year, and I can't say I've ever seen an out couple."

"You don't look at people." I hated the petulant sound of my voice.

He laughed. "I look more than you know. I hear everything."

"So, we hide. Until we figure out our own loopholes."

Touching his forehead to mine he asked, "If you find a loophole where I get new parents, let me know?"

"You can have my parents."

His gray eyes watched me, and in the eerie, snow-cast light, they took on a silver gleam. I brought my hand to his cheek and kissed him, wanting to forget about all the bullshit. If I could, I'd stay in here for days, letting him have my body, taking his. No them, no outside, just this room and those silver eyes, and two people who couldn't stop kissing even if they tried.

Camden rolled me onto my back, his heavy body weighing me down into the mattress. His famished lips feasted on my jaw, my neck, his hand reaching between us. I was hard for him already, the heat of his palm surrounding us both. My hips jumped at the contact and he moaned into my mouth. We were making up for almost an entire week of no touching, and with Kai still not back from break, we could be as loud as we wanted. Campus would be a ghost town until tomorrow, and I planned on taking full advantage.

I took his face in my hands, holding his mouth to mine, licking his lips, and rocking my body to the rhythm he'd created. I wanted this to never end, wanted him to take his time. As my hands fell down the sloped arch of his back, the smooth muscle beneath bunched under my fingertips. His jaw was clenched, his eyes slammed shut. Camden was close. Too close, he worked us both at the same time, his hot hand moving faster. Swearing under his breath, his brows furrowed, and he kissed me with urgent lips, a low growl in his throat as our hips started to move in tandem.

"Wait." I grabbed his hand. Breathless, he kissed my wet lips, and I whispered, "I want you inside me."

Camden met my heated gaze, his pupils dilating. He'd given himself to me in every way, and I wanted him to have this. I wanted to offer him my body, offer him my heart in its entirety, whole and heavy and wanting.

Lowering his mouth to the crook of my neck, his lips trembled against my skin. "I want that... I want you. But..."

"I'm ready, Camden."

My hands skated over his shoulder blades, down his spine, to the curve of his backside, and I pulled our hips together. He groaned, giving in, and pressed soft kisses to my chin, down my chest, my hip, on my stomach. I forgot to care about Liam, about hiding. All I cared about was the wet heat of his tongue, the pressure of his fingers. It didn't take him long, driving me crazy, I squirmed with need. Every inch of my body was awake, hot and sensitive to every one of his touches. His fingers sketched a long line up my inner thigh, over my hip, until our mouths collided again. I shivered, expectant, anxious, and ready for him as he parted my knees with his own. My fingers dug into the muscle of his back as he moved himself between my legs.

"Trust me," he whispered, and I did, with my name on his lips, reverently written against the skin of my throat, my head tipped back as he gradually slipped inside me.

Slow. God. So slow.

My grip on his shoulders tightened with every inch he took. The connection, it stole my breath, my ability to move, and once the pain of it subsided, once his lips coaxed mine to open, his kiss reminded me to breathe again. His hands cupped the back of my head, his fingers in my hair, and it was like speaking in tongues, the sounds he pulled from me, his lips working my lips with strong, demanding strokes.

The angle of his body, inside of mine, with every drive of his hips, he reached, hitting a spot that set my skin on fire. My eyes opened, and he broke our kiss, staring at me with fevered eyes as I begged him, in jumbled, inarticulate syllables. *There. Jesus. Please. Need you. Make me come.* Camden framed my face with his hands, his brows on mine, answering my plea with his silent touches, the tip of his nose touching my nose, his lips falling open, breathing me in. His thumbs rested against my cheek bones, and the pressure of his forearms on my shoulders, the lean muscle of his stomach as he pushed deeper, every point of contact, a buildup until the friction of it all set me off. Heaving in synchronized breaths, his heat filled me. Sweaty and sticky and perfect, Camden placed soft, feather-light kisses to my eyelids, to the tip of my nose, and to my upper lip. Being with him like this, he'd taken my body, as I had taken his. Equally captured in each other's arms.

"There's no walking away from this, from us," I said, my timbre touched with a shaky vulnerability.

He ran his palm down my chest. My body lit from the inside out, I shivered as he whispered, "I love you."

He drew me in with a lazy, distracting kiss, avoiding my statement all together.

A loud crash woke me. Bleary eyed, I stole a glance at the clock. It was only eight in the morning. Camden's arm pinned me in place, his hot breath on my neck, his chest to my back. Another loud bang, and a few aggravated expletives had me sliding out of bed as quietly as possible. Kai must've come home. I slipped on my boxer briefs and jeans and slowly walked to the bedroom door. I looked over my shoulder, staring, ogling— admiring Camden's naked body one last time before I had to open the door.

"Jesus Christ." Kai almost stumbled into the couch. "You fucking scared the shit out of me."

"Sorry, I didn't—"

"Fuck." He stubbed his toe on the coffee table, and I raised my hand to my mouth to stifle my laugh. "It's not funny."

"Keep it down, Camden's still asleep."

Kai stared at Camden's bedroom door, his eyes glassy, his speech—I realized—slurred as he said, "Oh, yeah." His lips curled into a sloppy grin. "You guys banging now?"

I disregarded his line of questioning for a more important one. "Why are you drunk at eight in the morning?"

"Why aren't you wearing a shirt?" He held up his hand to point at my chest and swayed on his feet.

"Kai, what's going on?" I took a step toward him, and he waved me away. He fell backward onto the couch and grunted.

Leaning forward, his elbows on his knees, his head in his hands, he mumbled, "Shit's too much to take."

"What shit?" I asked and sat down next to him.

He relaxed into the cushions, his head hitting the sofa. Kai closed his eyes. "Too many balls and only one court.

I laughed. "What the hell are you talking about?"

I'd seen Kai drunk, but not like this. When had he come back from break? Where had he been all night?

"My mom."

The two words wiped the smile off my face.

"She's got MS."

"Multiple Sclerosis?"

"Yeah." His head rolled to the side, and his eyes opened. "The rarest form. Primary Progressive."

I had no idea what that meant, and I could tell by his defeated expression he didn't want me to ask.

"No one here knows, well, besides fucking Ellis, no one here knows."

"What about Brie?"

"We're done."

"I'm..."

"Sorry, yeah. I know. Me, too." Kai stared at me, his foggy dark eyes unblinking. "My dad left. The bastard left, on Thanksgiving." *Shit.* "I knew it was coming, he's been fucking his old high school girlfriend for a couple of years, ever since..." He exhaled and it caught in his throat. "You don't want to hear this, shit. Go fuck your boyfriend. I'll put in those ear plugs I got."

"Kai. I'm your best friend. I want to know what's happening in your life. Even if I can't change it, I want to help."

"Help." He rolled the word on his tongue. "Can you help my mom walk?"

It was a rhetorical question, one that split my heart in two, but I answered it anyway, "I can't, but I'm here. Kai, if you need me, I'm right here."

He laughed and I hated the pained sound of it. "Thanks." He sat up. "I'm gonna pass out. Wanna lift later?"

"Kai."

He struggled to stand. "I just need a few hours and I'll be ready to go."

He was more likely ready to puke up guts.

"Promise me... promise me you'll stop drinking so much. I'm here, okay. Right here. You don't need that."

"I'm fine."

"For now. But it will catch up to you, and then what? Who's going to lead the team?" He shrugged, choosing to hit him where it hurt, I asked, "Who's going to help take care of your mom?"

"Fuck you."

He tried to walk by me, but I grabbed his hand. "I'm right here," I offered again.

"I see you."

"Do you?"

"I do." He dropped his eyes to our hands before he let go.

I watched his sloppy navigation as he made his way to his bedroom door and flinched when it slammed shut. All this time, and I had no idea, too wrapped up in my own crap. Guilt had me reliving our friendship, the last few months, in a different light. The girls, the late nights.

I wasn't the only one who'd been hiding.

Royal

Being in the wild with Camden, after getting a taste of what it was like to be open, having to hide my feelings for him, sucked more than I thought it would. Stacks was packed after we'd crushed Western Idaho in what had been our best swim meet of the semester. With only one more meet scheduled before finals, coming back from a long break, winning should've tasted even sweeter. But I was in a booth with my teammates, sipping crappy beer, watching my best friend get drunk, and I wasn't even allowed the simple luxury of holding my boyfriend's hand. It was safe to say I wasn't in a celebrating mood.

I tracked Kai as he walked across the room to the bar where a full pitcher awaited him. With his fingers gripped around the handle, he flirted with the new bartender. She leaned her elbows onto the countertop, her boobs basically falling out of her low-cut, V-neck top. She had dark chocolate hair, pink lips, and a small waist. Her makeup was too thick, hiding what probably could've been a pretty face.

"See something you like?" Dev asked, and I quickly turned my attention away from the bar.

I snorted. "Not hardly."

"What *is* your type anyway, O'Connell?" Corbin slugged down a gulp of his beer, and Camden shifted next to me. "I mean, you haven't hit shit this semester."

"Hit. Shit. This. Semester. Jesus, Corbin, you're so eloquent."

He raised his eyebrows and knocked Dev in the ribs with his elbow. "See, that's what I'm talking about."

Dev laughed and rubbed his side. I was lost. "What are you getting at?"

Corbin's eyes darted to Camden, then back to me. "I bet Dev you were gay."

I kept my cool. This was the usual smack talk I endured when I was out with these guys, but Camden, he wasn't used to this, and his body visibly stiffened. I almost risked resting my hand on his knee. But I doubted it would help calm his internal panic. If anything, it might've made it worse.

I chuckled, an attempt at nonchalance. "Why, because I haven't dated anyone?"

I had to give Dev credit, trying hard not to laugh, his shoulders shook as Corbin qualified his suspicions. "You don't date, or even hook up, and you say shit like *eloquent.*"

Dev lost his control and started to cackle, sputtering, "Bro, you sound so stupid right now."

Corbin elbowed him again and Camden relaxed.

"Ow, fucker, quit that shit."

"What if he was gay?" Camden's voice was level, smooth, and it caused the hair on the back of my neck to stand.

"I'd ask him how my dick measured up to his boyfriend's." Corbin, oblivious to those around him, snickered to himself before draining his pint glass.

I laughed abruptly, my nerves overflowing, and to my surprise, Camden laughed, too.

"It's smaller," I replied. "Much... smaller."

This earned me a few more laughs from the other side of the table, and made Camden's cheeks flood with color.

"Oh, damn." Dev held a fist to his lips. "That was cold."

"What was cold?" Kai asked, placing his pitcher onto the table.

Corbin rolled his eyes.

"Corbin's dick is smaller than Royal's boyfriend's," Dev explained, and I willed Kai not too look at Camden.

Kai only shook his head. "You guys are idiots."

Corbin and Dev started to quiz Kai about the girl at the bar, and I used the moment to meet Camden's gaze. If they only knew, I was dying to say, but there was no humor in his eyes, and I regretted taking the joke too far.

"Let's play pool," Kai suggested.

Dev slid out of the booth first. "You guys coming, Royal?"

"Nah, you go ahead."

"Lame." Dev shrugged, holding up his fist for me to bump. "Good to see you again, Camden."

Still pink in his cheeks, my boyfriend gave him a quick nod.

"We have weights in the morning," I warned Kai after Dev was out of ear-shot, and he narrowed his eyes.

"I'm aware."

"Maybe take it easy tonight."

He lifted the pitcher from the table with one hand and saluted me with the other. "Yes. Sir."

Kai plastered a smile on his face, but I could see behind his mask, see how much every minute cost him. His eyes glassy and bloodshot, already drunk, he turned toward the pool tables, and I wished I knew what to do, or what to say, to help him.

Corbin grabbed his beer glass, sliding his way out of the booth. He stood and paused next to the table, leaning down, he looked at Camden. "For the record, I wouldn't care. You do you, man."

He knocked on the table once and smiled before chasing Kai and Dev down. At first, I didn't say anything, my pulse had skidded to a halt.

"He's the first one to ever call me on it." Camden's eyes scanned my face. "You're pale."

I choked on a laugh. "Do you think he knows?"

"About us?"

"Yeah."

He didn't answer right away.

"No. But he definitely knows about me. I shouldn't have asked that question." His brows furrowed. "I hope that doesn't make things difficult for you."

I placed my hand on his knee, not caring who noticed. "You already know I don't care who knows."

He gently pushed away my hold. "Let's get out of here?"

I nodded and followed him out of the bar without anyone noticing.

The street was wet and empty, but the rain had stopped, washing away any last traces of the snow we'd had the other night. The temperature had dropped, though, making the sidewalk slippery enough we had to pay attention as we made our way back to campus in silence. Camden's breath floated from his lips in tiny white clouds. His cheeks and nose were rosy, the dark blue color of his sweater enhancing the pink hue on his pale skin. I couldn't help the smile that stretched across my face.

"What?" he asked, not looking in my direction.

My mouth felt sticky with the cold as I said, "I want to hold your hand, like the first time we walked home from Stacks."

He chuckled, finally giving me his big gray eyes. "You were drunk. People would've assumed I was just helping you home."

I took his hand in mine, laced our fingers, and pulled him closer. There wasn't a soul in sight. "Then I'll stumble a few times. If we see someone, let them think what they want."

His chilled fingers warmed against mine as we neared the campus gates.

"My mom called today," he said, reminding me there were some people who would never accept us.

"She did?"

"She said they might come for the Winter Festival Concert in Rockport."

"Do you think they will?"

He sighed. "I don't know. One of their friends, another St. Peter's alumnus, is the composer I'll be working with. Appearances have to be kept."

The Winter Festival Concert was next week, the last week before finals. I couldn't wait to watch him play in front of an audience again, but then I dreaded it, too. It meant the semester was almost over, and I didn't know where that left us for the long winter break. I'd almost asked him a few times since we'd been back if he wanted to go home with me again. Stay with my family until spring semester started, but I wasn't sure if it was too crazy of a suggestion. Winter break lasted almost five weeks. I spent all of my free time with him, and I hated thinking about him all alone, in Astoria, with his parents, for over a month. And the selfish part of me admitted I'd miss him too much.

"Did she ask you about fall break?"

He leaned into me. "No, not really. My mom asked if the cafeteria served the students who stayed on campus Thanksgiving dinner."

"What did you say?"

His laugh was mischievous and it made me smile again. "I told her they did, and that the food was terrible."

"So, she has no idea?"

"None."

"Wow."

"It's better this way. The less they're in my life, the less shit I have to deal with." He let go of my hand as we neared Garrison. "Are you staying with me tonight?"

"Only if we can break your no touching rule. If not, I'm dragging you to my place."

"No dragging needed." He smirked, which was rare, and I ate it up every time.

"*If* Kai comes home he'll be drunk anyway," I muttered.

"He's worse since we've been back. Did he say anything to you?"

I gave him a noncommittal shrug of my left shoulder. It was Kai's story to tell.

"You should talk to him."

"I will," I promised, hoping tomorrow during weight training Kai could hold himself together long enough to fool Coach.

I punched Camden's password into the keypad and opened the door. As usual, there was no one at the front desk after ten, and we made our way up the stairs to his suite. Once inside, with the door closed and locked behind us, I grabbed his wrist, pulling him toward me, chest to chest, and kissed him with needy lips. His fingers wound tightly into the fabric of my St. Peter's hoodie, his head falling back, inviting me to kiss him harder. My lips were swollen when I finally broke away from his addictive mouth, raw from the new stubble on his chin. I rubbed my thumb across the coarse hair.

"I'm out of razors." He dusted his knuckles across my lips. "Does it hurt?"

"Not too bad." I kissed his jaw, exploring the rough surface. "I like it."

"Well, get your fill because tomorrow it's gone, it itches too much."

We didn't bother turning on the lights inside his room, shedding our clothes within the safety of his four walls. In here, we could be whoever we wanted to be, love whoever we wanted to love. I pushed him backward onto the bed, crawling over him, pressing kisses on his thighs, his stomach, his pecs, saving my last kiss for his mouth. Camden brushed his lips against mine, his hands exploring the ridges of my stomach.

"What if I wanted you to come home with me again?"

His hand paused at my waist. "When?"

I pinned my bottom lip between my teeth, giving away my anxiety, I spoke faster than I'd intended. "It's a long time. I mean, if you think it's too much—"

"Oh." Camden swallowed. "You mean after the semester is over?"

"I don't like you being alone."

"That's a lot of extra burden to put on your family, Royal."

"My parents wouldn't mind, especially if they knew how shitty it is for you... with your parents."

"I'm not a charity case." He wouldn't look at me.

"I know that, Camden. I'm selfish, and I'll miss you too much, okay. That's my real motive." I rolled my hips into his, trying to reel him back in, and he met my gaze.

"What about my parents? They don't know you exist. They'd have too many questions."

"You don't owe them an explanation."

He exhaled a long, unsteady breath, his hands skating up my spine, he cupped the back of my head. "Five free weeks with you... If I could—"

"You can."

"There are things I need to consider. Let me think about it, alright?"

"Alright."

"Can I kiss you now?" His miraculous smirk showed itself again.

"You never have to ask."

Despite the bags under his eyes, the greasy hair, and the fact that he smelled like a brewery, Kai seemed to be holding his own this morning. I'd overheard him talking to his mom when I'd left Camden's room earlier. Kai had been on the couch in his boxers. I'd wondered if he'd slept there and hadn't heard much of what he'd said. Something about lawyer fees and money she didn't have, but I'd left it alone as we'd walked to the gym together. He appeared to be in better spirits now that he'd worked off some of the alcohol. The team had called it quits about twenty minutes ago, but Kai and I always stayed a little longer. We were alone in the corner of the weight room, all the questions I had spinning inside my head.

"I'm worried about you."

He groaned and dropped his weights to the floor mid deadlift. "Fuck, here we go."

"Tell me what I can do."

"Leave me alone, maybe?" He wiped his hand with a towel, throwing it over his shoulder, he shot me a glare.

"She's sick?"

His face crumpled. "Really sick."

"How long?"

He sat on the weight bench across from me. "Years, it's gotten worse these past two. She can't walk anymore, and my fucking dad..." He grit his teeth. "He wants a divorce. She depends on him, for insurance, and he knows, he fucking knows, she won't fight him. He'll leave her with nothing."

"You think he'd—"

"I know he would. He's a selfish prick. I tried to talk to him. He said some bullshit about giving her alimony, the house. How the hell can she afford the house? She's been a stay-at-home mom my whole life." He mumbled under his breath, talking to himself, "I'll take care of her. I always have anyway. One more year until I graduate. I'll work two jobs if I have to."

"What about family? Grandparents?"

"My dad's parents died a while ago. My mom only has her dad, and he's in a treatment center with dementia. Her mom died from pneumonia, she had MS, too." His dark eyes stared beyond me, at the wall, at all the loss he'd lived through already. "I sound like a bad country music song." He rubbed the back of his neck, his signature grin sliding center stage. "I'll get it figured out. I'll work as much as I can over break, get her the retainer she needs for a lawyer. I don't know, maybe I can talk some sense into my dad. Stop worrying about me, Royal, you have your own shit to deal with."

"I don't doubt you have it handled, but you have to lay off the alcohol. One more year, right? If you're too drunk to swim, you have no scholarship."

Kai raised his gaze, his eyes honest as he said, "I'll lay off."

I wanted to believe him.

I nodded my head and stood from the bench. "What happened with Brie?"

"Ugh."

"That bad?"

"She got drunk and screwed Sherman."

"No way?"

He chuckled. "Thought I was gonna kick his ass."

"Why didn't you?"

"Not worth it." He opened the locker room door.

Dev was the only one left behind, but he was already shouldering his bag. "See you guys tonight at practice."

He disappeared through the door and Kai punched me in the shoulder. "You and Camden, looks like the trip went well?"

I blushed, my smile creeping up my heated cheeks. "Yeah."

"Coming out anytime soon?" he asked, lifting his shirt over his head.

"Indie and I looked over the code of conduct again after we got back from break. There's nothing in there specifically targeting sexual orientation. But we did find a section that stated the college has a zero-tolerance policy."

"Zero tolerance for what?"

"Discrimination. Race, religion…"

"Sexuality." He smiled. "When you come out, do I get to wear a rainbow swim cap?"

"Sure, I'll have Indie make you one with washable marker."

"Har har." He threw his sweats at me. Disgusted and laughing, I dropped them to the ground. He went quiet as I pulled my shirt over my head. "She wasn't at the meet last night."

"Who, Indie?" He nodded, as I stuffed my sweaty shirt into my bag, and turned to open his locker. "Her end-of-the-semester project is due, she's basically living in the studio with Daphne."

"Makes sense." His mood had shifted again.

"Listen, Kai." He looked up from his bag. "You're going to be okay."

"It's the only choice I have."

Camden

Rockport's Winter Festival Concert was a big deal, at least, if you were a music major it was. To be asked to play, or participate, was a great honor. I'd played in the concert last year, but as a part of the orchestra. Professor Michelson, the Dean of Music, had asked me after the recital in October if I'd wanted to play a solo, as well as be a part of the orchestra this year. At first, I'd wanted to say no. The composer chosen to lead the festival was none other than Nathan Faust, a professor at Juilliard, who was handpicked because of his alumni status. He also happened to be the same professor, and a good friend of my mother, who'd convinced her Juilliard was the only college I should've considered. Apparently, he hadn't held as much clout as my mother had thought. I had been accepted to the school, but not offered a scholarship. I'd wanted to earn my degree on my own terms. St Peter's was my choice.

My Choice.

The walls of the dressing room seemed to narrow, sweat formed under my collar as I fixed and knotted my tie for the fifth time tonight. The orchestra had started to tune, the clashing medley of sound worming its way down the hall and through my brain. The laughter, the clacking of heels on the hardwood floor of the stage, and the harsh metal scrape of the chairs, moving this way and that, my head ached with the noise of it all. I stared at my reflection in the mirror. My gray-green eyes squinted against the bright light of the room. Where were my parents? Were they coming? It was like déjà vu.

I closed my eyes and whispered the words, "My choice, my life, my love." Over and over again until the throbbing in my head subsided. If they came, I'd tell them about Royal. If they came, it would be the last time. I was sure of it.

"Ten minutes," someone shouted into the dressing room and I opened my eyes.

I looked at myself again. *Really* looked this time, with open eyes, eyes that were tired of telling lies to the world, tired of hiding, and I saw a man who was proud of who he'd become. Proud of his accomplishments, his life. It didn't matter if Professor Faust was here, or if my parents actually showed up. I'd been chosen for tonight because of my talent, not because of him, not because of my parents' influence. The man had hardly said three words to me during the last three days of rehearsals. He was a guest, stepping into our theory professor's shoes in the final minute. I owed him nothing. I owed this honor to myself. Like Royal had told me last night, *this is for you, it's yours, and no one can take that from you.* I'd play like I was in my room, playing for him, playing with his lips on my neck, with my eyes closed—I'd play and the whole room would feel my love.

I buttoned the jacket of my suit and made my way to the stage. I was almost the last person in place, everyone was ready, flipping through their sheet music. I could have played without it. I'd memorized each song a week after we'd received the playlist. It wasn't arrogance. This was my world, and tonight, I wanted to own it.

For me.

Just for me.

The strings of the violins and cellos yawned as the curtain lifted, the lights blotting out the three mezzanines, a full house. People from up and down the Oregon coast traveled here every year for this concert, and the applause that seemed to hang in the air above us in expectation, quieted. Royal and Indie had gotten tickets for the third floor, right balcony, and even though I couldn't see them, I looked up in that direction anyway. I let a small smile form on my lips, and when the lights dimmed, and the soft tap, tap, tap of the conductor's baton echoed through the orchestra, I closed my eyes and felt the warmth of Royal's breath on my neck. I let the heat spread down my arms, to my fingertips, and transferred it to the keys, letting it billow through the room like a blanket of sound. Mixing and dancing with all the other instruments, it was elegant and safe and endless.

I didn't once open my eyes until someone announced my name for the solo. I heard a whoop from the third-floor balcony, and the audience laughed at the uncharacteristic cheer. A few of the people in the orchestra gave me dirty looks, but I didn't mind. I glanced to where my boyfriend and his sister were most likely sitting, staring up into a blank sheet of light and smiled. I'd chosen to play the Eric Satie piece, *Gymnopédie No. 1*. The same song that had played quietly in the background the night I'd given Royal my body and my heart. I hadn't meant to cry. I did so rarely, and never in public, but with each soft note *I remembered.*

I remembered what it was like to lose yourself in someone, to trust and to give your soul away, even if it'd been in shredded fragments. He'd scooped them up and made them his.

The entire building was silent when the last note played. I swiped my thumbs under my eyes, hoping to hide the emotion on my face, and lowered my chin. The minutes passed in slow motion, but in truth, it only took a second for the room to come to their feet, giving me a standing ovation. I stood and bowed my head in thanks, only lifting my eyes to look up and to the right. I touched my first two fingers to my lips and bowed my head again. The gesture spoke across a room full of people with a private message—*that was for us.*

The concert lasted ninety minutes, with one intermission, and when the curtain fell for the last time, I was ready for it. Ready to see him. I hadn't made it more than twenty feet from the stage when I heard my name called.

No more hiding.

"Camden," Indie squeaked and wrapped me into the same type of hug she reserved for her brother after his swim meets. She sniffled with tears in her eyes as she pulled away. "That was phenomenal. You are phenomenal."

Instead of letting my arms dangle at my sides while she attacked me, I ran with it, squeezing her back just as tight. Looking over her shoulder, into my boyfriend's light eyes, I admired how handsome he looked in the suit he'd borrowed from me. His hands were deep in the pockets of the tailored, charcoal slacks, the gray button-up stretching across his broad shoulders, and the green tie he'd chosen fit perfectly down the center of his chest. I liked that his hair still flopped over his forehead, though, his boyish charm all dressed up for the night.

"Thanks." I lowered her back to the ground, giving Royal a small smile.

"I mean it, that song... I felt it... It was so... red."

"Red?" I asked and Royal chuckled.

"Her feelings always have to have a color."

"It's how I paint," she explained.

"Feeling equates to color for you and to sound for me."

"We're artists." She raised her right brow and giggled.

Royal rolled his eyes. "And I'm the dumb jock."

"No." I shook my head and he stepped closer, glancing at the people hurrying past us. I took his hand in mine. "You're an artist, too." He stared down at our entwined fingers. "Water is your medium."

"I like that." His blue eyes scanned my face. "You didn't tell me."

"Tell you what?" I asked.

He looked at his sister. "Give us a second, Pink?"

"Sure, I'll be in the lobby." She popped onto her tiptoes and kissed my cheek. "Stunning work."

"Thanks for coming."

"I wouldn't have missed it."

She turned and waved over her shoulder as she left through the stage door.

"You didn't tell me you were going to play that song." He leaned in, stepping close enough I could feel the heat radiating off his body.

"It was a surprise," I whispered in a low tone, my eyes on his mouth.

He looked down the empty hall, his gaze following the faint sound of laughter. "Should we—"

"I don't care anymore who knows. I love you, and I'm tired of hiding it."

His lips spread gradually, the right corner lifting a little higher than the left. "You're serious? Why... I mean, when did you change your mind?"

"It's been a process."

He chuckled and touched his forehead to mine.

"After Salt Lake, maybe? I liked it too much, being with you without boundaries or fear. Once we got back... it was different. Like two flames trapped under a cup. Eventually, all those rules... Royal, they would have smothered us. Our flame would have died, and I don't want to lose you." I sucked in a breath, my voice gruff as I admitted, "I don't want to feel trapped anymore."

His lips were gentle, hesitant as he kissed me, waiting for me to change my mind. My hand slipped behind his neck, drawing him in closer, until my back hit the wall. His kiss burned, irresistible and earnest as his tongue slid against mine. Royal held my hips, pressing our bodies together. The world around us disappeared, and for a fraction of time, the universe granted us the freedom to live in the moment.

"This is what you want?" he asked.

I kissed his bottom lip, tasting the soft skin. "All I want."

He hummed as I pushed my fingers into his hair. "No more hiding."

I shook my head, and his mouth met mine with a desperate kiss. A few girls giggled as they passed us, the soft click of heels dancing across the floor, and I didn't flinch. His body was a shield, and all I could feel was his heat, his heart in the way his lips tenderly took mine, and my pulse ignited.

Royal's smile lit his cheeks, leaning away, he said, "I can't wait to show you off."

He linked our hands, and I was flat against the wall, trying to catch my breath, the smile on my face only for him, when I heard my name, in a voice that couldn't be real. Not now, not like this.

"Camden?" The two syllables were a gasped condemnation.

Royal's face drained of color as he watched the horror fill my eyes.

"What's... what's going on here?" She was audibly shaken.

He turned to face her. I didn't dare look.

"Camden Morgan, you will look at me this instant."

I was sixteen years old again. My hands trembled, and the room was too quiet. She stared at me, her eyes a cloudy shade of silver, biting and cold. That glare had pinned me to the sofa.

"Camden." His sweet voice didn't belong here, not in this empty house, this vacant, chilled space inside my head. "Hey, it's okay." It smelled like summer, and soap, and he squeezed my hand. "It's okay."

No more hiding.

My choice.

My life.

My love.

"I didn't think you were coming." I pushed as much confidence as I could into my scratchy voice.

"Of course we would be here." My mother's incredulity was comical. Her lips were pinched tight, her hair pulled back into an immaculate bun. My father, just another accessory she wore. "Explain yourself."

"I already did... when I was sixteen."

"Camden, don't be disrespectful," my father decided to chime in. "We drove all this way."

"Not for me you didn't." I found courage in the heat of Royal's hand. "Let's go."

I took a step, guiding Royal to come with me, but my mother wasn't finished yet.

"Young man, I don't know who you are, but you will let go of my son's hand. Right now." She leaned in, her jaw tense as she whispered through gritted teeth, "You will not embarrass me with this disgusting display. You were kissing him." Incredulous, her eyes widened. "Anyone could have seen. Nathan could have seen!" she hissed. "It's sick."

She grabbed Royal's arm, but he yanked away from her grip. "What the hell is wrong with you?" His voice thundered down the hall.

"Everyone, calm down," my dad begged. Placing his hand on the small of her back, he said, "Teresa, enough now."

"Don't tell me what to do, Bradley." She faced me again, her composure slipping on like a well-worn mask. "Say goodbye to your friend, Camden. We have some things to discuss." She smoothed her hands down the front of her black skirt.

"I have nothing to say to you that I haven't already said. I'm not one of your patients, Mom. You can't fix the gay away. This is my life, and I'm done living under your rules."

She laughed, the sound off-putting and hollow. "Is that so?" She took a step forward and Royal pulled me closer to his side. "You forget whose money is in your bank account, or how all I have to do is make one phone call to the head dean, and you and your friend will no longer be welcomed at St. Peter's." Her smile lay flat on her face, mirthless and unyielding. "Now, let's go."

"You're supposed to help people, isn't that what you do? As a psychiatrist?" Royal glared. "It's twisted, someone like you in that position. This is your son, you're supposed to love him. Unconditionally."

Unintimidated, her voice dripped with disdain, "You don't get to judge me."

"Teresa," my dad cautioned, trying to take her hand. She waved him off.

"But you can judge us? I love your son, and I'm not ashamed of it. I'm not ashamed of him. He's every..." Royal's voice cracked and he clenched his jaw. "He's everything that is good and beautiful, and you're an idiot if you throw that away."

I blinked a few times, trying to stave off the burn in my eyes. I held his hand tighter, the pulse in his thumb beating against my own. Fast and angry.

"She already threw me away years ago." I struggled to breathe as I watched the façade fall away from her features, leaving behind a sadness etched so deep I wondered if she even felt it anymore. My dad's eyes were red, his lashes wet. And I dreamed for a time when those eyes looked at me with love instead of loss. "Call the dean, Mom, and I'll show him the zero tolerance for discrimination policy I highlighted in the code of conduct."

She was motionless, like hard glass, as I moved past her.

"Camden, wait." My dad reached for me. "Don't do this, not to your family, we can work it out."

My boyfriend watched me, pride gleaming inside his irises. "Royal is my family now."

Royal

The definition of bravery, courageous behavior, didn't sit very well in my word-addled brain. Bravery was the man who'd cried himself to sleep last night. Though he'd been valiant and had stood up to his parents, he'd later admitted he'd never felt so small, so discarded by the two people who were supposed to love him without rules or conditions. Bravery was the way Camden had taken my hand and walked through an entire lobby full of his classmates, tears in his eyes, shaking from head to toe. Bravery was the man in my arms. The man who loved me enough to risk it all.

"Risk it all," I whispered into the soft spot where Camden's neck met his shoulder. I pressed my lips to the warm skin, trailing kisses along his jaw, and he curled his legs around mine. "I've got to go."

"Right now?" he asked with one eye open and a sleepy grin. "It's too early."

"I want to talk to Coach."

His smile faded and both of his eyes opened. His hand on my hip, I shivered under his touch.

"You're really going to do this... today?" he asked, his fingers drifting over my ribs to my shoulder. I nodded, and his brows dipped into an anxious crease. "Wait until after the last meet on Saturday."

"And do what? Leave a note under Coach's door thanking him for the semester and 'oh, by the way, I'm gay.'" I forced a smile but he didn't buy it.

"Wait until after the meet, that way he has time to think about everything over winter break."

"Camden... what you did last night... for us... Telling my coach, my team, pales in comparison. You gave up your family."

"They gave up on me." He exhaled a defeated sigh. "These guys... your team... you share a locker room with them, shower with them... it could get ugly."

I'd thought about all of that. A million times. And if I had Coach on my side, it wouldn't matter what anyone had to say.

"Coach won't let it."

"If he's okay with it. If he's not? What then? He could make things difficult for you."

"It's better to rip off the bandage. To tell everyone now. At least that way, I'll know who I have to watch out for next semester. I don't want to worry about it over break, Camden. I want to be with you. I want to be happy." He searched my eyes. "I can be fearless, too. For us."

He swallowed and bit the corner of his lip. "For us..."

"For you." The two words brushed against his lips as I kissed him.

Bravery was his smile—despite the concern in his eyes—and the way he held my face in his hands, whispering the promise we'd made the night before, "No more hiding."

His kiss was urgent and serious, his lips claiming mine like it was the last time he'd get to taste them. I had to force myself out of his bed, wearing my confidence like a jacket, I pulled on my sweats and a hoodie, wishing I could ask him to come with me. It was a weak thought, a chink in my armor, but after seeing how easily Camden's parents had turned him away, I'd started to doubt my own naïve beliefs. Maybe my family was the rarity after all, and the world was as upside down as Camden had always warned me.

"Meet me outside Beckett at seven?" I asked, hoping he couldn't decipher the slight tremor in my tone, the small seed of doubt trying to take root. "We'll go in together."

In the dark, from where I stood in the doorway, the light only illuminated half of his bed, hiding his eyes. Feeling anything but brave, I held on to the strength of his voice. "I'll be there."

I arrived twenty minutes earlier than usual, and as expected, the gym was empty. Kai's bedroom door had been shut, lights off as I'd snuck out of the suite this morning, and as tempting as it would have been to wake him and bring him with me for support, this was something I had to do on my own. Setting my bag onto the bench by my locker, I took comfort in the familiar, static sound of the radio drifting from Coach's open door. I heard him swear and laughed as a loud bang echoed through the locker room.

"Piece of shit," he grumbled as I approached his office.

"Coach?"

His head snapped up, his hand hovering over the old clock radio. "I didn't hear you come in."

"Trying to get the score from last night's hockey game?" I asked, closing the door behind me.

He chuckled, turning down the volume, he said, "I suppose I should give in and just look online." It was his morning ritual, listening to the college's radio sports highlights. He eyed the closed door. "You're early."

I took a seat across from him. "I needed to talk to you about something."

He sat up straight in his chair. "Everything alright?"

Coach's lips set into a grim line, and I placed my shaking hands in my lap. My tongue was fat in my mouth, desiccated and thirsty with anxiety. I thought about Camden, and how he hadn't backed down, not once last night, and resolved to see this through.

"Everything is great... actually." I attempted to smile. "I don't really know where to start..."

"I hear the beginning is always the best place."

I inhaled a deep breath, and he gave me a kind smile. One I hoped would still be there in about thirty seconds.

"I'm gay." His brows shot up at my abrupt admission, and I waited a few seconds for a response. His silence twisting my tongue, I continued, "I-I'm gay... well... What I wanted to tell you... Shit, this isn't..." I shook my head. "Sorry, Sir. I didn't mean to swear."

"Royal." He held up his hand. "Your private life is your business."

I trudged on, not really hearing him. "I had a girlfriend once, and it wasn't... didn't feel right... But, now I have a boyfriend and it shouldn't matter, because I can swim faster than Ellis and Dev, and I—"

"Stop, son, it's your business," he repeated like I'd missed the point.

We stared at each other until it finally clicked, the light bulb glaringly obvious. "You want me to keep quiet?"

His brows dipped in confusion. "Isn't that what you want? Privacy?"

"I want to be like everyone else," I clarified, trying to conceal my disappointment, my irritation. He wanted me to hide?

"Royal..." His features softened. "These boys... most of them are good boys. But some of them..." He rubbed the back of his neck. "They might not understand. You catch what I'm saying?"

I leaned toward the desk, my jaw tight, my throat aching, I asked, "What about you, Coach? Do you understand?"

He nodded, his posture sinking into his chair. "I understand people can be small minded. You can't help who you're attracted to, but not everyone will see it that way. In my opinion, your personal life shouldn't matter to everyone else." He knocked his fist onto the top of the desk. "We're a team, and you're a phenomenal swimmer. Tell the team, don't tell them. I'll support you either way. And if there's backlash, I'll deal with it."

"I have your support?" I asked, not quite sure I could believe it.

"You do." He nodded, his smile steady across his face. "You really do, kid. Anyone has anything to say, they can talk to me."

There was a knock on the door, but he didn't answer it. "Do you want to tell the team, or should I?"

"I think I should. Kai already knows."

"And?"

"He's my best friend."

"When you're ready, he'll have your back."

Another knock and the door opened. "Oh, sorry, Coach." It was Sherman. "When you get a minute, I—"

"Take a number." Coach laughed, and Sherman gave him a sheepish smile and shut the door.

"I better get out there," I said, pushing the chair back, I stood. "Thanks for... thanks for not tossing me off the team. For being cool with... everything."

His gaze was resolute as he stood. "You belong on this team. Remember that."

With glassy eyes, my nostrils flared, heavy sentiment clenching my jaw, I managed a tight whispered, "I will."

"You're going to walk in, holding hands?" Indie asked. Her bottom lip was trapped between her teeth, her blue eyes bouncing back and forth between me and Camden.

"Why not?" I asked. "We're a couple, couples hold hands. We should get to hold hands."

She grinned. "Yes, you should."

Camden's hand found mine. His warm palm easing my sprinting heart. "Last chance." His throat bobbed as he looked toward the cafeteria doors. "You sure? About this?"

"I'm sure about you."

He watched me, his irises filled with a mixture of love and alarm as Indie said, "I'll go first."

"Okay." His tone was even, steady, but I could feel how his palm had begun to sweat, clammy against mine. His other hand held a death grip on the strap of his backpack, as we walked behind my sister toward the door.

She held it open for us and I pulled him a little closer, walking past her. He looked perfect in his worn jeans and my St. Peter's swim team hoodie. He was mine, and I refused to feel small, to hide behind my sister. I wanted him to know how proud I was to have him at my side, and as we walked in, the heat of the cafeteria, the noise, swimming all around us, I whispered into his ear, "We're free."

let there be light

I could actually feel the relief wash over him as he relaxed at my side. At first, no one even noticed. We held hands through the food line, only letting go to throw two breakfast burritos onto Indie's tray. It wasn't until we were about halfway across the room that the murmurs began to spread like wildfire. I could feel the eyes on my back, burning holes through my skin. I gripped Camden's hand tighter when I heard a grumbled, "what the fuck?" The usual din inside the open room died down to a hushed thunder. Kai, Corbin, and Dev were already at our table.

Kai's eyes darted to our clasped hands and he immediately stood, his smile wide and welcoming. "About time." He bent down, lowering his voice, he said, "Coach talked to me after weights, told me you stopped by his office."

Camden let go of my hand, pulling out one of the chairs. The guys at the table stared at the familiar team hoodie he wore as he took a seat. Dev appeared to be confused, his mouth hanging open, his forkful of pancake paused mid-bite.

Corbin grinned like a hyena, and like nothing at all was out of the ordinary, he stole a tater tot from Indie's plate.

"Seriously," she protested.

Corbin shrugged, giving her his best innocent smile. "I'm hungry."

"Get your own, asshole." Kai pulled out the chair next to Camden, gesturing to me. "Have a seat, I was about to leave anyway."

"Stay," I whispered, and Dev averted his eyes.

Kai glanced around the table, his gaze lingering on Indie. Her head was tipped down, her attention on her phone. "You've got this," he whispered and clapped me on the shoulder.

"Where are you going?" Dev finally spoke.

"To the library. Finals next week, we can't all have silver spoons in our asses."

"It's mouths, dickwad, silver spoons in our mouths." Dev laughed and took another bite of his pancakes.

Kai grinned. "Whatever." He gave me a pointed look. "Come to practice tonight a few minutes early?"

"Why?"

Leaning in, he kept his voice down, "After this news spreads... better to be the first one in the locker room. You're here to stay, the sooner they realize that, the better."

I let his words swirl inside my head as he walked away, ignoring the glares coming from some of the students at the surrounding tables. Dev and Corbin were quiet as I took a seat and slipped my hand onto Camden's knee. His hand covered mine as his leg started to tap. I reached over to Indie's tray and grabbed our breakfast, trying like hell not to break, to keep my shoulders rolled back, my chin up, regardless of the tension building in the room, at this table, between Camden and me.

"I have a question." Corbin's voice sliced through the silence.

Dev groaned. "Please, for once in your pathetic life don't—"

"Is his dick really bigger than mine?" Corbin grinned, and I swear my sister almost choked on her potatoes.

Camden's leg stopped bouncing, and Dev's face fell into his hands. I huffed out a sputtered laugh, and I squeezed my boyfriend's thigh.

Dev mumbled into his palms, "Jesus Christ, Corbin."

"Hey, someone had to say something. And it's cool, whatever, they're a couple..." He held up his hand in mock horror. "But more importantly, the reputation of my manhood is at stake here. So... is it true?"

Dev looked up. "Do not answer that, O'Connell."

Camden exhaled, and I loved the full blush that painted his cheeks.

"I don't plan on it. My sister is at the table," I answered, taking a bite of my burrito.

Indie's cheeks were bright red, too, as she studiously ignored us.

Dev let a laugh slip, his eyes meeting Camden's, he said, "I don't know why any of us put up with him."

"Because I have the fastest freestyle on the team."

Dev snorted, a smirk hanging off his lips. "I'll tell Sherman you said that." Corbin flipped him off, and Dev pointed at Indie with his fork. "Dude, you better apologize to that man's sister."

"Sorry, Pink." Corbin gave her a toothy grin, and something warm flooded my chest at his use of my nickname for her.

I looked around the room, and a few residual stares and scowls met my gaze. But I was still Blue and she was still Pink and Corbin was still ridiculous. Nothing had changed, at least between us, the people who mattered. I tugged on the string of Camden's hoodie and Dev gave us a smile.

"This feels too easy," Camden whispered.

Maybe it was, maybe every step would get harder, or maybe this was how it should be.

That unknown warmth in my chest, it spread its way through my veins, muting the noise of the cafeteria, breathing its definition in my ear.

Bravery.

You belong on this team.

Acceptance.

Here.

Family.

With him.

Royal

"Good luck with your finals." Barb, one of the reference librarians, lifted a stack of books from the desk and placed them on the cart.

"Thanks, don't miss me too much over the holidays," I teased, shrugging my duffel onto my shoulder.

"I don't know how I'll manage." She laughed to herself, and my attention snagged on the way her red lipstick seemed to creep into the wrinkles around her mouth when she smiled.

This was my last shift at the library for the semester, and as I watched Barb disappear into the stacks, I took a few seconds to smell the books, the dust, and that ever-present scent of rain that never quite dissipated, no matter how sunny it was outside. I was going to miss this place. This place, these last five months, my world had completely changed. On my way to the door, I let my fingers drift across the wood surface of the desk where

I'd studied with Indie, the same desk where everything had begun for Camden and me. A nostalgic smile crossed my lips as I passed through the library doors and into the night air.

Everything was frozen, as if time had dusted the tips of the pine trees, holding them in a perpetual state of green. Ice crystals dangled from the gutters of the buildings after this evening's rain storm. The damp, chilled air clung to my lips, my breath—my bones—as I hustled toward the pool, dreading tonight's practice for more reasons than I wanted to think about. So far today, anytime I was with Camden, we'd chosen to hold hands. I'd even kissed him on the cheek after lunch, earning a few disgusted glares. There had been a few smiles, though. The smiles made it easier for me to believe everything would be okay. It was strange, being under a microscope, having people watch us like we were some weird circus act. We couldn't be the only gay couple on campus. It was a small school, but not that small. Maybe our coming out would eventually draw others out, too. Give them the courage they needed to step outside their own four walls. By the time we got back from break, no one would care, or remember. At least, that was what I kept telling myself.

I filed away all my concerns as I opened the large door and walked into the lobby with my head held high. I hadn't seen my team, beyond Kai, Dev, and Corbin, since morning weights, and if news had traveled as fast as Kai had thought it would, I had to walk into that locker room prepared with metal-forged skin. I was halfway down the hall, the smell of chlorine pulling its way into my lungs, when I heard Camden's voice.

Turning, I was greeted with his cute, shy smile, and all the anxiety I'd felt about ten seconds ago dissolved into the chemical-scented air.

"What are you doing here?" I asked, checking over his shoulder before placing a kiss on his lips.

His fingers pulled at the loose thread hanging from the hem of his shirt as he whispered, "You were there for me. With my parents." He lifted his gaze to the locker room door. "You're about to walk into a lion's den."

I gently grabbed the strap of his backpack and pulled him a few inches closer. "I'm not alone, Camden." I didn't doubt that if he could have, he would've come into the locker room with me. "And this..." I stared into his eyes, my lips dying for a kiss. "You coming here, for me, it gives me more strength than you know."

His eyes fell to my mouth, and the space between us grew almost insignificant.

"Be careful."

"I promise."

He took a step backward, my hand falling to my side as a few male voices resonated through the hall.

"I'll see you tonight," I said as I watched him leave. Mason and Max, two juniors on my team, passed him without a second glance.

"'Sup, O' Connell, you gonna chill in the hall all night? Or you here to swim?" Max held the door open for me, the grin on his face a good sign.

"Swim."

"Let's go, then. The pool ain't getting any warmer."

Half the team had already arrived, and I avoided their eyes, avoided looking at them all together. The conversation in the room lulled as I made my way to my locker.

"I thought I told you to get here early?" Kai asked, his stern gaze scanning the room.

"I got held up at the library." I set my bag on the bench. "How bad is it?"

He ran his hands through his hair as he kicked off his shoes. "Ellis has been talking shit all day."

"He knows?" I whispered.

"Everyone fucking knows." The anger in his tone was unmistakable. "His girlfriend saw you kiss Camden's cheek at lunch today."

Was Kai pissed at me?

"I'm sorry."

Repentant, he said, "You shouldn't be sorry. Ellis is an asshole." He looked over my shoulder. "As far as I can tell, most of the guys don't care. Or if they do, they know not to say shit. I've already told a few of them to get over themselves."

"You don't have to fight my battles."

"I do though." He pushed my shoulder, and his lips twitched, suppressing a smile. The tension in my muscles eased a little. He lifted his shirt over his head, his eyes finding mine again. "You'd do the same for me."

"I would."

"Shit." Kai threw his shirt onto the bench. "Incoming."

"What's he doing in here? This is fucked up. Where's Coach?" Ellis stared at Kai, his face red, and his hands balled into fists. "I'm not letting this faggot eye-fuck me while I'm changing."

The slur was like a punch to my stomach, knocking the air out of my lungs. Cold crept its way along my skin, blood draining from my face. Fury twisted itself into a knot inside every single one of my muscles.

Kai's jaw pulsed, but his lips split into a tight smile. "You're not his type."

"Thank fuck." Ellis took a step closer, and the tips of my fingers went numb. "You shouldn't be here. You don't belong in here. Coach—"

"Coach knows, asshole," I bit back, finding my voice.

Ellis smiled as if he'd gotten exactly what he wanted. "Coach knows..." His laugh was bitter. "You hear that, guys... looks like the pervert gets to stay."

"Chill out, Ellis," someone called out from behind him.

I risked a glance around the room. Dev and Corbin stared at me with sympathetic looks on their faces. I refused to feel embarrassed, refused to acknowledge Sherman's repulsion as he watched Ellis make a spectacle of me.

"Don't expect me to stay quiet about this." Ellis slid his narrowed gaze down my body, his face contorting like he'd swallowed something rancid. He spoke through gritted teeth. "You have no right to be here."

"Last time I checked, I clocked the fastest fly on the team. Pretty sure that gives me the right." I mustered as much poise as I could, letting my lips spread into a wide grin. "Maybe if you swam as fast as you ran your mouth, you'd have a chance at beating me."

He planted his palms into my chest with a shove. "Fuck you, O'Connell."

"In your dreams."

Kai put his arm between us. "Chill the fuck out. Both of you. Coach isn't going to put up with this shit." He put his fingers between his lips and whistled. "Everyone, listen up. You got a problem with this?" No one said a word, the room so utterly quiet I wondered if Ellis could hear my thundering heart. "We're a goddamn team. We stick together. We win. Everything else is bullshit." He shoulder-checked Ellis as he growled, "Now suit up."

Kai turned his back to Ellis and I followed his lead. The guys in the room slowly started to move again, the dead silence giving over to a murmured hum. My fingers shook as I tried to open the zipper of my bag. The anger I'd been holding on to faded into pure adrenaline, scorching its way through my veins, leaving exhaustion and sadness in its wake. This fight wasn't over. Liam had been right. Camden and I would have to constantly struggle to be who we were, to be together. I was in my head, letting my self-pity distract me, I hadn't noticed Ellis was still standing beside my locker.

"Didn't I tell you to get ready for practice?" Kai asked, more like demanded.

Ellis ignored him, animosity spilling off his rigid shoulders. "Tell me something, O'Connell. Is it biological?" He smirked. "I mean, it'd be a pity if your sister was a dyke, she's got a fuckable ass."

I wasn't given the chance to even process what he'd said. Kai threw his fist into Ellis's face, the force of it sending Ellis into the locker with a gruesome crack. His nose exploded, dark red blood pouring down his chin like a river. His eyes glazed with fury as he flung himself at Kai, both of them falling over the bench, Kai's back hitting the tile floor with a blunt thud. Ellis tried to use this to his advantage, his fists finding purchase against Kai's chest, his ribs—his face. My last vestiges of adrenaline kicked in and I grabbed Ellis by the back of his collar. Kai was perfectly capable of taking care of himself, though, and as I pulled, Kai kicked Ellis at the same time, sending us both flailing into the locker.

The back of my head hit the sharp knob of the metal lock, sending a shooting pain down my spine. The room went fuzzy. Something hot trickled down my neck, and I lifted my fingers to the back of my hairline. I hissed, the contact instantly making my head throb. I heard Kai's warning, or maybe it was another slur from Ellis, something about blood, I wasn't sure. Everything sounded like it resonated from of a tin can, and the last thing I remembered before I blacked out was the splitting pain right below my eye, and the cold, hard surface of the locker room floor.

I woke up on my back with a bright white light shining in my eyes.

"Welcome to the land of the living." An older man with a thick, salt-and-pepper mustache stood over me, a pen light in his hand. "That's one hell of a black eye you earned." He smiled, and I tried to smile back, but it hurt too much. "Half the swim team is outside, but your coach won't let them in."

Let them in?

Outside?

What was he talking about? I tried to sit up but the man placed his hand on my chest. "Now wait a minute. Don't get up too fast, you'll make yourself sick."

He grabbed my hand and helped me into an upright position. It took me a second to get my bearings. I hadn't left the locker room, or the floor. My head pounded, and my eye felt like it was about to pop out of my skull. I looked down at my fingers and a spike of fear jolted through me. Blood. On my fingers, my chest, my jeans. I swung my head to look for Kai, for Ellis, like the man had cautioned, nausea hit me like a truck and my mouth watered.

"Royal, take it easy, son."

Coach.

Tears brimmed over my lashes. A sudden rush of emotion I had no desire to control. Everything. This burden. It was too substantial. My shoulders shook as quick bursts, like a fast-moving reel of film, the fight replayed inside my head.

"Where's Kai?"

Coach's warm palm settled on my shoulder. "Kai and Ellis look like they fought ten rounds. Don't worry, they're going to be fine. Kai had to get stitches for his eyebrow. Dev and Corbin took him to the urgent care in town."

"Ellis?"

He shook his head. "Banged up. He'll live. But you... Jesus, you scared the hell out of me. Is he okay?"

The man nodded. "It's just a cut on the back of his head, no stitches needed. His nose is definitely broken, might need a scan to rule out a concussion." He kneeled down in front of me and held up his hand. "How many fingers am I holding up?"

"Three." I spoke in a rough whisper.

"What's your name?"

"Royal O'Connell."

He nodded his chin and asked me a few more questions. What was the day of the week? Who was the president? What year was it?

He seemed satisfied. "I think he's okay."

Coach shook his hand. "Thanks, Dale."

"Not a problem. Get some ice for that shiner." He gave Coach a look I couldn't decipher. "I'll be around."

"Who was that?" I asked, as the man left through the back of the locker room.

"Campus police."

"Police?" I let my face fall into my hands and winced.

"When Corbin couldn't get a hold of me, he sent one of the guys to grab Dale." He cleared his throat and I looked up. "He'll need to hear your side of the story before he can file any charges."

"I don't want to file charges. I don't want anyone to go to jail." My voice cracked. "This is all my fault."

"Not according to Dev, to Corbin. To Max." Coach held my stare. "Hell, I got fifteen guys out in that hall telling me Ellis provoked the fight. That you happened to get caught in the mix with an elbow to the face no less, and a locker to the back of your head."

"I don't want to file charges."

He sighed. "I'll talk to Dale." Coach handed me a towel and I used it to wipe my hands. The blood wouldn't come off. "The dean isn't going to let this slide, though."

"Camden," I said his name, trying to whisper him into existence, here at my side, his hand in mine. I raised my fingers to the bridge of my nose. If my face looked as bad as it felt, he would panic. And now the dean was involved. Everything he was afraid of had come to fruition. "Am I going to get expelled?"

Coach grumbled, "Not if I have anything to say about it. Listen... All of those guys out there are concerned for you. All of them willing to have your back."

"What about Kai? Is he—"

"He threw the first punch."

If Kai lost his scholarship, I'd never forgive myself.

"He was protecting me."

"Dean Thomlinson is an honorable man, he'll do what he thinks is right. I'll do my best, tell him what happened, that he defended you. Anything you can add, or remember will only help his case. It's going to be fine. You don't need to worry about it right now. You do, however, need to get a picture of that noggin, make sure everything's A-OK." Compassion lined his eyes as he stood, completely unaware of the connection between the dean and Camden's parents. He didn't understand how deeply hate could root itself inside a human heart, feeding on a man's honor, until there was nothing left. He had no clue how my best friend's life was about to be destroyed.

Because of me.

Camden

It wasn't abnormal for Royal's swim practice to run a little late, and certainly not before the last swim meet of the semester. But it was almost ten, and usually by nine Kai and Royal were strolling in with Chinese food. I played a few scales to try and quell my anxiety, letting one note trip into the next until I was creating something new. I stopped, my fingers pausing over the keys, when I felt my phone vibrate in my pocket.

"Hey." The word stretched itself out through the speaker of my phone, worn and weak. His breath hitched, and my heart sank into my stomach. "Can you come to my place?"

"What's the matter?" I was already grabbing my wallet, shoving it into my back pocket, slamming my bedroom door behind me.

"Don't freak out. I'm okay, but—"

My phone cradled between my shoulder and chin, my head down, as I pushed on my shoes, hopping on one

318

foot, I hit a human wall. The phone slipped and almost fell to the floor. I caught it, swearing under my breath.

"Sorry, I didn't realize you were... home."

My roommate's face was almost unrecognizable. A huge gash sliced across his brow, stitches straining to hold it together. A puffy, purple mask surrounded his eyes. His top lip was cracked, and blood crusted on his chin. The silence suspended itself over me, an anxious vacuum sucking away my breath.

Kai's mouth moved, his ruined brow dipping in concern, his hand reaching toward me, but it was Royal's voice, calling my name, faint, and far away, that broke through my quiet alarm.

"What happened?" I asked, my voice rising with panic.

"There was a fight." Royal tried to keep his voice even.

"I know."

"You know?"

"Kai just got home."

"Is he okay?"

"Are you okay?"

"I'm okay. Camden..." Royal stuttered through a wet breath. "Just get here, okay."

"I'll be there in ten minutes." With trembling fingers, I ended the call and pushed my phone into my front pocket.

"He's fine. Coach texted me when they were at the emergency room." Kai's voice held no emotion.

"Emergency room? What the fuck, Kai?"

He collapsed onto the couch, a grimace distorting his already gory features.

"Shit went down in the locker room." He closed his eyes. "Everything is fucked."

I didn't want to wait for him to sift through his own head for answers. If Royal looked as bad as... I couldn't let myself think about it. I couldn't breathe again, and that sinking feeling, where everything around me was closing in, and each breath I took was too loud, and the distance between me and Royal made my chest ache, my eyes hurt, and my mouth dry. Like a three-ton anvil was sitting on my chest.

"Kai, I—"

"Go. I'll be alright." He opened his eyes. "Tell Royal..." He swallowed and blinked a few times, and when he spoke again, the strength in his voice had faded. "Tell Royal I'd do it again, every fucking time."

Hot tears burned at the corner of my eyes as I nodded. I didn't know what had happened tonight in that locker room. I had no idea how badly Royal had been hurt, but I had a feeling I owed Kai everything.

It took me exactly six minutes to get to Warren House. I took the stairs three at a time, practically running down the hall to Royal's room. Indie's voice was the first thing I heard when I opened his door. The lights were off except for his bedside table lamp. She was on his bed, and when she turned to look at me, tears stained her cheeks. Her blue eyes broken open, her lashes wet—my knees hollowed. I fought not to sink to the floor. She was devastated.

"Camden?" he asked for me as he sat up.

I stood motionless, my mind helplessly trying to survey the damage. His nose was swollen, his left eye more purple than his right. The blond curls of his hair around the nape of his neck stained the color of rust. I felt every bruise.

"Oh, God." I heard myself say.

"It looks worse than it really is. More like a really bad headache, nothing I can't handle." Royal smiled, but I saw the wince he tried to hide. "Please don't cry."

I hadn't even realized I'd started to cry. I raised my fingertips to my cheeks and wiped away the evidence. He'd been strong for us tonight. I had to be the strong one now. Indie stood, leaned over, and kissed her brother's forehead.

"I'll call Mom back, just rest, okay. I'll let her know the doctor said there was no concussion." Royal kept his eyes on me as she wrapped me into a hug. "Take care of him for me..." She exhaled a shaky whisper. "Please."

It wasn't until I heard the click of his bedroom door that the noisy panic in my head finally subsided. We didn't speak, at first. Royal moved inch by inch, giving me room to lie next to him. I rested my head on his chest, the powerful drum of his heart, the best sound I'd heard all day, vibrated through me. His fingers ran through my hair, his feather-light touch an illusion trying to warm me to sleep.

"I was so naïve," he said, and the deep cadence of his voice rumbled inside his ribcage.

I lifted the weight of my body onto my elbow. His black eye was almost completely swollen shut. I leaned down and placed a kiss on his brow, to the bridge of his nose, to his parted lips. He cupped my cheek, the pad of his thumb sweeping away the moisture.

"This should have never happened," I whispered.

"But it did."

His hand fell from my face, and I listened to him explain how Ellis had picked a fight. How *Ellis* had thrown around slurs that made my blood want to boil. How *Ellis* had done everything in his power to provoke and incite, and in the end, he'd gotten exactly what he'd wanted. Every time Royal said Ellis's name, that thing inside me, the shame and guilt I'd carried around for so long, it changed. It morphed into something hard and angry. What had happened in that locker room threatened the very light I loved inside Royal. The light had already begun to dim. The golden melody of his voice waned, patched up and out of tune. Rough with the realities of hate and fear, and I wanted to fix it, fix the broken thing inside him, the same thing I'd once harbored inside myself.

"There will always be an Ellis, Royal."

"Like you said. Like Liam said. It will always be a fight."

"I know."

"I can't do that to you. What about the dean?"

"From what you said, there were more than a dozen witnesses. Thomlinson may be friends with my parents, but this is so much bigger than me or you, or their personal agendas. What happened tonight was a hate crime. He'd be an idiot if he tried to spin it any other way."

"And Kai?"

"He stood up for us. He did the right thing."

Royal closed his eyes, tears leaking under his lashes. I shifted, lowering my lips to the soft crease of his inner elbow.

I kissed his tattoo, each word, and read them, my lips dusting against his skin. "*Do anything, but let it produce joy.*" I raised my head and met his gaze. "You bring me joy. You showed me, Royal... You reached in, and took away the shame, you told me I didn't have to hide."

"What if I was wrong?"

"Does this feel wrong?" I pressed my mouth to his and he exhaled. Soft and sad, his lips opened for me. I tasted his shame, his fear, and it was bittersweet.

"No." His fingers were in my hair. "It doesn't."

I could see beyond the destruction of his face, down to that bright light, fighting to break through. "You give up, and the assholes win. Whatever happens, I'm here... with you."

He held my face in his hands, the heat of his palms dripped down my neck, and shoulders, filling my chest as he repeated, "Right here."

"For as long as you want me."

The corner of Royal's mouth lifted, and he chuckled as he winced. "Forever then?"

Forever was a Rachmaninov Concerto, sweeping and romantic.

His thumb traced the curve of my bottom lip and I smiled. "Forever works for me."

"How are you not nervous?" Royal bounced back and forth on his feet outside the dean's office.

"One of us has to stay calm, Blue." Royal's hand was sweaty, but I held it tightly against mine as Indie said, "If Kai didn't get kicked out, you won't either."

"She's right," I agreed and Royal rolled his eyes.

"He's on probation. They won't let him take his finals, and now he has to repeat this entire semester. Hardly an easy sentence. I'm scared."

Royal's bruising had barely started to fade over the weekend. But the swelling was gone, and his bright blue eyes were wide with anxiety.

"He got to keep his scholarship," I offered. "That's a good thing."

"Lost his position as captain." He stopped fidgeting. "It's not fair."

"It's not." I squeezed his hand. "But maybe keep that to yourself once we go inside."

The door opened as if the dean had been waiting for that very moment to reveal himself. He avoided my eyes, and spoke directly to Royal. "Come in, sorry for the wait. I just got off the phone with your parents."

"My parents?" Royal's grip on my hand was almost unbearable.

"Yes." He held out his hand, indicating we should sit. "Have a seat. And, uh… young lady, feel free to pull up a chair."

"My math final starts in twenty minutes." Indie gave Royal a quick peck on the cheek. "Text me as soon as you can." He nodded, and I thought I heard her wish him luck under her breath before she left.

Dean Thomlinson's office was overheated. The walls tipped inward, heavy with shelves, overfilled with books, his desk small, making him look that much bigger. I wondered if he'd done that on purpose.

He sat across from us, in a dark blue suit, his belly touching the edge of the desk as he folded his hands on its wood surface. He cleared his throat, the jowl under his chin vibrating as he said, "Firstly, on behalf of the entire faculty, I'd like to offer you an apology for what happened. We do not condone such behavior. I am sure, by now, you have learned the fates of your teammates?"

"Yes, sir." Royal spoke in a clear and strong voice, and I wanted to smile at the way Thomlinson kept darting his gaze to our linked hands. "Well, I mean, Kai told me... but I don't know—"

"Ellis has been expelled." The dean's forehead beaded with sweat. He grabbed a handkerchief from his coat pocket and blotted his brow. "We have zero tolerance for discrimination here at St. Peter's. And like your parents reminded me this morning, a hate crime is punishable by law, and Ellis is lucky you didn't press charges... As for Kai, he was the first one to act in violence, but he held true to the loyalty we hold dear at this school, and I am aware he was defending his teammate and friend. But because of that violence, there had to be some repercussion."

"And for me?" Royal asked, and I could feel his pulse thrashing against my palm.

"Your professors and I decided you should be exempt from taking your finals, based on the severity of your injuries, both physical and emotional." The dean lowered his gaze to our hands once more. "I hope that in time, you both will feel safe here at St. Peter's." For the first time, since I'd stepped into the office, he met my eyes. "There are people in this world who see everything in concrete, straight lines. I am not one of those people."

Royal's grip relaxed. "Is there anyway Kai could..."

"I know it seems unfair. He defended you. But he didn't have to act in violence. You are all lucky no one was gravely injured. 'An eye for an eye will only make the whole world blind.'"

"Mahatma Gandhi," Royal whispered and the dean smiled.

"Your father said you were a smart boy."

The smartest, I wanted to say, but didn't. I was still reeling from his speech about straight lines. Could he really be okay with this? With two boys holding hands, kissing in his halls, loving each other in his dorms?

Thomlinson pulled a small card from a side drawer and pushed it across his desk with his finger. "If either of you have any problems in the future, this is my personal contact information and office hours."

Royal let go of my hand and picked up the card, placing it in his coat pocket. "Thanks."

"Good luck to you, Mr. O'Connell. I hope your holidays are well."

He walked with us to the door, and before I stepped over the threshold, his hand landed on my shoulder. I turned to face him and was greeted with a sincere smile. "I hope you can see me as... an ally."

He lowered his hand and all I could think to say was, "I hope so, too."

I caught up to Royal as he opened the front door, and the winter day poured into the building. The sun was hidden behind the clouds, the gray sky making all the color around us pop. The dark greens of the tree needles, the chocolate brown wood grain of the buildings, and the deep blue of Royal's eyes sparkled as he faced me, his lips as pink as his cheeks and nose.

"Is it terrible I feel relieved?" he asked, taking both of my hands in his.

"Why would it be terrible? Because of Kai?" He nodded, and I remembered I'd forgotten to tell him something the night of the fight. "Kai... that night, before I came to your place. I was so freaked out I completely forgot. Kai said, 'Tell Royal I'd do it again, every fucking time.'"

"Of course he would." Royal's laugh was light and unburdened.

"I love that sound."

He let go of my hands only to tug at the sides of my jacket, aligning our bodies, his gaze fell to my mouth. "What sound?"

"Your laugh."

His knuckles grazed the side of my cheek. "I love this," he whispered before placing a soft kiss to my lips. "Where do we go from here?" he asked.

"Indie and I take our finals, and we all head home for Christmas."

"Together?"

"Together."

"I love the sound of that."

His lips lingered over mine, tasting, until all the world went quiet, leaving behind a blank sheet of music.

And the first note.

Would be a drum.

The sound of my heart finding his.

Royal

The blue lights of the Christmas tree cast a silvery glow across the living room. It hadn't snowed yet, but the clouds teased the skyline, thick and looming, waiting for the right moment to wash the city in a clean palette of white. Camden's haunting rendition of *O Holy Night,* played reverent, and humble, floating through the room until he had captured everyone's attention.

Indie was curled on the couch, her legs tangled with Mom's. My cousins sat on the floor nearby, Ava softly singing the words, my Aunt Kelly singing with her, and I caught Quinn smiling as he watched them. My dad leaned in the doorway of the kitchen, his arms crossed over his broad chest, pride in his eyes as he observed Camden at the keys. My Uncle Kieran and his wife were still sitting at the dinner table, their hands linked at their sides.

"He's good," Liam said as he sat next to me on the floor by the Christmas tree.

"He really is."

Liam crossed his ankles, resting his inked elbows onto his knees. "You haven't been by the shop." I didn't respond. I'd avoided my uncle since I'd been back. Avoiding the '*I told you so,*' I was sure he'd slap in my face. "Your dad told me what happened."

"And... you want me to tell you what? You were right?"

He flinched, and I immediately regretted my sharp, whispered words. But, everything that had happened had continued to weigh on me. It didn't help that Kai hadn't answered any of my texts since he'd left campus.

"I shouldn't have said what I did." I looked at him, his dark brown eyes were gentle. Vulnerable. "Royal, I'm not the best with words, but I'm sure as hell good at pushing people away. I'm scared for you. Scared for what you both will have to go through. What you've already had to deal with." He stared at the bruising around my eye, more of a pale green now. "I swear to fuck, if I wouldn't get arrested..."

I chuckled, despite the way his jaw pulsed. "I wouldn't hold you back."

He knocked his knee into mine. "I'm old, and Kelly would kick my ass before I ever got to lay a hand on the kid."

"She so would." I laughed, a little louder than I should have, and my sister shushed me.

"If he's worth it to you, then he's worth it to me."

"He's my family."

"Then he's my family, too."

Liam didn't smile, but he knocked his knee into mine again, and we both turned to listen to Camden play. I could see my father standing in the doorway out of the corner of my eye. He'd watched us the whole time. As Camden hit his final note, and the room broke out in applause, the attention made him blush more than I ever could.

"I love it when you blush," I whispered into his ear as he sat down next me.

Liam covertly stood, giving us privacy, and joined the rest of my family in their debate of what they were going to make Camden play next.

"*Silent Night,*" Ava shouted and Quinn groaned.

"Jesus, something more upbeat."

"*Rockin' Around the Christmas Tree?*" my mother suggested.

"I'm not playing that," Camden said deadpan, and everyone laughed.

I slid my hand in his, his eyes perceptively tracking Liam across the room. "How'd that go?"

"Really well, I think." I kissed his cheek.

"I heard from my dad this morning."

"You did?"

"Yeah... he texted me." His tone turned sardonic. "*'Missing you today. I'm here when you're ready.'* Like it's my fault. Ready for what? Ready not to be gay?"

"Did you text anything back?"

He looked at me and then around the room. "I wasn't going to. But being here with you and your family..."

"Our family."

"Our family," he corrected himself with a lopsided grin. "I felt like I should be the bigger man."

"What did you say?"

"Just 'Merry Christmas', but it's something." He leaned into my shoulder, his gaze drifting to the window. Giant, fat, white flakes danced in the wind as he whispered to himself, "It's a start."

The End...

Acknowledgements

To the reader, thank you so much for reading this book. It took me eight months to write, and I'm so grateful you stuck around to read it. Without you, my words would sit alone in a corner, thank you for dusting them off and giving them love =)

Thank you, Kirk, for sharing your story with me and answering my questions.

My editing team, Elaine and Kathleen, you guys rock my socks off. Can we have martinis now?

My ENTIRE beta team/ARC team, you guys are amazing. If your eyes have graced these pages pre-publish you are a Godsend, and I could have never typed THE END without you. Buckle up... Kai is coming.

Thank you, Cornelia, Anna, Ari, Haley, and Jodi. Please send your therapy hours billed to my Kaysville address.

Becca, you are the solid ground I walk on every day.

Dumbledore's Army—Jaimee, Kristy, and Tracey, never let them see you sweat.

Indie ladies, you are my gurus and I heart you immensely.

AJ's Crew, best group on the interwebs.

Amy, Laney, Cornelia, Mel, and Taylor #GoStars

My friends, if you are in my life, you know who you are, and you know I would side hug, maybe even boob squish the hell out of you.

Aaron, you better pick a boy.

Last, but not least, to my children, remember who you are and what you stand for. Fight for the rights of others. Stand up for what you believe in.

Acceptance and Tolerance and Hope.

Mom loves you no matter what.

Love is love.

Amanda~

https://www.thetrevorproject.org/

Visit the address below for the playlist for *Let There be Light*.

https://open.spotify.com/
user/12150951606
playlist/4E2npGodIi7NcVHgukklyi?si
=JNScFWSgTJutmt1Farl98g

About
The Author

Amanda lives in Utah with her family where she moonlights as a nurse on the weekends. If she's not busy with her three munchkins, you'll find her buried in a book or behind the keyboard where she explores the human experience through the written word. She's obsessed with all things Austen, hockey, and Oreos, and loves to connect with readers!

Stay up to date by signing up for her newsletter here
http://bit.ly/NewsLetterAMJBooks

Connect with her online
https://www.facebook.com/AMJOHNSONBOOKS/

Instagram @am_johnson_author

Other Books by A.M. Johnson

Manufactured by Amazon.ca
Bolton, ON

38657982R00206